Midnight Masquerade

MARCIA LYNN McCLURE

Published by Distractions Ink
P.O. Box 15971
Rio Rancho, NM 87174

Published by Distractions Ink
©Copyright 2013 by M. Meyers
A.K.A. Marcia Lynn McClure
Cover Photography by ©Andrey Kiselev/Dreamstime.com and
©Francisah/Dreamstime.com
Cover Design and Interior Graphics by Sandy Ann Allred/Timeless Allure

First Printed Edition: July 2013

McClure, Marcia Lynn, 1965—
Midnight Masquerade: a novel/by Marcia Lynn McClure.

ISBN: 978-0-9889582-3-4

Library of Congress Control Number: 2013932011

Printed in the United States of America

To Clara Jean Elorrieta Tucker,
A blessed and continual mentor in my own "Hero's Journey"

And to Abby, Kara, Kathleen, Laura, and Victoria,
The Healing Princesses in My Life!
Thank you, my five little angels of mercy!

***To Andrew, Brigham, Cody, Dallas, Dillon,
Hayden, Jonas, Keagan, and Max-Slash-Kyle,***
True heroes already.
I will be watching your heroic deeds
and adventures from afar—always.

CHAPTER ONE

She was tired—oh, so very, very tired. Never, not in all her life, had Evony Elorietta known such thoroughgoing fatigue. As she trudged out of the dark woods still veiled in the shadows of early sunrise, out across the expanse of cold, dew-drenched grass, and onto the main road of the village, Evony wondered how she would ever endure a day that was only just beginning. Every bone in her body ached; every muscle throbbed in misery; every inch of her flesh begged for respite. Yet there would be none—at least not until she had finished her stitching—finished the near thirteen hours of sewing she now faced under the ever-observant, incessantly critical eye of seamstress Agnes Teche.

After such a long, chilled, and sleepless night spent in watching, peering through the darkness and into the rooms of the inn in the woods until her eyes were too dry to watch any longer—after listening to the shallow, often vile conversations until her ears hurt from the foul ferment of it—Evony dreaded sewing for Mrs. Teche more than ever before. The woman was a banshee of an employer. And yet she was grateful Mrs. Teche had had the keen eye to recognize Evony's superior skills with needle and thread—for how else would Evony have managed to feed Mikol and Tressa, to shelter them, to keep them hidden?

Certainly she was not able to feed her young brother and sister *well*. In truth, many nights found only enough coin in Evony's pocket for the price of three potatoes or half a dozen eggs. Yet food was

1

food, whether or not it was scant and plain to the palate. And as for their shelter—indeed, there were larger hovels to be had but none so insignificant, and thereby less perceptible, than the one Miss Lovie had helped Evony to procure. The small dwelling kept Mikol and Tressa warm and hidden, and it was comfortable enough. Thus, Evony was thankful for it—thankful for Miss Lovie and the measure of safety they all knew there.

Evony sighed, wondering what in all the world would have become of Mikol, Tressa, and herself had they not been inadvertently discovered by Miss Lovie that day in the outer courtyard of Abawyth Castle. What would have been their collective fates if not for the kindness of a stranger? Would they have "disappeared" as their mother had? Yet in her soul, Evony knew their consequences would have been nothing less than dark, secret imprisonment deep within the castle's bowels—especially for Mikol.

Hence, not a day had passed since in which Evony did not graciously and sincerely express gratitude to the diminutive, sweet old woman, Lovie Wiggin, for her benevolent charity. Tenderhearted, aged, and bent with long years of work that was too hard, Miss Lovie was no less than a guardian angel. Even now, as Evony stepped onto the muddy main street of the village, she could see Lovie making her own way to meet her. No doubt Mikol and Tressa had begun to worry about their elder sister and begged Lovie to go in search of Evony. She smiled as Miss Lovie tossed a wave to her and quickened her step.

As the comforting aroma of baking breads and pastries wafted from the baker's shop to weave an invisible veil over the alleyways and streets of the village, Evony's stomach moaned with hunger. If she hurried, she would have just enough time to purchase food for breakfast, return home to cook for the children, and perhaps freshen herself a bit before hurrying to Mrs. Teche's.

"Good morning, Simon," Evony greeted the young boy holding a basket of fresh eggs as he stepped in front of her.

"Good morning to you, miss," Simon responded with a smile and a nod. "It's eggs for breakfast today then, miss?" he asked.

"Yes, Simon," Evony answered, smiling. Simon was younger than Mikol's ten years. She fancied he was perhaps just older than Tressa's six years. Yet he often spoke with the manner of a matured man and sold his mother's eggs with admirable determination.

"The usual number, miss?" Simon asked.

"Yes. Six."

Evony watched as Simon selected the six largest eggs in his basket. "Be watchful, miss. We wouldn't want them breaking and robbing you of your meal this morning, now would we?"

"Indeed not," Evony giggled, pleased by sweet Simon's concern and amused by the adult intonation of his voice. Carefully placing the eggs in her front apron pocket, Evony pressed a coin into Simon's outstretched hand and said, "Thank you, Simon. I hope you fare well today."

"As I hope you do, miss," Simon said with a lingering, pleased smile.

As Simon hurried off in search of others in want of his fare, Miss Lovie arrived, breathlessly announcing, "Oh, Evony! Another man has failed." Shaking her white-haired head with distress, she continued, "That brave young lord from Pariveth. The strange stupor of the castle claimed him each of these past four days, and this morning when he woke…the king dismissed him."

"Of course the king dismissed him," Evony grumbled. "The king is waiting for a man to arrive far wealthier than the young lord of Pariveth." Lowering her voice as she noted Simon glancing back to her, Evony added, "Or the even greater possibility to my mind is that the king does not want the mystery solved."

Lovie nodded. "As long as the princesses are kept weak and overcome with fatigue so much of the time, no one in the kingdom will question King Standwood's sitting the throne of Abawyth."

"Just as no one will question the steward he placed in Elawyth," Evony added. She shook her head. "Great fatigue, blistered heels, and puffy eyes," she sighed. "Why is it all that any physician can determine is wrong with the princesses? Any subject of this kingdom could determine that."

Lovie again shook her head. "And it does no good that each physician called upon bleeds them nearly dry with leeches."

"Bleeds them with leeches?" Simon exclaimed, suddenly appearing at Evony's side.

Evony forced a smile and tousled Simon's straw-colored hair. "Oh, do not worry, Simon," she fibbed to soothe him. "Miss Lovie and I are only making up stories with which to entertain ourselves."

"So the princesses will be healed...even though no physician can explain their blistered feet and weary ways?" Simon asked, looking to Lovie hopefully.

"Of course," Lovie reassured. "If no physician can heal them, then love will." Lovie smiled at the boy. "It is just why King Standwood has called for suitors for the princesses...called for champions to come from far and near, to endeavor to solve the mystery of our sleepy princesses. Somewhere there is a man from a kingdom who will triumph over whatever plagues our twelve princesses of Abawyth with weariness."

"Good," Simon sighed. "We are yet mourning the loss of our dear queen. What despair would fall upon the people if the princesses were lost?"

"Yes," Lovie agreed. "What despair indeed?"

A church bell echoing in the distance drew Evony's attention back to the tasks before her. "Oh! I must hurry, Miss Lovie...lest my dear ones go hungry all the day long."

Realizing that the sun had risen far higher in the east than she had realized, Evony retrieved the eggs from her apron pocket in favor of cradling them in her hands to ensure they did not jostle together and become cracked.

"I must hurry," she mumbled to herself as she darted into the street toward home.

"Evony!" she heard Miss Lovie cry out, an instant before the surprised whinny of a horse echoed—an instant before she turned and looked up to see an enormous black gelding rearing just before her.

Screaming with the realization she was about to be trampled, Evony leapt backward. An immediate and sharp pain stabbed her ankle. She tumbled to the muddy street, barely escaping the horse's powerful hooves as they slammed into the ground before her.

Even for the pain in her ankle and the mud that now covered the seat of her skirt, it was the sight of the broken eggs lying next to her on the ground that brought tears to Evony's eyes—for she had not one more coin with which to purchase others. Her young brother and sister would go hungry until Mrs. Teche paid wages to Evony when she'd finished her work that evening.

"Whoa there, Bromius!" a deep voice ordered as the horse stomped twice at the ground before Evony.

Evony heard the rider's heavy boots hit the mud as he dismounted—heard his deep, commanding voice ask, "Are you injured, miss?"

But she could not answer. She could not move but instead only stare at the shattered eggs seeping into the mud next to her.

"Evony!" Miss Lovie cried as she knelt beside her. "Are you hurt, my darling?"

At last Evony was able to pull her stare from the miserable sight of the wasted eggs to look at her friend. "They'll be so hungry, Miss Lovie," she muttered as tears escaped her eyes to begin streaming over her cheeks.

"You have my sincerest apologies, miss," the rider's voice offered. "You were so quick into the street that I could not rein him any faster. I truly feared Bromius would trample you...however unintentionally."

At last Evony looked up to the man. Instantly her long-withheld tears of fear and fatigue and frustration increased to profusion—for she knew at once why the man had come to Abawyth, and it inexplicably pained her heart.

It was obvious he was a noble—a lord, perhaps. It might be he was even a royal, a prince of some kingdom, come to solve the mystery of the princesses of Abawyth—to claim the hand of one of the twelve princesses in marriage as reward. Dressed as a man of wealth and title, from his black boots of the finest leather to the heavy fur cape he wore, the man's bearing was intimidating—and wildly affecting. Yet it was not so much his manner of dress and bearing that spoke to Evony of his importance and power, but rather the perfect comeliness of his features and face. He was, by any measure, the most handsome of men—broad-shouldered, square-jawed, blue-eyed, black-haired, and entrancingly attractive in every means in which a man could be attractive.

"You've come to win the hand of a princess of Abawyth," Evony remarked.

Yet the man seemed not to hear her—or chose to ignore her statement—for he simply asked, "Are you injured, miss?"

"No," Evony answered as the man took hold of her arm, placed one of his own around her waist, and began to assist her to stand. Yet the instant Evony attempted to bear her own weight, the sharp pain in her ankle dreadfully reminded her that she had indeed been injured. "Ow!" she gasped, wincing.

"You *have* been injured," the man growled, frowning.

"No, no," Evony argued. "I only twisted an ankle. I am well enough, sire." Of a sudden, Evony remembered Mrs. Teche and her sewing. "And I must hurry, lest I be tardy and lose my position with the seamstress."

"You will not be laboring for your seamstress today," the man stated, effortlessly lifting Evony into the cradle of his powerful arms.

"Oh, but I must!" Evony cried in desperation. Wiping tears from her cheeks, she added, "I will lose my position if I do not work even one hour of what I am meant to. And I do not need two good ankles in order to stitch and sew well."

"It is true, sire," Lovie ventured to the man. "Agnes Teche will not hold the girl's position...not even for reasons of illness or injury."

The man's frown deepened, and he said to Lovie, "I will see to it myself that this young woman does not lose her position with the seamstress." He looked to Evony then, and she found that the stunning blue of his eyes caused her tears to increase once more for some reason she could not fathom. "I nearly cost you your life, miss," the man explained. "I will certainly see to it that I do not cost you your employment with this Agnes Teche." He paused a moment, glancing down at the broken eggs lying in the mud. "And I will make recompense for your loss there, as well."

"Oh no, no, no! Please!" Evony argued. "I have no desire to be indebted to you, sire."

Again the frown furrowing his handsome brown increased. "You? Indebted to me?" The man looked to Lovie inquisitively and then back to Evony. "My horse nearly trampled you, miss. He and I robbed you of not only your breakfast and a day's wage but nearly your life. Why would you think yourself indebted to me for making whatever recompense that I am able?"

But as Evony could only linger speechless in the man's strong arms—bathe in the unfamiliar warmth emanated by his body and the furs he wore—Lovie answered, "She is near feverish with fatigue, sire," Lovie said. "Not a wink of sleep during the night and looking to a full day of stitching ahead of her."

"Miss Lovie!" Evony quietly scolded. "I am full well enough and—"

"Where is this seamstress…this Agnes Teche?" the man interrupted, glancing around him to the village shops lining the street. "Surely when I explain the situation, Agnes Teche will be understanding and compliant."

"She is just there," Lovie said as she gestured toward Agnes's shop. "She is the one of the queen's favorite seamstresses." Pausing, Lovie added, "Well, she *was* one of the queen's favorite seamstresses."

"Come then, miss," the man ordered as he began striding toward the shop, still carrying Evony in his arms. "Bromius! Follow," he commanded his horse.

"Sire, please," Evony began to plead, "I promise you that Mrs. Teche will show me no mercy. Please put me down and allow me to go my way."

"Nonsense," the man grumbled. "She will not be so callous once she has seen how injured you are."

Evony glanced over the man's broad shoulder to Lovie as she followed them. Yet Lovie only shrugged aged shoulders and shook her head with uncertainty.

Without hesitation, the man pushed the door of the seamstress's shop open with one booted foot. Stepping into the main room, he called, "I am looking for Agnes Teche."

But Evony had seen Agnes the moment they had entered the room—had seen her left eyebrow arch with disapproval the way it so often did. She watched as Agnes quickly studied the man from head to toe, obviously surmising he was nobility, for she pasted on one of her false and wicked smiles as she approached him.

"Good morning, sire," Agnes greeted. "I am Agnes Teche."

"And I am Stavos Voronin," the man began without pause. "My horse nearly trampled this girl in the street only moments ago, and she has sustained injury. I understand she labors under your employ, and I have come to ask that she be given the day to recover from the injuries I have inflicted upon her."

Again Agnes Teche offered a counterfeit smile of sympathy. Yet she was a hard woman—a heartless woman—no matter who addressed her.

"I cannot afford the loss of labor," Agnes explained. "Not one day. I will have to replace her, sire."

The man inhaled a deep breath, exhaling slowly as if struggling for patience. He looked down into Evony's tear-streaked face and asked, "Are you able to stand for a few moments, miss?"

"O-of course, sire," Evony whispered.

Gently the man removed his arms from the crook of her knees, allowing her feet to gently settle to the floor before releasing her altogether.

"I have explained to you, Mrs. Teche, that the girl's injury is no fault of hers, but rather mine," he stated, striding closer to Agnes.

"Sire—" Evony began. She could work well enough without her ankle, and she could not afford to lose her position with Agnes.

Panic was welling in her, yet the man raised one hand to indicate she should be silent.

"How much loss will come to you, Madame, if this girl is absent for but one day?" he asked the seamstress. "You will keep her wages, no doubt. So what is your loss?" He stepped closer to Agnes, yet Agnes stood firm and unwaveringly careless of Evony's situation. "I have nearly killed this girl, and I mean to make recompense for it by any means necessary," Stavos Voronin continued. "How much do you stand to lose in profit?" Evony watched as the stranger reached into a small pocket in his trousers and produced a gold coin.

"No, sire!" Evony gasped.

Yet the narrowed eyes—the icy stare of warning that Agnes Teche glared at her—silenced her at once.

Without hesitation, Agnes Teche reached out, plucking the gold coin from the man's fingers. "One day," she mumbled. "She may have today to rest her injury. But if she does not return tomorrow…"

Retrieving another gold coin from his pocket, the man offered it to Agnes. "Three days she will rest it, and you will hold her position for her…else I will not be so obliging when next I step into your shop, Madame."

Again Agnes did not pause to snatch the coin the man offered. "Agreed," she said.

Near instantly, Evony found herself swept up into the man's arms once more. She was astonished into silence—that the man would offer Agnes Teche more than a fortnight's profit in return for three days to allow Evony to recover. She could not conceive it at first.

As the man, Stavos, began to stride from the room to exit the shop, he paused. Turning toward Agnes Teche once more, he commented, "I understand you were one of the queen's favored seamstresses."

Agnes Teche smiled with pride, straightened her posture, tipped her nose higher into the air, and said, "Yes, sire. I was."

"Then your seamstressing must be far more favorable than either your countenance or moral character. Good day, Mrs. Teche," Stavos Voronin said.

As Evony's mouth hung agape with astonishment, the man strode over the shop's threshold and into the street once more.

"How do you tolerate that old crone?" he grumbled, scowling as the intensity of his blue eyes captured the as yet astonished green of her own.

"Sire, you just gave Agnes Teche more wages than she earns in a fortnight," Lovie explained, "and you presented offense as you retreated."

"I know her breed," the man responded. "Coin is the only thing that moves her. Not even criticism will wound her…as long as there is money in her pocket." He glanced down to Evony again, and she was surprised as she felt a blush rise to her cheeks. "So your name is Evony," he stated.

"Yes, sire," Evony affirmed.

"I am Stavos," the man offered. He then looked to Lovie and asked, "And you, milady, are?"

"Lovie Wiggin, sire," Lovie answered, also blushing. "Widowed citizen of Abawyth, friend of Evony…and foe of Agnes Teche."

Stavos smiled at Lovie, amused by her response. "Very well, Lovie Wiggin, foe of Agnes Teche. Where does this injured kitten of yours reside?"

"Kitten?" Evony quietly exclaimed with mild indignation.

But Lovie only laughed as she answered, "This way, sire."

"Bromius! Follow," the man commanded. Again the enormous gelding snorted and then followed his master through the streets of Abawyth.

"This is where Evony and her young siblings reside," Lovie explained as she gestured toward the door leading to the hovel Evony shared with Mikol and Tressa. "I live in the rooms just next to these," Lovie continued.

"Sire…please put me down," Evony pleaded. "My brother and sister are not used to strangers entering our home. I wouldn't want them to—"

"Ah, but they know me as well as if I were their grandmother," Lovie interrupted. "I'll go in first."

Again Evony felt herself blushing—this time with humiliation—and she was disappointed with herself for such feelings. The rooms in which she, Mikol, and Tressa hid and resided were warm and comfortable for the most part, and she was grateful for them. Yet something in her did not want this Stavos to see how humbly they existed. He was obviously a very wealthy man, and she knew he was not used to such dismal circumstances. Furthermore, she knew he would think she and her family were far beneath him—and what he thought of them concerned her more than she wanted to admit to herself.

"Darlings!" Lovie called as she opened the door before them and stepped into the hovel. "I've brought your sister and a kind man we met in the village just this morning."

"Oh, Lovie!" Tressa exclaimed, leaping from her chair before the hearth and dashing toward the door. "We are so glad you have returned! Mikol and I are near starving to death—I swear it!" Yet the moment Stavos stepped into the room carrying Evony, Tressa gasped. "Evony! What has happened to you? Are you well?"

"I am," Evony assured her little sister.

"Lands! Look at that animal!" Mikol exclaimed then, dashing out the door to better see Bromius. "Is he yours, sire?" he asked, glancing up to Stavos a moment.

"Yes," the man answered, grinning at Mikol's delight.

Mikol shook his head with admiration. "He's a wonderful horse!" he noted. "Look at his stature."

"This is my brother, M-Michael," Evony stammered. "And my sister, Tess."

"I am honored to meet you both," Stavos said, looking first from Mikol and then to Tressa.

11

"The honor is ours, I assure you, sire," Tressa responded, dropping a polite and very graceful curtsey.

"Certainly," Mikol greeted, offering a hand to Stavos.

Even though the man still cradled Evony in his arms, he managed to awkwardly accepted Mikol's handshake. "That's a firm grip you have, Michael," he chuckled.

"Thank you, sire," Mikol said with a proud nod.

"But what happened to you, Evony?" Tressa asked once more.

"Oh, nothing to speak of," Evony lied. "I was not being careful when crossing the street and Mr....Lord...Mr. Stavos's horse startled me. I twisted my ankle a little is all."

"I, however, have robbed your sister of not only a day's wage from that old crone she stitches for," Stavos began, smiling as both Mikol and Tressa giggled at his calling Mrs. Teche a crone, "but also of your breakfast." Striding to one of the chairs sitting before the hearth, Stavos deposited Evony into it and continued. "Therefore, I was wondering if perhaps the two of you, along with your friend Miss Lovie here, might see to your sister's ankle whilst I return to the village to acquire a replacement for the eggs Bromius and I destroyed."

"Of course we will see to her, sire," Mikol assured the man. "But there is no need for you to worry over the eggs. We have plenty." It was an untruth, of course—that they had plenty. Mikol well knew there would be no breakfast for him and Tressa without the eggs. But he was ever the young gentleman.

"Yes, please, sire," Evony interjected. "Please do not heighten the weight of my debt to you. I cannot make recompense as it is, and—"

"You owe me nothing, miss," Stavos interrupted, however. "Your injury and loss of wages—and the loss of your breakfast—they are all my doing, and I will see that I make amends."

"Sire, please," Evony pleaded, new tears filling her eyes. It was so gallant of him to do all he had done—to offer more. But Evony feared his good deeds had already drawn too much attention to her, Mikol, and Tressa. If King Standwood were to hear even Evony's name spoken...

Evony was rendered breathless, however—all thoughts and fears scattered from her mind—as the man suddenly knelt before her, taking her hands in his own.

"I know there is more here than my eyes are seeing, Miss Evony," he said in a lowered voice—a voice that was reassuring and warm, like heated milk and honey just before bed. "And I promise I will speak of none of this…not to anyone. I swear it to you. But I pray you let me remain honorable. Allow me to replace your meal. It is the very least I can offer."

"Please let him bring us the eggs that were broken, Evony," Tressa begged, putting a comforting arm around Evony's shoulders. Then she whispered, "I'm so terribly hungry," into Evony's ear.

More tears welled in Evony's eyes—tears of fatigue, of pain from her injury, and of hunger—tears of defeat for the sake of Mikol and Tressa.

Meeting Stavos's insistent gaze, Evony nodded. "V-very well."

"Thank you," Stavos said, exhaling a heavy sigh. He smiled and asked, "How many eggs were lost?"

"Six," Evony admitted.

Rising to his full, towering height, Stavos smiled. "Then I shall return shortly." He looked to Tressa, saying, "And you shall have your breakfast." Striding toward the door, he paused. Watching Mikol study Bromius a moment, he then said, "Would you be willing to keep him for me while I retrieve the eggs from the village? He's had a long ride and could use some rest."

"Of course, sire! Of course!" Mikol exclaimed with sheer resplendence brightening his countenance. "I'd be very honored."

"Thank you, Michael," Stavos said. "I won't be long."

Mikol nodded.

Stavos chuckled and tousled the boy's dark hair. "May I speak with you a moment, Lovie Wiggin?" Stavos asked Lovie then.

"O-of course, sire. Of course," Lovie agreed.

"Tressa," Evony whispered to her sister, "quickly, go and listen to what the man is saying to Miss Lovie!"

But Tressa gasped with righteous indignation. "Evony! I can't! Eavesdropping? Mother says it's terribly bad manners to eavesdrop!"

"I know, darling…I know," Evony agreed. "But you remember how different things are now? The danger we're all in? I need to know what the man is saying to Miss Lovie about us…if he suspects anything."

"Very well, Evony," Tressa sighed with disappointment. "But please…don't ever tell Mother I've eavesdropped."

Evony forced a smile, simultaneously heartbroken and moved by Tressa's enduring hope where their mother was concerned. "I promise I won't tell anyone…not ever."

With another exhaled sigh of disappointment in herself, Tressa rather trudged toward the front door. Yet the moment she saw Mikol stroking the velvet nose of Bromius, the memory of the task Evony had given her was as fleeting as a snowflake on an ember.

Evony sighed with defeat, though she couldn't help but smile as she watched her brother and sister stroke the magnificent horse— speak to him in the kind, reassuring voices that only children owned.

"Thank you, Lovie Wiggin," Stavos said, pressing a gold coin into the woman's wrinkled palm. "And not a word to your friends, eh?"

Lovie Wiggin nodded. "Not a word, sire." She looked up into Stavos's face then, and he was struck by the deep emotion he saw in her faded blue eyes. "You are very kind, sire…especially for a nobleman."

Stavos chuckled. "Kind? Maybe," he said. "But I have all too many faults and failings, Lovie Wiggin. Let us hope you never discover those, that they cause you to forget my more praiseworthy qualities. Hmmm?"

Lovie Wiggin smiled, nodding at him. She turned then to return to the home of Evony and her siblings. Stavos watched her go a moment. She was a kind woman, and obviously a loyal friend—loyal enough to confess to Stavos that Evony and her young brother and sister were in dire need of food, yet also loyal enough not to reveal too much to him concerning their history, of how they came to be parentless and living in a hovel in the kingdom of Abawyth.

But Stavos Voronin was not as blind-eyed as many nobles and royals. Evony's physical gestures—even the simplest movement of her hands—revealed that she had not always been destitute. The same was true of the children—of their polished manners and the boy's knowledge of horses and tendency to be bold and fearless of strangers.

Ah yes, Stavos enjoyed a good mystery. After all, interest in the inexplicable circumstances surrounding the royals of Abawyth was the very thing that had lured him to the kingdom—the enigma of Abawyth's twelve sleepy princesses. And yet now—now his mind was all the more intrigued. Not only was the obscurity of what had caused the profound and baffling torpidity of Abawyth's princesses laid out before him, but also he found his curiosity intensely piqued over the riddle surrounding the very lovely Evony and her siblings.

Evony herself was quite beautiful—hair the color of roasted chestnuts and eyes that shimmered like polished jade. She was thin and weary—obviously from lack of nourishment and from miserable labor under the seamstress's crow-like eyes. But her beauty and grace were fully evident still, no matter how she had tried to hide them under tattered clothing. No—Evony had not always labored hard at stitching for the old crone Agnes Teche.

As he strode toward the butcher's shop, Stavos's mind began to concoct scenarios of her possible history. Was she the daughter of a once-wealthy lord who had squandered his riches on women and wine and then died to leave his children in poverty? Were she, her brother, and her sister in truth this Lovie Wiggins's illegitimate grandchildren, born of some nobleman's immoral escapade with a chambermaid yet raised by governesses who taught them the ways of nobles?

As Stavos strode through the village resting on the outskirts of Abawyth Castle, his mind reeled with possibilities. In fact, so overtaken was he with thoughts of this Evony and her young siblings that it was not until he entered the butcher's shop in search of a ham for their breakfast and heard the patrons speaking of the young lord of Pariveth being dismissed by the king early that morning that his musings were drawn back to why he had come to Abawyth at all—to solve the conundrum surrounding the twelve beautiful princesses of Abawyth kingdom—to solve the seemingly impenetrable crux and thereby win the hand of one of Abawyth's princesses, as his father, King Letholdus of Ethiarien, had commanded.

CHAPTER TWO

"He is very kind and sincere for a nobleman," Lovie remarked as she studied Evony's already bruising ankle. "He lacks the air of arrogance boasted by most men of his station. Yet his posture is full as straight and stiff…and he is quite intimidating. Don't you think?"

Evony nodded, even as she winced when Lovie pressed at her ankle. "He is a formidable presence, to be sure," she agreed.

"And as handsome as the world is wide," Lovie added with a giggle. She winked at Evony, and Evony could not help but smile with accord.

"Yes," Evony breathed. "He will make one of the princesses of Abawyth a fine husband indeed."

But Lovie shook her head. "If he can manage to avoid the stupor the castle seems to cast over any man who tries to discover what it is that is ailing the princesses."

"He will avoid the stupor," Evony stated. "And he will succeed in aiding the princesses."

Lovie frowned, however. "And what makes you think this Stavos will succeed where so many men have failed? What makes you so certain he will be the one to succeed?"

Evony was silent for a moment—a long enough moment to cause a silent answer to the questions to spark in Lovie's own mind.

Lovie's eyes widened with understanding. "You mean to take him into your confidence!" she gasped with astonishment.

"No," Evony countered. "At least not entirely. But I do mean to help him be successful in putting an end to all this misery and deceit…to the evil that has slithered its way into the halls of Abawyth Castle."

"B-but what if he fails…even with your help?" Lovie asked. "What if he succumbs to the malicious stupor that overtakes any man who enters the castle to try and resolve the…the whatever it is?"

Evony sighed with determination, however. "I haven't said anything to you as yet, Miss Lovie," she began, "but I…I think I know what causes the stupor that overwhelmed those who have tried before…including the young lord of Pariveth that King Standwood dismissed this morning. It came to me in the night. I woke up having suddenly remembered something."

"Remembered what?" Lovie asked in a whisper.

Evony drew a deep breath in an attempt to calm herself before making the accusation she was about to—even if the accusation was only to be heard by Lovie. "I think—no—I *know* the stupor is the doing of the princess Kathleen," she confessed in a whisper.

"What?" Lovie gasped in astonishment. "The princess Kathleen? But…but how could Princess Kathleen cause a stupor the likes to overcome the men who have been allowed to try to help her and her sisters?"

Evony gulped, feeling traitorous in her quiet blame of Abawyth's eldest princess, Kathleen. "Kathleen is well learned in alchemy. It has been her greatest interest since she was a child."

"Alchemy?" Lovie repeated as her eyes narrowed. "So it is the princess Kathleen who somehow induces this stupor that all the men are lost to for days at a time?"

"I think so, yes," Evony admitted—regretfully.

"But why?" Lovie asked then. "Why would she do such a thing as that? She is one in misery…she and all her sisters. Why would she not wish to be healed or helped? Why would she act as saboteur instead of helpmate?"

Evony shook her head. "I don't know," she mumbled. "But if my suspicions are founded—no matter how disloyal they may seem—

then I may be able to help this Stavos Voronin who has come to us this morning. I may help him to avoid the stupor and thereby discover what it is that plagues Abawyth's princesses."

A sudden chill caused Evony to shiver—though she could not determine from whence the chill came. Was it the slight draft breathing through the room? Or was it because she'd only just accused one of Abawyth's princesses of questionable doings?

There was more Evony had not revealed to Lovie—more she had discovered only several nights before. Yet she had no explanation to accompany her discovery—no reasoning as to why she had seen what she had seen during the past few nights. Until Evony owned a better understanding, she would hold her tongue, even keeping secrets from dear Lovie. After all, it would do no good for Lovie to worry and wonder more than she already did—for though Evony was grateful she, her brother, and her sister had been given such a loving guardian angel as Lovie Wiggin, she feared that some harm would befall the sweet old lady because of them. It was a dangerous undertaking, helping to hide Evony and her siblings from those who may wish them ill. And Evony worried near constantly about Lovie's safety.

Therefore, to Evony's thinking, it was best to keep Lovie innocent of some things she had discovered—at least for the moment. That way, if suspicion were to fall to Lovie for any reason at all—if she were questioned—she could truly claim innocence where awareness of certain details was concerned.

Lovie smiled then. "You must be quite smitten with this handsome stranger…to take him into your confidence so quickly."

Evony blushed but tried to ignore it. "I have a strange feeling, some sort of inner sense…a dark, ominous shadow that lingers in my heart, Lovie—a sense that time is short where all of this is concerned. I feel that if I do not discover what is at the center of this darkness surrounding Abawyth…my mind whispers to me that lives will be lost, more than those that may already have been."

"*May* already have been?" Lovie inquired, her faded eyes narrowing with curiosity.

But Evony simply shrugged, sighed, and shook her head as if she had merely misspoken. "I suppose I'm like Tressa. I just haven't given up hope that…that someone's disappearing might not necessarily mean they are dead."

Lovie smiled with sincere compassion and heartfelt sympathy. "Oh, my sweet girl," she sighed, reaching up to tuck a stray strand of Evony's hair behind her ear. "I admire your hope…as much as I admire your strength and resolve. And you make a very good point. Just because someone has gone missing, it is no reason to assume the worst."

Evony and Lovie both startled as Tressa suddenly burst through the door and into the room. "He has returned!" she exclaimed. Mikol followed her into the room. "He has come back to us, true as his word! And look what he's brought for our breakfast!"

The stranger Evony had met only that very morning—the handsome and compassionate nobleman, Stavos—then strode into the room. In one arm he held a basket filled with not just eggs but also warm bread, wrapped in a cloth. The heavenly scent of the bread breathed into the room like a warm ambrosia. In his other hand, Stavos clasped a large ham—enough to feed them all three meals a day for a week!

"I have replaced your eggs that were broken, Miss Evony," Stavos announced with a smile. "And I pray that the bread and ham will serve as further apology for the inconvenience and discomfort I caused as well."

"Here," Mikol said, taking the ham from Stavos. "Allow me to assist you, sire."

"The bread is still warm, Evony!" Tressa giggled in a whisper, throwing her arms around Evony's neck and hugging her tightly with happiness. "And I saw a brown paper in the basket too," the girl added, "the kind the baker wraps butter in!"

"Butter?" Evony asked, returning Tressa's affectionate embrace, even as she glanced up to Stavos. "Surely not, Tess."

"Surely yes!" Tressa giggled, however.

"We are…we are indebted to you, sire," Evony stammered. Indebted—a word she did not like—and a circumstance she was loath to find herself in.

"Not at all, Miss Evony," Stavos assured her as Mikol returned to retrieve the basket of bread and eggs, having placed the ham on the small table in one corner of the room. "I should yet be on bended knee before you, begging forgiveness," he said as he nodded his thanks to Mikol.

"No…no, it is we who are indebted to you, sire," Evony assured him once more. "And I do not enjoy lingering in such a state. You must allow us to…to somehow repay your kindness."

"No," Stavos answered firmly, however. "I am grateful to *you*. You did not scold me with even one discourteous word for my having nearly let Bromius trample you to death…not to mention the fact I have cost you two days' wages from that old crone—I…I mean your kind employer, Mrs. Teche." He gestured toward the tabletop now laden with good things to eat. "It is a minimal offering of thanks…quite pitiful now that I consider it further."

"Will you at least stay and breakfast with us, sire?" Lovie inquired. "Please, do us the honor of your company at our meal…the meal you have so graciously provided."

Evony's cheeks were ember-hot with humiliation. She was certain the man had never lowered himself to take food and drink in such a hovel as theirs. She knew Lovie was only being kind and polite in inviting him, but it shamed her all the same, for some reason.

"I would be honored, Mrs. Wiggin," Stavos answered. He was smiling—not as if he were amused at being invited to such a humble gathering but rather as if he were sincerely pleased at the prospect.

Lovie giggled like an adolescent girl who had only just received the attention of a would-be suitor. "Then let me be about preparing our meal, sire. And I thank you for providing such wonderful fare for it!"

"I am only honored, Mrs. Wiggin," Stavos began, "that you would have me at all after all the difficulty I've caused this morning."

His attention then returned to Evony. She found that her breath caught in her throat as the piercing blue of his eyes settled so thoroughly on her face. She still had not drawn a breath when he then, very unexpectedly, dropped to one knee before her, took her bare foot in his hand, and pushed the hem of her skirt up above her ankle as he studied it.

"Good Lord!" she heard Mikol exclaim in a hushed voice. "He's touching her bare skin, Miss Lovie!"

Evony blushed as Stavos glanced up at her, grinning with amusement at Mikol's astonishment.

"Fear not, Michael," he said as his attention returned to Evony's ankle. "I've seen a good many battles—tended to many wounds exacted upon myself and on others. I only want to determine the seriousness of the injury I have inflicted on your pretty sister."

"It is bruising quickly, sire," Lovie offered from her place before the fire. "I think it is not so bad…just a wee sprain."

"Hmmm," Stavos mumbled as his free hand roamed freely over Evony's bare ankle in determining the extent of the damage done her. "I agree," he said at last—though his fingers brushed over her foot several times in a slow stroking motion that Evony thought felt as near to a caress as anything she'd ever known. As her body rippled with goose pimples, she hoped he did not notice the slight tremble that had overtaken her—the tremble caused of delight from his touch.

He looked up into her face once more, smiling as he said, "A day or two of resting should suffice."

"Th-thank you, sire," Evony stammered, nervously taking the hem of her skirt and endeavoring to cover her foot with it, even for the fact he had not yet released her.

"My pleasure," Stavos said, however, as he raised her foot a bit, placing a quick kiss to the top of it.

The gesture caused a slight gasp to escape Evony's mouth—and the quiet exclamation of "Good Lord!" again to tumble out of Mikol's—as she quickly pulled her foot from his hand, covering her feet with her skirt.

A low chuckle rumbled in Stavos's broad chest as he stood. "But I do think you should elevate it somewhat," he commented, as if his having kissed the top of Evony's foot were the most natural gesture in the wide world. "First, let's sit you back a bit." Evony gasped again as his hands slipped under her arms and he lifted her a little in order to position her further back on the bed. Retrieving one of the down-filled pillows at the head of Evony's bed next, he said, "Here. Rest your foot on this." Positioning her injured ankle on the pillow, he then loosened the tie at his neck of his fur cloak. Flinging it wide, the fur settled over Evony, instantly warming her with the residual heat it had gathered from Stavos's body.

"Oh no, sire. I assure you, I-I—" Evony began to stammer.

"Tess," Stavos interrupted, however. "It seems to me that you might make the best nurse in the village. Will you therefore see to it that your sister stays quite tucked in warm and safe for the rest of the day, for me?"

Tressa giggled, curtsied, and answered, "Of course, sire."

"Good," Stavos sighed with contentment. "Then after our breakfast together, I will be on my way and about my business…leaving you all to some well-earned peace."

"Your business," Mikol began. "Would it be that you have come to heal Abawyth's princesses…or at least to attempt to do so?"

"Michael," Evony quietly scolded, "his business is his own. We shouldn't press him to—"

"That is my business exactly, Michael," Stavos answered, however, "to discover what is causing their illness…and more, if I am able."

"And to win the hand of one of the beautiful princesses in marriage," Tess finished, smiling with delight.

"Yes, Miss Tess," Stavos admitted at last. "If I am wise enough, discerning enough, and in the end fortunate enough to do what your king has asked…then, yes, I hope to win the hand of one of Abawyth's princesses."

A sickening wave of nausea overtook Evony in that moment. She felt tiny beads of perspiration begin to manifest on her forehead. She wondered if perhaps the pain of her injured ankle were worse than her conscious mind wanted to admit. She found she couldn't speak—couldn't begin to stop Mikol before he asked another question of their guest.

"What is your title, sire? Lord? Duke?" Mikol asked.

She watched as Stavos revealed a handsome grin, admiring Mikol's boldness, before he answered. "I am Stavos Voronin…and at my father's bidding, I rode from Ethiarien to attempt to aid the twelve princesses of Abawyth."

Mikol smiled. "You are *Prince* Stavos of Ethiarien," he stated. "I have heard stories of you. It is said you are a great soldier…a warrior whose men follow with confidence and without question. It is said that you are yet to meet your equal in swordplay, as well."

Stavos shook his head and laughed. "And how is it one so young knows so much about such things, hmmm?"

"H-he hides behind the inn in the village and listens to the wild tales the men tell," Lovie awkwardly offered as Evony finally managed to aim an expression of warning to Mikol. He had said too much—revealed that he knew far too much about a royal from a distant kingdom.

It was desperation to divert any further suspicion of Mikol that helped Evony find her voice at last. "I can help you," she rather blurted. "I-I can help you on your quest to win an Abawythian princess as your bride."

"Is that so?" Stavos asked, gazing at Evony with amused suspicion.

But Evony only nodded. "I can," she answered. "I am indebted to you, sire—Prince Stavos—indebted far deeper than I can ever amend. And as my pitiful offer of recompense to you, I will tell you how to begin to solve this mystery of Abawyth's sleepy princesses. And I promise that my help will take you much farther than any other man who has tried."

Stavos's smile faded. His handsome brow puckered into a frown as he said, "You owe me nothing. There is no debt to pay, Miss

Evony. Your injury, your loss of wages…it is all of it my fault, and I—"

"I can help you," Evony interrupted, however. "Truly, Prince Stavos, I can—"

"Stavos, please," he likewise interrupted. "I do not like to hear my name preceded with that title."

Evony frowned, puzzled. Wasn't it true that every prince wanted his title announced as loudly as possible when addressed or heralded?

"She *can* help you, sire," Lovie offered. "She can help you to succeed."

"How so?" Stavos asked, his frown deepening as he rather glared at Evony.

Again she felt perspiration at her forehead—felt her stomach wrench with nausea and fatigue.

"Please, sire…allow me a moment to rest while you breakfast with the others," she begged him as she leaned back against the wall, suddenly overcome with dizziness. "Allow me just those moments, and then…then I will tell you how to begin if you hope to decipher this mystery that no other man has been able to resolve."

"Are you all right, Miss Evony?" Stavos asked then, leaning toward her. The sincere concern on his face, combined with the inexplicable sense of nervous fluster his nearness rained on her, caused such disquiet in Evony's soul, she could feel tears beginning to well in her eyes.

"J-just tired, your highness," she whispered. "I only need a moment of rest, and then I will…I will tell you what I will."

Stavos straightened, however. "She is not well," his voice boomed. "A physician must be summoned, at once."

But when Lovie, Mikol, Tressa, and Evony simultaneously exclaimed, "No!" Stavos inhaled a deep breath, exhaling it slowly to calm himself.

There was so much laid out before him that he could not discern. And yet his sense told him to be patient—that all would be revealed to his mind if he could but muster his patience.

Thus, he said, "Very well. We will share breakfast and allow you to rest, Miss Evony. Then, provided you are feeling better, I will hear what you have to say. I owe you that…in the very least of it."

It was obvious Evony was experiencing some sort of deep duress that had little or nothing to do with her injured ankle, and for the very first time in all his life, Stavos was nearly overwhelmed with a sense of helplessness. There were secrets in the humble home—perhaps dark secrets—and there was fear. And even as every part of his body and mind wanted to help the pretty girl Bromius had near trampled, he did not know how, and it far more than irked him—it pained him.

Yet Stavos was a master at masking his true feelings and concerns. Thus he sat at the table with Michael, Tess, and Lovie Wiggin and enjoyed a fine breakfast—a breakfast that afforded him more satisfaction than any meal he could ever remember eating. Lovie Wiggin and the children truly and thoroughly enjoyed the ham and fresh bread. And Tess's reactions to the small slab of butter were akin to pure euphoria. It pierced Stavos's heart with both joy and despair. Butter—something he had always enjoyed yet never fully appreciated before. It was a humbling experience—such a simple meal shared with such sweet company. Stavos found himself more acutely aware of how lavishly he lived in comparison. A great guilt began to settle in him, and he was determined to help the besieged family and their friend Mrs. Wiggin, no matter the cost.

Several times during the meal, Stavos glanced to where Evony sat convalescing on the nearby bed. It seemed her eyes were in constant filled with tears—that her thoughts were somehow haunting.

Again his curiosity was piqued to near frenzy. What was it that she knew concerning the mystery of Abawyth's princesses and their ailments? He was convinced she knew even more than she had implied. She had offered to assist him in winning the hand of one of them, and Stavos's mind was ablaze with wondering how she could manage it. It was not so much the possibility of succeeding that lit the fire of interest in him as it was the wondering of how Evony could help.

Thus, once the meal was at an end and the pleasant conversation with the children and Mrs. Wiggin had settled, Stavos rose from his seat at the small table and strode to the bed where he had placed the lovely Evony to nurse her tender ankle.

"Will you be able to rest?" Prince Stavos of Ethiarien inquired as he brazenly took a seat on the edge of Evony's bed. "Or will your worry over your position with Agnes Teche keep your mind from any easement?"

Evony forced a friendly smile—though the prince's nearness offered her anything but peace. "I am admittedly very tired," she answered. "I will rest well, I think. Once you are...once..."

Prince Stavos smiled with understanding. "Once I take my leave?" he finished.

Evony felt the blush heating her cheeks as she nodded. "It would be very difficult for anyone to sleep in the presence of a prince."

Stavos exhaled a rather dissatisfied sigh. "I suppose," he mumbled. He chuckled, adding, "I guess it's your fear of snoring in my presence that would keep you from settling, eh?"

"I do not snore!" Evony defended herself—albeit as playfully as he had offered the suggestion.

The prince of Ethiarien again chuckled. Evony found that the sound of his amusement caused a bubbling of delight to burble in her bosom.

"Well, no one *admits* to snoring, now do they?" he teased.

"No," Evony agreed. "But I do not snore."

"Very well then," Stavos forfeited. "Then if you do not plan to sleep while I'm here and desire for me to exit so that you may sleep peacefully—snoring or not snoring—tell me how it is that you think you can assist me in helping the princesses of Abawyth, and I will take my leave."

Evony's smile faded instantly, her hands beginning to tremble where they lay in her lap. "I-I must have your word, Prince Stavos," she began.

"Stavos," he mumbled in correcting her.

Again Evony was struck by the oddity of his not wanting to be addressed by a title.

"Very well, Stavos," she managed. "I must have your word that what I confide in you must never be revealed…not to anyone…not ever."

Evony was rendered suddenly breathless as the ever-so-handsome man unexpectedly took her hands in his, kissing the back of each one and vowing, "You have my word. I will not reveal whatever it is you offer to me—not to anyone—unless you wish me to reveal all at some future time." Evony was yet unable to speak as he frowned, clasping her hands firmly between his own and mumbling, "Your hands are far too cold."

Again overwhelmingly affected by his touch, Evony attempted to distract herself from the wild elation washing over her and hurried to tell him what she first must. "You must not go to the castle yet," she told him. "Not today…not tomorrow. First you must insinuate yourself into the goings-on at the inn in the woods nearby."

Stavos frowned. "Why?" he asked plainly. "And what goings-on?"

Evony leaned toward him, lowering her voice so that Mikol and Tressa could not hear from their place at helping Miss Lovie clear the table and put away the food.

"There *are* goings-on there," Evony whispered in confidence. "I am trusting my intuition in confiding this in you, sire. But there are goings-on at the inn in the woods, and you have my vow—I swear it to you—that what happens there is woven as tightly with what is wrong and evil at Abawyth Castle as madness is woven with an impassable labyrinth."

"What do you mean?" Stavos asked.

"I must ask you to go to the inn in the woods. It is called the Hungry Horse, and it is a known meeting place for both those of wealth and means as well as paupers and villains," she began to explain. Evony was, in truth, astonished when Stavos did not argue or question her in that instant but only waited in silent interest for her to continue. "You must register there…procure a room. Do not tell the innkeeper nor anyone you meet *why* you have come to Abawyth. Only pretend you are a traveler and that you are interested in any sort of entertainment the village, inn, or surrounding area might offer."

It was then that Stavos released Evony's now warmed hands—that he drew a deep breath and exhaled it slowly as his eyes narrowed in studying her.

"There is more to this," he began, "but you do not fully trust me as yet, do you? I can see it in your pauses…in your trembling."

"I-I am only weary, sire," Evony responded. After all, she was weary. She had been up all the night and had injured her ankle; she was more than weary. And yet he had read her countenance. She had told him far too much already, and she paused in offering more.

"I am a stranger, after all," he said. Grinning, he added, "A stranger who nearly trampled you to death in the street only a short time ago."

"And she needs her breakfast," Lovie announced, arriving with a plate heaped with good food. Smiling with the compassion and care of a mother, Lovie placed the plate on Evony's lap. Then, looking to Stavos, she said, "Perhaps you could return later in the day…after our Evony has rested and her mind is not so foggy from fatigue."

Stavos rose from his seat on Evony's bedside. Again his eyes narrowed as he studied her, and Evony felt the beads of nervous perspiration caused by his attention beading on her forehead.

"You have offered me a start, Miss Evony," Stavos said. "And I see now that I must be patient…that I must earn your trust. Therefore, I am off to discover this inn in the woods—this Hungry Horse—wherein I will procure a room and tell no one of my true purpose here. Then, upon the morrow, I will return. And perhaps, after some rest, you will be inspired to share more confidence with me."

Evony held her breath as Stavos leaned down, placing his face near to her ear. "I know there is more to you, Miss Evony…more to all this than is evident by appearances. And I will keep your secrets safe…cache them away so as you do not worry. I promise."

He straightened to his full height once more, smiled at her, and said, "Now eat your ham and eggs. You need your strength. Goodness knows that old hag Agnes Teche will work your fingers to the very bone with stitching for her once you are well enough."

Evony found she could not speak but only wipe at the tears escaping her eyes—wish she were not so fatigued that her emotions lingered so weak and near the surface.

"There is one thing more that I would bid you, Prince Stavos," Mikol interjected unexpectedly.

"And what might that be, Michael?" Stavos asked. He grinned and teased, "You aren't planning to try and barter Bromius away from me, are you?"

Mikol smiled, shaking his head. "No…though I would if I could," he answered.

"Then what is it tasks your mind?" Stavos asked.

"Well, I do not know how you came by the knowledge of Evony's name, but if you have reason to refer to her or to address her further, I would ask that you address her as Miss Edith…and not Miss Evony."

Evony's eyes widened as another measure of fear gripped her. How could she have been so careless? Of course Stavos must address her as Edith! Just as she had told him Mikol's name was Michael and Tressa's was Tess, so must no one hear him refer to her as Evony!

Frantically she thought back over the morning's events. Had he addressed her as Evony in Agnes Teche's company? She was sure he hadn't, and she sighed with relief.

"Miss Edith it is then," Prince Stavos agreed, "at least outside the realm of your home. I cannot give up Evony entirely. It is such a beautiful name."

"Agreed," Mikol said with a nod.

Stavos looked about the room then. "What a pleasure it was to take my breakfast with you all," he said, taking Lovie's hand in his and gallantly stooping to kiss the back of it. "Michael, thank you for caring for Bromius for me, and, Tess, thank you for being such a gracious hostess."

Tressa giggled and dipped another perfect curtsy as Mikol offered his hand to Stavos. "You are a good and generous man, Prince Stavos," he said as Stavos accepted his handshake. "We are grateful for your help."

"It was my pleasure," Stavos said. "Indeed, my honor." He turned to Evony once more. "I will return tomorrow morning, Miss Evony. And in the meantime, I will endeavor to further earn your trust."

"You have already, sire," Evony managed as more tears brimmed in her eyes. Then as he made to take his leave, she remembered his fur cloak—the one he'd covered her with to warm her. "Prince Stavos!" she exclaimed, causing him to quickly turn on his heels. He wore a worried, rather puzzled expression. "Your...your cloak."

Yet as she began to move the plate of food on her lap in order to remove the cloak beneath it, Stavos raised a hand. Shaking his head, he said, "No, please, miss. Keep it through the night. I will sleep better knowing you are warm enough beneath it. Tomorrow will be soon enough for me to retrieve it."

He smiled once more, nodded to Miss Lovie, and crossed the threshold, closing the door behind him.

"He knows we are not who we pretend to be," Mikol announced with a heavy sigh. He looked to Evony, scowling somewhat. "I hope you are right to trust him, Evony."

Even for the anxious trembling that once again overwhelmed her, Evony nodded. "It is my soul that trusts him...not my mind, Mikol. My soul tells me Prince Stavos is the champion the princesses require. If all this treachery is to ever end—if evil is ever to be driven out of Abawyth and Elawyth—we cannot do it alone. That much has been before us from the beginning."

"Eat something, Evony," Lovie encouraged. "You are weak and tired and hurt. Eat and rest." Then looking to Mikol and Tressa, she added, "We will see what tomorrow brings. But for me...I trust your sister's instincts, Mikol. And so must you. Evony's intuition has saved you all before, and it will again. Mark my words. It will again."

Mikol sighed and nodded. "You're right. I will do my best to trust this prince, Evony." He paused a moment and then smiled. "After all, what is there to doubt in a man who would own such a horse?"

Evony smiled—even felt a giggle of amusement rise in her famished throat. And as the first bite of wonderful, nourishing, savory ham touched her tongue, her soul whispered to her that Prince Stavos Voronin of Ethiarien had indeed been led to them—to her and Mikol and Tressa—to Miss Lovie—and to her cousins, the twelve sleepy princesses of Abawyth.

CHAPTER THREE

Mikol was such a good boy—so helpful and thoughtful. He would make an exceptional king one day—that is, if King Standwood did not succeed in having him imprisoned or assassinated. Evony was grateful Mikol had stoked the fire again before retiring himself. Though she was cozy and warm (ethereally warm) beneath the soft sable cloak Prince Stavos had left for her, the added warmth in the room made Evony feel as if she were bathing in pure luxury.

The comforting glow of the fire, the soft shadows it created, dancing above her on the ceiling, the crackle of the burning wood—all of it attempted to soothe Evony's worried mind and tired body. She was still weary, even for having slept the most part of the day. Yet now—now in the late hours of the cold night, her thoughts followed a turbulent venue once more.

Should she have trusted Prince Stavos? Even though she had not revealed anything of great importance to him, should she have trusted him? Evony's heart and soul assured her that she was doing right by taking him into her confidence. It was only the fear rooted in her mind that caused her to doubt. Still, fear was such a brutally powerful thing, and Evony yet worried.

Unable to find respite through sleep for the sake of lingering worry and self-doubt, Evony tried to twist her thoughts to the day weeks before, when she first fully understood the danger she and her siblings (especially Mikol) were in.

It seemed an age ago that she and Mikol and Tressa had quietly abandoned their kingdom of Elawyth in search of assistance. When Abawyth's queen had disappeared—followed shortly by the disappearance of Elawyth's queen—Abawyth and Elawyth, being sister kingdoms, had both fallen to the rule of Evony's step-uncle, Kind Standwood Warde.

Queen Raina Thaybwyn Lardosean Warde of Abawyth had gone missing nearly two months before. Only seven days later, her twin sister, Queen Charmaine Thaybwyn Elorietta of Elawyth—mother to Princess Evony, Prince Mikol, and Princess Tressa—had also vanished. Both kingdoms were thoroughly searched, as were all outer kingdoms, but nothing was to be found—nothing save the dead and stiffened body of Queen Raina's small dog, Dirkish.

It seemed Queen Raina had left the castle to wander with Dirkish in the east gardens one cool late winter morning. It was the last time anyone had seen the beautiful queen—the queen of Abawyth, the queen who had borne six sets of twin girls of her beloved first husband, King Albert (who was killed in a tragic hunting accident some years prior).

Many suspected that Queen Raina's second husband, King Standwood Warde, was responsible for Queen Raina's disappearance. Standwood's thirst for power was no secret to the subjects of Abawyth, and the whispers in both kingdoms placed blame on King Standwood.

Yet when Queen Charmaine of Elawyth vanished only seven days after her sister, the whispers turned a bit, from King Standwood to superstition and witchery. How could Standwood have had any hand in the vanishing of Elawyth's queen?

Evony and her siblings had been devastated at the loss of their beloved mother, their father King Thomas having died only two years before of consumption. Evony worried that some dark evil might come upon them without their mother's powerful rule to protect them Naturally, the servants were loyal enough, and her mother's counselors. Yet a feeling of impending doom mingled with her despairing state of mourning her mother's loss. Even when messengers had promptly arrived from Abawyth, bearing promises from King Standwood that all would be well, Evony's misgivings heightened instead of lessening.

Mikol, being only ten years of age, was considered too young to rule Elawyth in King Standwood's proud opinion. Thus, when the rule of both kingdoms fell to Standwood, he sent with his messengers a lord to stand as steward over the kingdom of Elawyth until Mikol reached the age of twelve and could more easily claim the crown. Her mother's own counselors felt Standwood's appointment of a steward was wise. And after all, Mikol would be twelve in less than two years, at which point he could take the crown and rule Elawyth.

But it was near immediately after Lord Rothvern's arrival in Elawyth that Evony determined the lord was loyal only to King Standwood. He had no respect nor care for Queen Charmaine's children—especially her only son and male heir, Mikol.

When a loyal kitchen cook confided in Evony that Lord Rothvern had ordered a strict diet be fed to Mikol of only broth, bread, and water—for Lord Rothvern's physician claimed Mikol was at an unhealthy pudginess—Evony's fears mounted. Mikol was a slender youth, with the veracious appetite expected of a growing boy. Yet Lord Rothvern would himself stand sentry over Mikol at mealtime. And when Evony awoke late one night with an eerie sense that she should check on her brother, upon entering his bedchamber, she found that someone had opened all his windows, allowing the cold of the dead of winter to turn the room in which he slept to a frigid temperature. His fire had been snuffed as well. It was then that Evony knew Mikol was in danger—perhaps she and Tressa as well, for Evony would inherit the throne of Elawyth if Mikol were lost to some tragedy. Tressa would inherit if Evony were then lost. Yes, the discovery of Mikol's open windows and snuffed fire confirmed to Evony that they were not safe in their own kingdom.

Therefore, though she disliked her step-uncle, King Standwood, her suspicions fell first to Lord Rothvern. She wondered if perhaps he meant to kill all of Queen Charmaine's heirs and then somehow claim Elawyth for his own when she, Mikol, and Tressa had all been vanquished.

And so, with assistance of a few loyal servants, Evony had spirited Mikol and Tressa away from Elawyth, hoping to find safety and aid in Abawyth.

Evony turned in her bed—pulled Prince Stavos's warm, soft sable cloak more snuggly around her shoulders. Exhaling a heavy sigh of discouragement at the memory of what had awaited her and her siblings at Abawyth Castle, she continued in her reveries, wondering how much of it all she should reveal to Prince Stavos when he returned on the morrow—if he returned.

King Standwood had seemed sincerely concerned when Evony, Mikol, and Tressa had first appeared before him to explain why they had fled Elawyth and Lord Rothvern's stewardship. He had embrace them all, professed his love and concern, and promised to help them—to remove Rothvern from his position as steward of Elawyth. After all his promises to help and protect were made, King Standwood summoned one of Abawyth's twelve princesses, the princess Patrice, to escort Evony and her siblings to a nourishing meal and warm bed chambers.

Yet when Princess Patrice led Evony, Mikol, and Tressa not to bedchambers of their own but to the large and lavish chambers Patrice shared with her eleven sisters, the true evil of what had become of Abawyth's and Elawyth's vanished twin queens began to be revealed.

"I want you to take Tressa to Miss Lovie's when Prince Stavos arrives, Mikol," Evony tenderly instructed her brother. "If he arrives, that is."

Mikol frowned. "He is an Ethiarien royal, Evony," he grumbled. "Of course he'll arrive." Mikol's frown deepened as he studied his elder sister from head to toe a moment. "And you should not be on your feet, Evony. Your ankle needs respite."

Evony smiled and tousled Mikol's dark hair. He was so protective of both her and Tressa—and even Miss Lovie now. She could see the weight of responsibility already settling on his shoulders, even though he would not be king of Elawyth for near two more years. In that moment, Evony felt tears brimming in her eyes, for as much as she loved Elawyth, its beauty as it nestled in the foothills of the mountains—as much as she loved the subjects of her kingdom, desperately wishing for a kind, concerned, and protective monarch to rule them—she loved Mikol so much more and wished she could somehow whisk him away from the responsibility he would one day know. Tressa too. If Evony's deepest wishes could be granted, she would wish Mikol, Tressa, and herself to some distant, warm, green place where the responsibility of an entire kingdom did not rest on them.

But she further understood duty to birthright. And as much as she wished for safety and a less public life for the children of Queen Charmaine Elorietta, she did not wish to see the people in her kingdom suffer under the stewardship of Lord Rothvern, nor the rule of King Standwood.

Exhaling a heavy sigh, Evony told her brother, "My ankle does not pain me so much as you might think, Mikol. I think the long day and night of rest truly did the necessary healing. I should well be able to return to Mrs. Teche's shop tomorrow."

A growl of irritation rumbled in Mikol's throat as he angrily mumbled, "Wonderful."

The firm rapping on the door startled them all, Evony's heart leaping into her bosom with anxiety of a sudden.

"I'll answer it," Mikol offered. Striding to the door with the sure posture and determination of a captain of the guard, Mikol asked, "Who is there?"

"Stavos Voronin," came the deep, booming voice of Prince Stavos of Ethiarien.

"Very well," Mikol called as he lifted the heavy bolt he had drawn across the door the night before. As the door swung open, he greeted, "Good morning, Prince—I mean, Stavos."

Stavos smiled, nodded to Mikol, and greeted, "Good morning, Michael."

At the very sight of him, Evony gasped, her heart skipping erratically in her bosom. There he stood—tall, black-booted, wearing fitted gray trousers and a crisp white shirt, black cravat, and red vest.

Evony gulped down the lump that had accompanied the quiet gasp in her throat and forced a friendly smile as he looked at her and greeted, "Good morning, *Edith*."

"Good morning, Prince—good morning, Stavos," she managed.

Tressa dipped a curtsy and giggled, "Good morning, Stavos. Did you sleep well?"

"Like a rock," Stavos answered, smiling at the little girl.

"But where's Bromius?" Mikol asked, peering out the door and into the street with disappointment.

"I stabled him in the village," Stavos answered. He looked to Evony, adding, "My thinking was that perhaps I should not be so obvious in my comings and goings to your home…lest I draw too much unwanted attention."

Evony blushed under his piercing gaze and alluring smile. "Thank you for that," she said in a lowered voice. "I-I am sorry you must be so inconvenienced."

"It's no inconvenience," Stavos assured her. His smile broadened as he added, "And if it were…what matter is a little inconvenience when the solving of a mystery and a princess's hand in marriage may be the rewards, hmm?"

"Mmm hmmm," she mumbled, momentarily distracted by the perfect shape of his lips—the thin, whiskerless outline around his mouth between his lips and his two or three days of whisker growth. His upper lip was so flawlessly formed with a faultless V shape in its middle that Evony's fingers began to twitch with wanting to reach up and trace it. By contrast, his lower lip was full, but not exaggeratedly so—just full enough to make Evony unconsciously bite her own lower lip as she wondered what it would feel like to have such a masculinely perfect set of lips press a kiss to her cheek.

"Come with me, Tess," Mikol said then, rattling Evony from her mesmerization with Stavos's mouth. "Miss Lovie is waiting for us to help her with…uh…with the wash."

"But I want to stay here with Evony and Prince Stavos," Tressa quietly whined.

Stavos chuckled. "How about I make you a promise, Miss Tess?" he began.

Tressa smiled, of course, delighted with his attention.

"How about I promise that I will not leave without lunching with you, hmmm? Let me have a bit of time alone to talk with your sister about some things…then we will all enjoy a luncheon. All right?"

Tressa smiled. "All right," she agreed. Then with one more curtsy, she clasped Mikol's hand. "Let's go help Miss Lovie," she said. Then lowering her voice to a giggling whisper, she added, "I wonder if I might convince him to treat us to a pastry at the baker's shop."

"Hush, Tess! We don't want him to think we're beggars," Mikol quietly scolded.

As Mikol closed the door behind them, Evony felt every nerve in her body begin to ingle with a mingling of anxiety and excitement. She was alone in the room with a man! And not just any man—the most handsome of men to walk the earth!

"You were right," Stavos began as he strode to a chair near the hearth. "The Hungry Horse is a place of very diverse patronage." He took a seat in the chair and looked up at Evony with obvious expectation. "Not the sort of establishment one enters carelessly."

Stavos dwarfed the chair upon which he sat. Where it had once appeared as big as any other chair in the world, it now looked as if it had been fashioned for a child.

"Indeed not," Evony agreed as she moved to join him in a chair sitting opposite his.

The man frowned as he watched her take her seat. "Your ankle is well enough that you are walking already?" he inquired.

"Mmm hmm," Evony assured him with a grin of pride in her quick healing. "I should be more than well enough to sew for Mrs. Teche tomorrow."

"Wonderful," Stavos grumbled, frowning. He inhaled slowly, exhaling as if he were more than just a little irritated. However, at last he began. "Well, Miss Evony, I have done what you asked of me…taken a room at the Hungry Horse Inn in the woods and told no one of my purpose here. Have I earned enough of your trust that I might bid you share with me a bit more of what you know about this…this enigma plaguing the kingdom?"

"Did…did the innkeeper…did he mention to you anything…well, anything that seemed strange? Very out of the ordinary, I mean?" she asked in response.

Stavos's eyes narrowed. "I did as asked in this regard as well…inquiring of the innkeeper of what sorts of entertainment Abawyth might offer a traveler."

"And?" Evony prompted as the rising anxiety and hope in her began to quicken the rhythm of her heart.

"He said nothing," Stavos answered. But when Evony's shoulders slumped with visible disappointment, he leaned toward her, adding, "Until I placed a piece of silver on the table before him."

"And then?" Evony breathed in a whisper of renewed optimism.

Stavos grinned the most handsome grin Evony had ever enjoyed from a man as he said, "Well, apparently there is to be a dance tonight…late tonight. In fact, it does not begin until near midnight, and I swore on peril of my life never to reveal a knowledge that this dance even exists. He called it the Midnight Masquerade and promised me that I would enjoy myself thoroughly." Stavos sat back in his chair. "He then reminded me that I would wake to find my throat being cut in the middle of the night if I ever revealed the existence of this Midnight Masquerade to anyone."

"He threatened to kill you?" Evony asked in horror.

"He did," Stavos confirmed, "though he presented the information and invitation to participate with a friendly enough smile…and an assurance that I would find the evening well worth the risk."

But Evony was already trembling with such fear for Stavos's safety—and guilt for having brought him to edge of such danger—that she silently considered telling him to run, to escape Abawyth and the evil lingering in it, before he came to any harm.

Nevertheless, Stavos was nothing if not observant and instantly sensed her disquiet. Reaching out, he leaned toward her again, taking her trembling hands in his warm, steady grasp.

"Tell me what I need to know in order to help you, Miss Evony," he said. His voice was low—soothing as a breeze through the supple leaves of bedecked summer trees. "What is this Midnight Masquerade? And why would this vile innkeeper tell me of it, only to follow up the sharing of knowledge with such a serious threat?"

"I-I think you should not…" Evony began.

But as Stavos's hands released hers—as he reached up, cupping her face firmly—she could not think of what she had been about to say.

"I have come to Abawyth to solve this wild mystery surrounding her princesses. And at my father's bidding, I have come to win the hand of one of them…to win a bride," he explained. "But having met you—your Michael and Tess and Miss Lovie—I am now determined to assist you and yours as well. I know there is much you are not telling me…that you're all hiding. I know you must be in danger. And I will help you. I am no coward, Evony. If you are in distress or danger, I will champion you and your siblings, as eagerly as I will champion Abawyth's twelve sleepy princesses. So do not let your own courage fail you now. Do not worry for my sake. I am more capable than I perhaps appear to you."

So overcome by the euphoria induced by his touch, however, Evony could not immediately find her own voice. As her trembling did, indeed, begin to diminish a whit—as the heat of his palms seemed to travel from her cheeks to fill her entire body with a much-desired warmth—she could only stare at him a moment, eventually managing a slight nod in response.

"Very well then," he said. "Tell me more of what you know—or even suspect—and I will do my worst to solve this plague on this kingdom…and free you from whatever it is you're hiding from."

"I-I suppose…I suppose I should begin at the beginning," Evony stammered.

Stavos sat back in his chair, relaxed, folding his arms across his broad chest as if he would wait a lifetime in order to hear what Evony had to say.

"Usually the best place to begin," he agreed.

Evony gulped down the lump of anxiety that had taken up residence in her throat. Then sighing in an attempt to settle her nerves, she began, "Do you know the story of Abawyth?" she asked. "The history of Abawyth and its sister kingdom, Elawyth? Of the twin queens…the twin daughters of the great ruler, King Rowan Thaybwyn?"

"Yes," Stavos answered, "though I think I would like to hear it again…if you please. To refresh my memory."

And so, being that he bid her to tell him the story, Evony continued, "King Rowan Thaybwyn was a meritorious king. He ruled his kingdom Abawyth with wisdom, compassion, and yet a powerful sense of protection of its people. Still, no sons were born to Rowan Thaybwyn and his queen Aylethia—only two daughters, twins, and the queen named them Raina and Charmaine.

"The twin princesses of Abawyth grew in beauty and were loved and cherished, not only by their parents, the king and queen, but also by all the subjects of the kingdom. Far and wide Princess Raina and Princess Charmaine were loved…from the castle of Abawyth here to the far reaches of the beautiful city at the foot of the mountains, Elawyth, that marked the northern border of the kingdom.

"All of Abawyth knew that one day King Rowan would pass away—being that death is, after all, inevitable—and that when he did, Abawyth would have a dowager queen in Aylethia (if she survived him) and that the crown would pass to Princess Raina…her being the first of the two twin princesses to be born."

The grin that slowly spread across Stavos's face caused Evony to blush as he studied her—and to wonder what it was he found so amusing in her story.

"What?" she asked. "Am I forgetting something in the telling?"

But Stavos shook his head, his grin broadening. "Not at all. I'm simply noting how truly the story resembles a folktale or some such thing."

Evony smiled with relief, nodding with agreement. "It does, doesn't it?"

"But please…forgive my interruption and continue," Stavos bid her.

"Very well," Evony said. "Yet, even as his daughters both grew strong and began to manifest all characteristics of one day being kind and wise leaders themselves, King Rowan worried that the kingdom of Abawyth had grown too broad for one monarch to rule successfully. Therefore, on his deathbed, he bisected the kingdom of Abawyth, naming Princess Raina as the queen and ruler of Abawyth and crowning Princess Charmaine queen of the smaller kingdom of Elawyth.

"King Rowan's desire was that Elawyth be fortified with its own monarchy, royal guard, troops, and everything else the farthest reaches of the once north border of Abawyth required. When the heralds announced King Rowan's demands, all of Abawyth cheered, for they knew that the kingdom had grown vast and therefore that the farthest stretches of it stood vulnerable. Thus, with its own queen, its own castle, guard, and soldiers, Elawyth would be safe, and Abawyth could rest easier. And besides, each kingdom would have a queen beloved by the people. And all was well…for a time."

Stavos sighed when Evony paused. "For a time, for more than twenty years…until just months ago, when both the queen of Abawyth and the queen of Elawyth vanished without a trace or explanation and this plague of lethargy overtook the twelve princesses of Abawyth," he offered.

"Yes," Evony admitted. She continued, "Upon their father's death, as crowned queens of their sister kingdoms, Queen Raina of Abawyth married Prince Albert Lardosean of faraway Mariamwim, and Queen Charmaine of Elawyth was wed to Prince Thomas Elorietta of Breac. Both queens were fortunate to love and be loved by their spousal kings.

"Now, once wedded, it soon became apparent that Queen Raina of Abawyth had inherited the blessing of bearing sets of twins as progeny and heirs. Over the course of a mere eight years, Queen Raina bore six different sets of twins…all surviving and every set a pair of girls."

"The famed twelve princesses of Abawyth," Stavos offered, shaking his head with astonished admiration. "Six sets of twins. It's nearly unfathomable."

"Yes," Evony agreed. "And yet Queen Raina retained her beauty and strength. She ruled Abawyth as her father had, with only concern for the welfare of her people. And when her beloved King Albert was killed in a tragic accident, Queen Raina recognized that it had weakened her emotions and strength. And for the sake of her people—for she imagined a new king would stabilize their worries…her worries—she married Standwood Warde, a widowed lord of Mariamwim and distant cousin to King Albert.

"Though not blessed with twelve children, Charmaine of Elawyth did have children, including a male heir that would one day rule Elawyth just as Queen Charmaine's father had once ruled all of Abawyth, with wisdom and strength for his people. Yet Queen Charmaine knew tragedy as well, for she lost her own beloved, Thomas, to consumption…and only six weeks to the day after Queen Raina lost King Albert."

"A tragic story," Stavos mumbled, "that both queens lost their lovers."

"Yes," Evony whispered, willing the tears brimming in her eyes to dissipate. "And it was only the span of a few months following Queen Raina's second marriage to Standwood Warde that the rumors began to spread."

"Rumors?" Stavos asked, slowly sitting straight in his chair. "What rumors? I have heard nothing of this part of the history."

"And you won't, not from many, for few knew of it—of the rumored intentions the sister queens had of reuniting the kingdom of Elawyth with her mother kingdom of Abawyth."

"What?" Stavos asked. "The queens meant to reunite the kingdoms? Why?"

Lowering her voice, Evony whispered, "To save both Abawyth and Elawyth from the tyranny and greed-driven rule of King Standwood."

Stavos frowned. "But…but there are twelve heirs to Abawyth's throne…and at least one male heir to Elawyth's." He paused, his eyes narrowing as understanding settled in his mind. "Unless it was supposed that King Standwood would take Abawyth for his own."

But Evony only shrugged. She could not reveal too much of what she knew or suspected. "It *is* what the rumors circulate in the hushed parts of both kingdoms." She paused a moment, captured Stavos's gaze with her own, and then breathed, "And then, all at once, within mere days of one another…both queens mysteriously disappeared. And shortly thereafter, the twelve princesses of Abawyth were overcome with the strange lethargy that seems to consume them."

"And you think Standwood is at the center of it?" Stavos asked.

But Evony began to fear she had already revealed too much. And so quickly she reminded, "I think I can help you to solve what ails the princesses of Abawyth and to win the hand of one of them for your bride."

Again Stavos's eyes narrowed, and he studied her for a moment. "Which will give Abawyth an ally…my father's kingdom of Ethiarien."

Evony felt her brows pucker into a frown. "I-I hadn't thought of that…but yes!" she exclaimed with sudden realization. "It would!" She couldn't keep from smiling, for Abawyth certainly was in need of an ally.

"You hadn't thought of it?" Stavos inquired with obvious skepticism. "Then your intent was not to gain an ally for this kingdom?"

"No…though I will not deny it is something to be considered, is it not?" Clearing her throat, Evony rushed on. "I have seen this Midnight Masquerade at the Hungry Horse Inn," Evony interrupted, even though it was bad-mannered. She did not want Stavos to follow the line of thinking he had begun. Rather, she wanted to turn his attention from why she had been so overjoyed at the prospect of winning a powerful kingdom the likes of Ethiarien as Abawyth's ally and back to the evil presence lingering in Abawyth Castle.

"You have?" Stavos asked, astonished.

"I-I have," Evony admitted. "And I admit now that it is why I sent you there—why I asked that you procure a room there...and that you not share your true reason for being here with the innkeeper."

Stavos frowned. "I am growing...unsettlingly curious with the fact that you ask me to do these things and then give me no reason...no explanation of how you have come to own such knowledge or how it is that you can help me with my quest to solve this mystery."

Evony nodded, humbly, and with complete understanding. He meant he was impatient, not simply curious. Stavos had stepped into the dark, somehow having mustered enough confidence in Evony's countenance when he met her to trust her. She must stop holding in all the secrets she knew. She must share them with him—or at least share a great deal of them with him.

"You have been very valiant in what you've been willing to do...and only on my word and promise of help," she told him. Then, inhaling a deep breath in an attempt to settle her nerves, she continued, "Every night at the Hungry Horse Inn, the innkeeper holds a ball...a dance of sorts in a large room that is cut off from the inn's guest chambers and eating establishment. Each night there arrive in this room, and by way of a path through the forest and a hidden door leading to the room, more than twenty young women. These young women enter already dressed in lavish ball gowns and with masquerade masks hiding their eyes, noses...to hide their identities. Once in the large room, a spinet begins to play, and the young women are then approached by men, also masked. Once a man chooses a young woman, the innkeeper collects coins from the man, and only then is the man allowed to dance with the young woman of his choosing. They dance to two musical pieces, and then he leaves his partner to choose another young woman, pressing coins into the innkeeper's hand before the music starts again."

Stavos noted the pretty pink blush that rose to Evony's cheeks as she described the scene she had witnessed—men paying to dance with women. He knew she was uncomfortable speaking of such indecent goings-on, yet he needed to know more—especially if he were to infiltrate this Midnight Masquerade. Furthermore, though he suspected the reason, he wanted affirmation as to the connection between the Midnight Masquerade held in such secret at the inn in the woods and the mystery surrounding the lethargy of the twelve princesses of Abawyth.

And so he asked, "Is there only dancing that the innkeeper is paid for, Evony?" He watched her eyes widen as horrible understanding washed over her.

"Of course!" she answered far too quickly, and with far too much certainty—certainty he could see she did not fully own. "They would never…the women never endure more than…more than…perhaps…a wandering hand from her partner now and again."

"A wandering hand now and then?" Stavos asked.

Evony's blush deepened, and she glanced away for a moment. "It is all I have observed," she nearly whispered in response.

"And why is this Midnight Masquerade so important that I need to know of it? To involve myself at the Hungry Horse and its secret debaucheries?"

He watched as Evony's small hands began to tremble where she clasped them in her lap. Yet she straightened her posture, looked him squarely in the eyes, and, with a quivering lower lip, answered, "Because…because twelve of the masked women who are dancing with the innkeeper's patrons in order to line his pockets with coin are the twelve princesses of Abawyth."

CHAPTER FOUR

Evony watched as Prince Stavos's alluring eyes narrowed, not with astonishment but with an expression of deep concern—or even perhaps anger or vexation.

"And you know the princesses are some of the women how exactly?" he asked.

"I-I've seen them unmasked," Evony stammered. "I followed them through the forest one night once this wicked Midnight Masquerade the innkeeper manipulates had ended. I had seen them leave the back rooms of the inn. They were moving toward the castle…and had removed their masks. All twelve were present."

Stavos exhaled a heavy, rather worried sounding sigh. "And why are the princesses involved in such a disgraceful business? Why would they choose—"

"I don't think they have chosen this, sire," Evony answered. "I think they are being forced to…to participate." Evony swallowed the nervous tickle in her throat and added, "The truth is…I *know* they are being forced to these ends. It's why I can help you to—"

"What do you mean, you *know* they are being forced?" Stavos nearly growled. Evony watched as every visible muscle in his body tensed. "You've known all along that the princesses of this kingdom are being forced to such measures, and yet you've told no one?"

"But I haven't known all along!" Evony defended herself, fearfully. As tears leapt to her eyes, she experienced a sudden sense of panic—panic not for the sake of the princesses' well-being, the safety of her own cousins, but panic in the growing fear that Prince Stavos Voronin of Ethiarien would think less of her than he may already. "I only just discovered the princesses' involvement in the Midnight Masquerade some seven days ago," she explained. "Before that…I only knew that the missing Queen Raina is not dead—that she is most assuredly alive—and I likewise began to hope that Elawyth's Queen Charmaine is also still—"

But Stavos was on his feet now. "What?" he nearly roared. "You know that the missing queens are alive?" He was angry, and the expression on his face—the sheer countenance of him—was overwhelming in its intimidation.

"I know Queen Raina is alive…but I am only speculating over her sister, Queen Charmaine," Evony managed to answer.

"But why have you not told someone?" Stavos asked in frustrated unawareness. "Why have you allowed the queens' disappearances and the princesses' involvement in—"

Leaping to her feet as well, Evony cried, "Because I think the queen is still in danger! I think the innkeeper at the Hungry Horse knows where she is…and that he, perhaps, is using his knowledge of her whereabouts to manipulate the princesses into doing his bidding. I can fathom no other reason or explanation for their behavior!" Wiping tears from her cheeks, she continued, "And I *am* telling someone. I'm telling someone *now*. I'm telling *you*." Her words seemed to calm him somewhat, and as he inhaled a deep breath to further settle his temperament, Evony added, "And there is more. I fear this wickedness goes much deeper…has roots spread throughout the entire kingdom."

"Why is that?" Stavos asked.

Evony gulped with still lingering fear and brushed more tears from her cheeks. "Because…of the more than twenty women I witnessed participating in that despicable Midnight Masquerade, at least half of them, including several of the princesses, were wearing dresses that I recognize as coming from Agnes Teche's shop." She looked up into his smoldering blue eyes, wishing he were not frowning so severely at her. "Three of the dresses were made by *me*."

"So your hag of an employer is somehow involved, hmmm?" he mumbled.

Evony watched then as, in the very next moment, Stavos's frown softened, his handsome brows arching with astonishment as he breathed an incredulous laugh. "I have to admit to you, Miss Evony, when I arrived to meet with you this morning, I could not have fathomed you would reveal all *this* to me. I thought that perchance Abawyth's princesses were being slowly poisoned somehow—that some malignancy were plaguing them. Indeed, I assumed you had somehow come by a knowledge of it. But I never could have imagined all of this—to be forced into improper associations with strange men, in order to somehow protect their mother? It's unbelievable."

"But you do believe me, don't you, your highness?" Evony ventured. "I swear on my own life that—"

"I believe you, Miss Evony," Stavos assured her. "I am not so ignorant as you might presume to such goings-on as this—to evil men manipulating women." He paused, shaking his head in awe. "But this…to be brazen enough to involve royalty. The Hungry Horse's innkeeper is a fool for this Midnight Masquerade undertaking…and an utter imbecile to involve royals in such a scheme."

Evony exhaled the tightened breath she'd been holding. He believed her! Prince Stavos truly believed her! The realization not only brought a sensation of relief and hope to buoy her spirits but also filled her body with renewed vigor.

"The man is a fool…and far from a master strategist, I am sure," she offered.

"Exactly," Stavos agreed. "I've met this miscreant. He could not have conceived this entire plot, let alone implemented it…not on his own. No, the Hungry Horse's owner—this Ewan Happer, they name him—he is not the most intellectual of men. But he is obviously filled with malevolent intent. As maliciously greedy as he is dimwitted."

Exhaling another long sigh of relief in hope, Evony smiled. "I knew I could trust you," she confessed. "The moment I had my wits about me after nearly being trampled by your Bromius…I somehow knew you were the man to help Abawyth and its princesses."

Stavos grinned, unexpectedly stepping toward Evony and gathering her yet trembling hands in his own. "I'm pleased that something, or rather most likely a *divine* something or someone, prompted you to trust me, Princess Evony Elorietta."

Evony gasped in astonishment and returning fear at hearing Stavos address her by her royal title. But before she could respond otherwise, Prince Stavos dropped to one knee before her, raising her hands to his lips and placing a lingering kiss to the back of each one. The backs of her hands felt as if they'd only just been delightfully branded! A warm, tingling sensation traveled from the place where he'd kissed each one, up and over Evony's arms, until her neck, face, and ears burned with delight.

She knew it would be pointless to deny her true identity any longer. Therefore, she simply stammered, "H-how did you know?"

Stavos chuckled, still kneeling—still clasping her hands in his.

"The moment I stepped into your home and saw your brother's countenance, your sister's proper curtsey, and heard them repeat your name once more, as Miss Lovie had…*Evony*." He arched one handsome brow as he studied her a moment, adding, "Evony. It is not so common a name as you might think. And besides, Michael— or should I say *Mikol*—is not the only prince who was forced to study and memorize royal lines by his tutors."

Evony blushed, feeling foolish, even as she worried over how easily Prince Stavos had recognized her and her siblings. If he had so easily noticed the details that revealed their true identities, how easily might others suspect?

"But…why then did you not call us out at once?" she asked.

Stavos's smile faded as a look of concern overtook his expression. "I knew something was amiss…foul indeed if it found two princesses and a young heir prince in hiding as the three of you are. I further sensed that if I revealed my suspicions to you, you would not trust me with what you knew, or what you stood in need of, whether it be for your cousins' sakes or your own."

"Are we so terribly transparent?" Evony asked, still very concerned.

Stavos grinned and raised her hands to his lips, kissing the backs of each once more. "Only to a fellow royal who is known to be wildly observant and curious."

He released her hands an instant before he rose then, and Evony was astonished by the disappointment the absence of his touch caused to settle in her.

Stavos returned to the chair across from her and, after having taken his seat once more, asked, "And now that so much is revealed between us…why not reveal it all?" He paused, winking at her with reassurance.

"I don't know it all," Evony sighed with defeat as she rather slumped back down in her own chair.

"Then tell me what you do know," Stavos prodded, "and we'll speculate from there. All right?"

Evony nodded. "All right," she agreed, hoping she could explain what she knew as understandably as she could.

Drawing a deep breath, she began to tell the handsome Prince Stavos of Ethiarien of all she had come to know. "It was not long after Abawyth's Queen Raina vanished that Elawyth's queen—my mother, Queen Charmaine—vanished as well," Evony explained. "I- I saw her that morning at breakfast, just before she set out to walk in the southern gardens of Elawyth Castle." Hardly aware she was doing so, Evony raised her hand and placed her fingers to her right cheek—the place her mother had kissed her that morning before setting out for her walk. "She kissed me, told me we would take lunch together as usual, and went off." Brushing tears from her cheeks, Evony whispered, "It was the last time I saw her." Then sitting forward in her chair and suddenly pulled from her sad reverie to the memories of Lord Rothvern's arrival, she hurried on. "Almost instantly, my step-uncle, King Standwood, sent Lord Damian Rothvern to Elawyth and placed him as steward over Elawyth and my brother, my sister, and myself—even though I am well old enough to serve as steward and even Mikol to be crowned king if it is found that my mother is dead." Evony shook her head at the memory of Lord Rothvern. "Lord Rothvern ill-treated us…especially Mikol," she continued. "And it was not long before I began to realize that Lord Rothvern meant for Mikol to…to expire…to deprive him of nourishment and subject him to the cold, wet elements of autumn night in the mountains. In my soul, I knew he meant to vanquish the heir of Elawyth."

"No!" Stavos breathed. "Truly?"

Evony nodded. "Yes. And so we escaped…abandoned our kingdom and our people in hopes we would find respite and help in Abawyth." She continued, "Several loyal servants assisted us, and we disappeared into the dark night, traveling to Abawyth in search of aid from King Standwood. I thought surely my step-uncle would provide us safe haven and send soldiers to remove Lord Rothvern from the throne room of Elawyth."

Stavos exhaled a disgusted breath and asked, "But you found no ally here?"

Evony shook her head. "No. Well, yes…at least I thought we had…at first."

"Go on," Stavos urged. It was apparent by the blaze of mounting detestation in his eyes that he was far more than mildly interested in the tale Evony had to tell—the whole of it.

And so she did as he bade her do and continued. "Mikol, Tressa, and I were escorted into the throne room to be presented to King Standwood," she explained. "I thought…I thought we had managed to find safe harbor and was elated to have Mikol and Tressa there, where I knew they would be well-fed, protected…"

She paused a moment, and Stavos patiently waited for her to persist, his gaze never leaving her face.

Evony blushed a bit under his rapt attention yet said, "King Standwood looked sincerely surprised when I told him of Lord Rothvern's actions and attitude…of his apparent attempts to put Mikol in peril. The king roared with disgust and rage at hearing we had been so ill-treated by a man he had set as steward over Elawyth. He assured me that we would be cared for, that Mikol would eat well and be protected as Elawyth's heir. Then he summoned my cousin Patrice and asked that she show us to our chambers…see that we were well fed and given fresh clothing and warm fires in our hearths. As we left his presence, King Standwood swore to me that he would remove Lord Rothvern from stewardship in Elawyth and see him punished. He also gave me his promise that the search for his wife, Queen Raina, and my mother, Queen Charmaine, was still in full force—that every royal guardsman and soldier that could be spared was hunting everywhere for the missing queens.

"Kind Standwood bid us good night and promised to meet with us at breakfast the next morning. Then he sent us away with Patrice to lead us." Evony felt new tears gathering in her eyes as she then began to reveal to Stavos the whole of what had happened the night she and her young brother and sister had arrived in Abawyth seeking safety and help.

"No sooner had we left the throne room, with the doors closed firm behind us, than Patrice took hold of my arm and whispered, 'Come with me, Evony! At once!' It was obvious Patrice was in great distress…frightened. She was trembling like a wet kitten, and her eyes were wide with panic. She told me that King Standwood meant to harm Mikol…meant to harm us all if he could find a way. She said that he had set Lord Rothvern as steward over Elawyth and that she and her sisters believed it was King Standwood himself that had ordered Mikol ill-treated. She said that we could not linger at Abawyth Castle…that we had gone from the one danger straight into another."

Evony paused and studied Stavos a moment. He wore no expression of doubt, only that of intense interest. He nodded to her—a gesture that she should continue.

"Patrice led Mikol, Tressa, and me to the large bedchamber the twelve princesses of Abawyth share. There we sat in quiet conference with Kathleen, Laura, Abbitha, Karamelle, Victoria, Patrice, Diana, Anne, Jewel, Opal, Elspeth, and Isabella—our cousins, all twelve princesses of Abawyth—all twelve assuring us that it was King Standwood himself that meant us harm…especially Mikol."

Stavos's frown deepened. "Your little brother…the only male heir to the throne of Elawyth and therefore the only one who could argue King Standwood's rule of Abawyth now that her queen has vanished."

Evony nodded. "Yes. If Mikol were to be crowned king of Elawyth, he could indeed challenge Kind Standwood's right to sit the throne of Abawyth…for the kingdoms are still sister kingdoms, after all."

"So Standwood means to rule both sister kingdoms," Stavos said, nodding with understanding. He quirked one handsome brow then and inquired, "Yet how did the Abawythian princesses come to know of Standwood's malicious intent?"

But Evony shook her head in not knowing. "I do not know it all, your highness," she answered. "As quickly as they could, my cousins literally whisked Mikol, Tressa, and myself away from the castle and out into the woods. They told me nothing…save that Mikol, Tressa, and I should fear for our lives and attempt to find a hiding place of sorts. They knew of none."

"And so you hid in plain sight?" Stavos asked.

"I-I had planned to find safe passage for us to the estate of a distant cousin of my father's," Evony explained. "But it was what my cousin Kathleen said before leaving us in the forest that bade me risk ourselves to stay in Abawyth."

"And what was that? What did your cousin Kathleen tell you?"

Evony gulped the large lump of fear and anxiety that seemed to have taken up permanent residence in her throat. "Kathleen told me that their mother, though vanished, was not dead, that she and all her sisters knew this to be true, and that they suspected the same was true for my mother…though they offered no proof." She brushed tears from her cheeks as she rambled, "I begged Kathleen for more information…to tell me how she knew her mother was still alive. I begged them all! But amidst their fearful, tear-filled eyes, I saw only panic and dread! My cousin Laura…at last she said, 'We are terrified slaves to a secret that even we do not fully understand.' And then she promised me that it was the truth…all of it…that Queen Raina is alive, that King Standwood meant us harm—for his greed and lust for power are insatiable. They hurried me on, telling me to run—to take Mikol and Tressa to safety and never to contact any of them again…for our own safety. And then they hurried off, all twelve in a row, but not back in the direction from whence we'd come. They hurried away in the opposite direction. And my hope for my mother's life, and uncertainties where my twelve cousins were concerned, could not be quenched."

Evony exhaled a heavy sigh. She felt as if she'd only just finished an entire day's work for Mrs. Teche. The confession—the telling of all she knew, though it seemed even less now that she had repeated it aloud—had entirely drained her of any liveliness.

"And so instead of making for your father's cousin's estate, you came to Abawyth's village and found respite in hiding…of sorts," Stavos sighed.

"Of sorts, yes," Evony admitted. "It was Miss Lovie who saved us. We three had never been out and about on our own in an unfamiliar place." Evony paused, smiling as she remembered the first moment she'd seen Miss Lovie. "At first I thought certain Miss Lovie was some magical being. The three of us had endured a long, dark, and very cold night. And when we first stepped into the village the next morning, Miss Lovie approached us. Her smile was so kind and inviting, and my heart knew at once she could be trusted." Evony gazed at Stavos a moment, a smile spreading across her pretty face. "Much the same way it knew that you could be trusted as well, Prince Stavos."

He grinned, obviously pleased, yet proceeded onward in questioning. "And she did not find it strange? Three royals plodding out of the woods one morning?"

"We were dressed as townsfolk," Evony explained. "We had left Elawyth in secret and did not want any suspicion to befall us as we traveled. Thus we dressed quite comfortably as plain traveling folk."

"And Miss Lovie Wiggin took you in," Stavos said.

Evony nodded. "She did. And it was Miss Lovie herself who found me means to provide for Mikol and Tressa by way of working for Mrs. Teche…though Miss Lovie fed and sheltered us until I had earned enough for this place, this room next to hers."

Stavos sighed again and relaxed against the back of his chair, stretching his long legs out in front of him. "And how, pray tell, did you become privy to this Midnight Masquerade in the first of it? To your cousins' involvement?"

"Once my thoughts and fears had settled a bit, due in great to part to my deciding to finally confess all to Miss Lovie," Evony began, "my mind was constantly drawn back to the moments in the woods when my cousins had brought us out of the castle by one path but left us by another. I kept wondering why in the world my cousins had taken the path they had that night, for it does not lead back to the castle in any manner but rather deeper into the woods.

"The twelve princesses of Abawyth and I had grown up together, always playing about in the woods, having grand, imaginative adventures of being rescued from the clutches of villains by handsome princes and such other things that young girls imagine. I am closest in age to Victoria and Patrice, but all of us enjoyed playing together among the pines and other trees of the forest, and therefore I knew the woods well. So why did my cousins not simply return whence they had come? To Abawyth Castle?

"And so, one night after a long day in Mrs. Teche's vile company, I did what any curious soul would do, and I wandered to the wood…to the very spot where my cousins had left us after leading us out of the castle. I found the second path the princesses had followed that night and followed it for as long as I could with only the moon and stars to light my way. It was then that I came upon the Hungry Horse Inn…rather that I came upon the backmost rooms of it. I peeked through a window, and I saw the dance—the Midnight Masquerade, as *you* have discovered it is termed."

"And there you saw the dresses you had labored over for Agnes Teche," Stavos offered. "And that is when you followed your cousins…saw them unmasked and began to suspect that something malevolent is at work here in Abawyth, something other than simply the power-thirsty King Standwood."

"Yes!" Evony exclaimed, having been suddenly overcome by a sense of wild relief. "Oh yes!" She felt an odd giggle bubble up in her throat, something akin to euphoric senselessness. "Forgive me, sire. I don't know what has come over me! I feel as if…as if in telling you all that I know, I have somehow been forgiven all my sins or something."

Stavos smiled as he studied the pretty—oh, so pretty—princess sitting across from him. "I cannot imagine one such as you owning any sins at all, Princess Evony."

He felt his smile broaden as her pinking cheeks revealed that she was pleased by his compliment.

"Well," she sighed then, leaning back in her chair as if having just had a heavy-laden yoke removed from her shoulders, "there you have it, Prince Stavos. There you have all that I know about the Midnight Masquerade and the twelve sleepy princesses of Abawyth."

He arched one admiring brow and said, "Well, you certainly know more than anyone else in Abawyth…save that old crone Agnes Teche."

Stavos was thoughtful for a moment—distracted by the light of the hearth fire reflected in Evony's eyes. He thought about the quest his father had sent him on—to solve the mystery surrounding Abawyth's enigmatic royals—of the king of Ethiarien's command that Stavos assist the princesses of Abawyth and marry one of them. In that moment, he thought that, if there were no command from his father to marry an Abawythian princess, his desires could well settle themselves on the princess Evony of Elawyth. He admired Evony's courage, her devotion to her siblings, her cousins, and her mother, her willingness to sacrifice everything in protection of her brother's life and to unravel the evil tapestry binding her cousins. She was strong of character, as well as beautiful, and Stavos tried to ignore the sudden ache of regret that was rising in his chest.

"So," he began, leaning forward as he forced his mind to the matters at hand. Using his fingers to enumerate as he went, he vocally listed, "We know the princesses are being manipulated by Ewan Happer, proprietor of the Hungry Horse Inn and overall evil-doer. We know that Queen Raina is alive, which likewise nearly ensures that your mother, Queen Charmaine, also lives. We know that King Standwood plans not only to claim Abawyth's throne for his own but also to rule over Elawyth as well. We know that Agnes Teche is in league with Ewan Happer."

Evony watched as Stavos smiled, his eyes widening with what she could only deem was excitement at a looming challenge.

"I see our course very clearly, Princess Evony of Elawyth," he exclaimed.

"You do?" she asked—for she certainly did not see a clear path before her.

"Of course!" he assured her with infallible confidence. She watched as he again began to use his fingers to enumerate. "First we must infiltrate the Midnight Masquerade—rather, I must infiltrate it," he explained. "And that was your scheme in the first place. Brilliant, by the way."

Stavos winked at her, and Evony's heart leapt with delight in her bosom.

"It is paramount to this mystery, I am certain—this vile Midnight Masquerade. This is our initial path—to infiltrate the Midnight Masquerade, wherein I may be able to gain the trust of one or more of the princesses of Abawyth. Likewise I will befriend Ewan Happer…pick over his thick, and probably very small, brain and see if he gives up any information without realizing it."

But Evony was growing anxious. "But what of me?" she asked. "I must be allowed to assist you! I cannot simply sit here in this room wondering all the while!"

"You, my lady, must be patient," came his answer.

She felt a frown pucker her brow—wanted to purse her lower lip like a pouting child.

Still, before she could argue the point with him, Stavos added, "And you must quit your employment with that hag Agnes Teche."

Evony smiled, giggling a little. "I cannot quit Agnes Teche," she offered, amused that he would even make such a suggestion. "How in all the world would I provide for Mikol and Tressa? What would we eat? The walls of our meager home? Our furniture?"

Stavos shrugged. "That's effortless enough to answer. You'll simply become my mistress—my kept woman—and I will provide all that you and your brother and sister require. Let's toss Miss Lovie into the pot as well. She looks like a woman who deserves to retire to a more comfortable life."

Evony's mouth hung agape. "B-become your…your mistress?" she squeaked in astonishment as she blushed to the tips of her toes. "I-I should slap your face for even suggesting—"

But Stavos burst into laughter. "Evony!" he chuckled. "I'm only being playful."

"Oh…oh, of course," Evony breathed with relief—though mildly disturbed by a slight sense of disappointment weaving through her.

"Although, now that I consider on it further, it might benefit us both if you actually were to—" he teased.

Evony fairly leapt from her chair, blushing as red as a summer radish. "I had no idea you were such a…such a rapscallion, Prince Stavos," she scolded, mildly.

"Oh, fear not, lovely princess," he laughed, still smiling with amusement at her reactions. "I only possess a tendency to be over-playful at times. I would no more take you as my mistress than I would Miss Lovie," he told her.

"You wouldn't?" Evony exclaimed with unexpected and abrupt distressful offense.

Again Stavos laughed. "No, no, pretty princess…you misunderstand. I meant I would never take *any* woman as mistress— for I would never keep a mistress. I am not such a man as that."

"Oh, I see," Evony sighed, trying to mask her relief.

"No," Stavos continued. "I will only ever take a woman to wife. And, in fact, I mean to solve this nonsensical sleepy princesses conundrum and have one of the twelve princesses of Abawyth as my prize. And so…I will join this appalling Midnight Masquerade tonight! And then, my dear Princess Evony, we shall both be on the path to discovery and reward. Yes?"

"I hope so, sire," Evony answered. She forced a smile as she noted the excitement of facing a challenge flashing in his beautiful blue eyes. Yet something in her—and it was deeply seeded in her— was unhappy as well, unhappy at the thought of Prince Stavos taking one of her twelve cousins to wife instead of taking…

"But I do promise you this," Stavos began then. "If ever I do become a miscreant and decide to take a woman as my mistress…" He stood and stepped closer to Evony—so close she had to crane her neck to look up into his face, so close she could feel his breath on her forehead. "Well then, Princess Evony of Elawyth…I promise that *you* shall be the first to know."

Evony blushed and forced her eyebrows into a frown, even for the wicked delight that leapt in her bosom at his teasing her once more.

"If you'll excuse me a moment, Prince Stavos," she said, however. "I'm certain that Miss Lovie and the children are quite beside themselves with curiosities over our meeting."

She started toward the door leading to Miss Lovie's rooms but paused when Stavos said, "You will quit Mrs. Teche." It was not a question, nor was it a command. It was a statement.

Turning to face him again, her limbs suddenly feeling limp and weak as she looked at him, she said, "I cannot. It would draw suspicion if I were to suddenly and intentionally leave her employment. She knows I have no other way of providing for myself."

Stavos of Voronin grinned at her, however—an alluring, teasing, nearly seductive grin. "Well, as I said, there is another way for you to—"

Putting up one hand to stop his teasing, Evony could not help but smile at him as she said, "You know I am right. I cannot leave Mrs. Teche. And besides, perhaps I might glean some information that would be helpful to our plight…just as we hope you will glean something from an association with Ewan Happer."

"I suppose you are right to stay with her," Stavos admitted at last, "for the time being, that is." She nodded at him with approval. Yet in the next moment, he added, "But I will not have you and yours doing without. You must gather your strength, Evony—all of you—for we do not know what challenges await us on this path we intended to tread together. Mikol must be well fed and strong, as must you and Tressa. Therefore, you will not want for food and warmth. That I will not waver on."

Evony knew he was right. Likewise, she knew that she, Mikol, and Tressa had become weakened over the past weeks. Meat had been scarcely affordable with the pitiful wages Mrs. Teche paid her—milk as well—and Evony could not foresee what travels the three of them might be forced to make. It was best to remain humble enough to accept Stavos's command in this regard.

Therefore, she nodded and offered a meek, "Yes, sire."

As she again made for the door leading to Mrs. Lovie's rooms, Stavos called, "And, Evony…my name is Stavos. I am not your king…so please disperse with the formalities. It greatly discomforts me."

She smiled and offered, "Yes, sire…Stavos."

The sight of his smiling at her caused a wave of butterflies to flutter in her stomach the likes she had never experienced before. Yet he was here not for her but for adventure and to win the hand of one of her cousins. She must keep the fact ever in the forefront of her mind, lest she risk losing her wits and sensibilities when, for her brother's and sister's sake, and perhaps even for her mother's, she could not risk losing them.

"We will find Queen Raina and free your cousins from Ewan Happer's hold over them, Evony. And if your mother is with her sister, we will find her too. I promise you that. And I will see King Standwood pay for his crimes against you and yours as well. That I swear to you."

Indeed, hope did swell within her at the strength of his words. She nodded to him and then proceeded to open the door leading to Miss Lovie's—for she was certain both Mikol and Miss Lovie were fraught with curiosity and worry.

Prince Stavos Voronin of Ethiarien had made a promise to the princess Evony of Elawyth—sworn a prince's oath to her—and he meant to champion her. He'd discovered much more malevolence slithering through Abawyth than he had expected to find, but it would not deter him in any way. He would see it all through to its end, no matter the consequences, for he found that his soul cringed at the thought of failing Evony Elorietta—almost as powerfully as it reveled in the thought of pleasing her.

Stavos's mind could not be settled. As Evony disappeared into Miss Lovie's adjoining rooms, it seemed that Evony's revelations of what she knew of the mystery of the twelve sleepy princesses of Abawyth did more to inflame his curiosities than to satisfy them. Question after question, silent inquiry after silent inquiry, leapt about in his brain like a thousand hurtling javelins. Who had captured the missing queens in the first of it, and how? If they truly were alive, then where were they? And why had every man who had tried to assist the Abawythian princesses failed? What was the strange stupor that was rumored to overtake any man who accepted the challenge of attempting to solve the mystifying mess?

Of one thing Stavos was certain, however: Evony could not be pressed for more information in that moment, even if she owned it, whether consciously or subconsciously. She was spent—worn out from the telling of it all. Stavos knew that with each step she took in telling her tale to him, she had somewhat relived the horrors of the past months over again. It might be that there were small details she had heard or witnessed that could help him sort out the conundrum—help *them* sort it out. But she was too taxed for one day, and he would not press her further.

It was no more than a few moments before the young Princess Tressa of Elawyth came skipping into the room. Mikol was just at her heels, followed by Miss Lovie, and lastly Evony.

"You promised to stay for luncheon, Stavos," Tressa cheerfully reminded him.

As the little girl smiled coyly at him, battering her eyes like any older, more accomplished coquette, Stavos chuckled and gathered the child onto one knee. "I would not miss lunching with you today, Tressa...not for anything."

Tressa giggled and threw her arms about his neck in an affectionate embrace of delight. "I'm so glad, Stavos!"

"And once we've had our meal...I think it best if I returned to my room at the inn for a little midday napping," Stavos said. Looking to Evony, he added, "For tonight promises to be fraught with sleepless adventure, does it not, Evony?"

Evony could not have kept from smiling at Stavos, even if she had wanted to—which she didn't. He truly meant to do it; she knew he did. The prince, Stavos Voronin of Ethiarien, sincerely meant to help her—to help them all. He honestly intended to infiltrate the vulgar Midnight Masquerade held in secret each night at the Hungry Horse Inn to more fully comprehend the mystery surround her sisters, her aunt, and hopefully her own mother.

"Indeed it does," Evony answered. Of course, she had no intention of confessing to Stavos that she meant to attend the Midnight Masquerade as well—as a silent, somehow concealed witness.

The moment Stavos had said he would attend the lurid dance, Evony had decided that she would, as invisibly as possible, journey to the inn that night and peep through the small windows of the inn's hidden rooms. Just as Stavos had claimed he would not miss lunching with Tressa for anything, so Evony would not miss being witness to Stavos's infiltration of Ewan Happer's torment of her cousins. Naturally Stavos would never know of her being witness to it all—but she would be.

"Perhaps you should rest as well, Evony," Miss Lovie suggested, "especially if you truly intend to return to Agnes Teche's employ tomorrow."

Evony saw the understanding bright in Miss Lovie's eyes. Though Stavos did not suspect Evony's plotting to follow and observe him, Miss Lovie knew Evony all too well.

"Yes," Mikol agreed, unsuspecting, but caring. "If you have to work for that old crone, at least you should do it well rested."

"Absolutely," Stavos agreed, "especially in light of your refusing my suggestion of alternate means of being kept sheltered and fed." His blue eyes danced with mischief as he winked at Evony, sending her heart leaping with delight and her arms and legs racing with goose pimples.

"What other means?" Mikol asked.

"It is of no consequence, Mikol," Evony answered. "And besides, even Prince Stavos agrees that I need to remain in Mrs. Teche's employ...at least for the time being. We don't want to draw any unwanted attention to our situation, and if I suddenly had no employment but was still able to provide shelter and food..."

"Ah, yes. I do see the wisdom in it," Mikol admitted. He frowned. "However, I am entirely frustrated that I cannot be the one to provide for us." He sighed with discouragement.

"Mikol," Stavos began, "you are right to feel as you do. And the day will come when you must provide for not only your sisters but also an entire kingdom. Meanwhile, I am here to help your sister. And though she has refused to quit Mrs. Teche for the moment, I will see to her welfare as far as she will allow it...and to yours, Tressa's, and Miss Lovie's."

Still, Mikol frowned. "And then I will be indebted to you forever, for my kingdom could never repay such valor and—"

Stavos's understanding laughter interrupted Mikol's selfless thoughts. "I do understand, Mikol. But remember...there is benefit to me in the end. If I can help your sister solve this damnable mayhem surrounding your twelve cousins, I will be given my choice of a bride from amongst them. Furthermore, I will have returned home having fulfilled the quest my father sent me to complete. Therefore, you see now—that it is I who will be indebted to you, yes?"

Mikol sighed with relief and smiled with some thread of respite from worry. But Evony did not. At the reminder that Stavos would choose a bride from amongst her Abawythian cousins should he succeed, she felt anger and nausea rise in her stomach. Yet what right had she to feel the stirrings of jealousy? He meant to do all he could to champion Evony and her family. Should not his reward be the choice of an Abawythian princess as bride, as well as glory? In the very least it should! So why could she find no joy in the contemplation of it?

"Let us share our midday meal together then," Stavos offered. "What would you have me fetch from the marketplace, Miss Lovie?"

"Oh my, Prince Stavos!" Miss Lovie exclaimed with a delighted blush. "Why...we've plenty enough ham from your goodness to us yesterday, sire...if ham two days running is acceptable to you, of course."

Stavos smiled at the elderly woman. "To be honest, Miss Lovie, I prefer ham to beef...or any other meat, for that matter."

"Well, fine then...ham it is," Miss Lovie giggled.

Evony watched, still awed not only by Stavos's wildly handsome features of face and form but also by his apparent integrity as well. She deemed him truly honorable and envied whichever of her cousins would win him as her husband.

Yet though Evony had had acquaintance with Stavos only a brief while, the thought of his marrying somehow disheartened her near to tears. Thus, she made busy in assisting Miss Lovie in preparing their meal—tried not to linger on thoughts of how one simple glance from Prince Stavos Voronin caused goose pimples to spring up all over her.

CHAPTER FIVE

Evony was grateful for the bright moonlight—for the cloudless winter sky that allowed its silver glow to light her way through the forest. The frost that already sparkled in the treetops gave the world of Abawyth's woods a mystical wonder. All the scents of night among the trees were crisp and clean on the air—frost on barren winter branches and a carpet of cool pine needles littered on the ground—and the scent of the hearth fires in Abawyth perfumed the air with a warm, woodsmoke essence that caused Evony to yawn and long for the softness of a bed and quilts.

All around there was silence, save the quiet crunch of Evony's footsteps and the occasional hoot of an owl somewhere in the distance. Not even a breeze moved the stiffened branches of the trees around her. It was a serene scene—rather it would have been if there were not so much toil and danger afoot.

As Evony approached one small window on the outer rim of the inn's secreted rooms, she was relieved that Ewan Happer had not yet discovered the tear in the curtain that was meant to mask it. The tear in the curtain at the window was how Evony was able to witness the Midnight Masquerade in the first of it. Though someone had taken great care to hang heavy curtains or draperies over the panes of each window of the secreted rooms, the covering at the small, neglected window had been torn at some point, allowing Evony to peer through the darkness and into the improvised ballroom. She was thankful, as she had been every night since discovering the Midnight

Masquerade, that once again no one had seemed to detect the flaw. No doubt the window was considered too insignificant to bother with.

Slowly she stepped up to the window and peered into the dimly lit ballroom beyond. She could see Ewan Happer standing near the door on the opposing wall. The very sight of his rotund belly, yellow teeth, snarling smile, and long black and gray hair caused Evony's stomach to churn. It seemed all the evil intent and ugliness that resided in the loathsome innkeeper's soul were manifest in his outward appearance as well. Ewan Happer was not a man Evony ever cared to be any closer in proximity to than she was at that very moment.

Attempting to distract herself from the nausea Ewan Happer's appearance had caused to settle in her, Evony studied the physique of each man currently involved in dancing with a woman on the ballroom floor. Each patron of the Midnight Masquerade, both women and men, wore a mask—the sort of masks Evony had once seen as a child while on a holiday in Venice of Italy. The masks hid the foreheads, eyes, cheeks, and noses of everyone in the room— save Ewan Happer, the one person whose face Evony wished covered. Only lips and chins were revealed. Thus, Evony began to search for Prince Stavos by studying the shapes and lines of each male attendants' body.

She spied Stavos nearly at once, however, for he stood apart from the other men like a red apple lying in a drift of new snow. Stavos was taller, his shoulders broader, than any other man. His long legs and the manner in which his breeches hugged the contours of his seat caused that he was far more easily recognizable than he perhaps knew.

At having discovered Stavos's position in the room, Evony's heart leapt with sudden exhilaration. Even the mere sight of him caused such a physical reaction in her that she again wondered if something were indeed wrong with her. He was simply a man—albeit a fantastically handsome and charming man. But should a man cause such a thoroughgoing thrill to prevail over her?

But Evony's thoughts were scattered as she then noticed the euphoric smile so blatant on the face of the woman Stavos led in the dance. In fact, Evony recognized the woman, her chestnut hair almost perfectly the color of Evony's own. Evony recognized the elegant, graceful movements of her cousin, Princess Patrice of Abawyth.

At once, Evony felt moisture gather in her eyes. *It should be me dancing with him!* her mind silently cried out. Yet Evony's good sense inwardly scolded her—for she knew that were she herself to choose from among her cousins the young woman who would be most worthy of Stavos Voronin, it would be Patrice. Patrice was not only beautiful but also kind, compassionate, loving, and, above all, blessed with a rare and sincere humility.

Still, as she continued to watch Stavos lead Patrice in a dance—one that found their bodies far closer than propriety would approve—as she watched Patrice smile up at Stavos, seem to giggle at his comments—Evony began to ache in a manner she did not find at all familiar. Futhermore, Stavos appeared to be as resplendent in Patrice's company as she was in his, and the fact caused Evony's unfamiliar ache to worsen.

"He is not here for you," she whispered aloud in reminding herself. "He is here to help them and to find his bride…not for you, Evony Elorietta." But even reprimanding her heart and mind did nothing to ease the discomfort taking root in her bosom.

Yet just as she thought she could endure no more of Stavos's and Patrice's apparent felicity, the music ended, and they stepped apart. Evony watched as Stavos then strode to another woman, offering his hand in an obvious request to obtain a dance with her. Evony studied this new partner of Stavos's. Was she also one of the twelve princesses of Abawyth being manipulated by Ewan Happer? Upon observing this woman's grace and movements, her ebony hair and slender figure, Evony determined at once that this partner to Stavos was Princess Diana of Abawyth.

Sighing with a relief she did not herself fully understand, Evony felt a smile spread over her face. Diana, though very beautiful and an exquisite young woman, did not seem to draw the same response of countenance from Stavos that Patrice had. Therefore, Evony was somewhat soothed for a moment and, in being so, began to study the other patrons of the contemptible Midnight Masquerade.

"There is Kathleen. I am certain of it," Evony whispered to herself as she saw another tall, raven-haired young woman dancing with a short, round, gray-haired man. "And Anne."

One after another, Evony identified her cousins. "And there's Laura and also Abbitha...Karamelle, Victoria. But where is...ah! There is Elspeth...and there's Jewel, dancing with a fair-haired fellow. And...let's see...yes! Opal and Isabella also."

It was true, just as it had been on all the previous occasions that Evony had spent the dark hours of the night peering through the tear in the curtain at the small window. All twelve of the princesses of Abawyth were present—all twelve dancing with strangers who, more often than not, held them inappropriately and forced familiarities that were lurid to say the least.

Evony's eyes filled with tears for the sake of her dear, beloved cousins. Each one owned a piece of her heart. Each one had been her playmate, comrade, cousin, friend, and confidant—most near to all her life! It was a despicable display! And yet it further assured Evony that Queen Raina was still alive, for never would the twelve princesses of Abawyth find themselves in such dire and desperate circumstances unless it were true.

Further reassured that her own mother was also alive, Evony exhaled a heavy sigh. Stavos was there now—there participating in the Midnight Masquerade. He was, she knew, her only hope of saving her own mother and her aunt and twelve cousins.

Still, as Evony watched Stavos continue in his dance with her cousin Diana, she could not squelch the irrational jealousy that kept rising in her throat—and it frightened her.

"Wherever did you find these girls, Happer?" Stavos asked, smiling as he accepted a tankard from the miscreant of an innkeeper. "They're charming! Though I do admit to preferring some over others. Are they local wenches?" He paused, winking at Ewan Happer conspiratorially. "Regardless of where you dug them up, each one of them does bring a man a measure of scandalous pleasure."

Ewan Happer chuckled. "That they do, sir…that they do." He looked to Stavos, adding, "And I'm glad to see you're enjoying yourself. The Hungry Horse Inn offers more, shall we say, amenities than any other inn you've visited, eh? I'm willing to bet my bottom on that fact."

"Indeed," Stavos confirmed. Though his stomach turned at the very sight of the idiot next to him, he knew that stroking Ewan Happer's ego—lulling him into a false sense of success—was paramount. Yet he wondered what fool or blind man on the face of the earth would ever accept a bet wherein Ewan Happer's bottom was involved.

"In fact," Stavos said, drawing several pieces of silver from the pocket in his vest, "I've enjoyed myself so much this evening that it seems to me you've more than qualified for a little extra remuneration." He dropped the coins into Happer's eager, grubby, filthy hand. "Provided that I am allowed to continue to enjoy myself, you understand."

"Of course, sir," Happer assured him, studying the coins a moment, his eyes boggling like a toad's. "Of course…and at your leisure." Ewan surveyed the room—studied the few girls who were not already involved in dancing with a man at the moment. "In fact, might I suggest you give the little chestnut-haired chit another whirl around the floor? It seems to me that you fancy her, sire."

Again Stavos forced a smile. "Indeed I do, Happer. Indeed I do. I see you are as observant as you are cunning in…business matters."

"I try, sir. I do try," Happer laughed.

Stavos was more than happy to leave Ewan Happer's side for the company of the "little chestnut-haired chit" standing in one corner. The man was nauseating! Not only was his character the stuff of compost, but his breath and body stunk like something that had laid rotting inside a dead dog for three days!

Even still, Stavos had learned much during his first evening in attendance at the Midnight Masquerade. In the first of it, he had easily discerned which of the rather enslaved women were in truth Abawyth's princesses and which were not. Twelve of the women had each given the same response when he had thanked them for a dance: "My pleasure, sire." And as if their synonymous verbal responses to being thanked for a dance had not given them away to him, their profound grace, elegance, and proper manner of speech had.

The entire condition was revolting to Stavos, to the point of churning his stomach. Whether princesses or common ladies in dire need of wages, it did not matter to him; no woman deserved such treatment. It was more often than not throughout the evening that Stavos observed other male patrons of the inn taking improper liberties with the girls of the Midnight Masquerade. In truth, all the night long he'd found himself thinking of Evony—grateful that it was not she who was finding a strange man's hand sliding downward to linger on the curve of her posterior—grateful she was safely tucked away in her quiet little room with her sister, her brother, and Miss Lovie.

Yes, indeed, Stavos had learned much during his first night at Ewan Happer's monstrous exploitation—not the least of which was the fact that the perimeter of the ballroom was much smaller than the outer perimeter of the hidden part of the inn. It led him to pondering that the improvised ballroom was not the only space at the Hungry Horse Inn that most patrons were not aware of. The fact sent his mind to racing over what other ghastly endeavors Ewan Happer had plunged his filthy, greedy hands into.

Evony wondered what it was that the innkeeper could have possibly said that would cause Stavos to laugh. And what in all the world could possess Stavos to give Ewan Happer several pieces of silver? It was painfully frustrating to be unable to hear their conversation—to only watch and wonder, to imagine what was being said.

And then, when Stavos left Ewan Happer to stride determinedly toward none other than Patrice, Evony's frustration was almost intolerable! For a moment, she tried to convince herself that the reason Stavos seemed to be frequenting Patrice's company more than any other woman's was because Patrice was the Abawythian princess that bore the most likeness to Evony herself. Since birth, Evony and Patrice had resembled one another—both with nut-brown hair and green eyes. As grown young women, they were exactly the same height. However, their personalities were nearly in opposition. Patrice was very soft-spoken and demure, very graceful and skilled in music, while Evony was more prone to an interest in literature and stitching. In truth, Patrice was content in her music and slow meanderings, but Evony had ever sought adventure of sorts.

She remembered then the summer she and Patrice had uncovered several earthworms while playing in the south gardens at Elawyth Castle. Patrice had run away sobbing, having been startled and disgusted by the wriggling, flesh-colored little things. But Evony—Evony had been wildly intrigued! So intrigued, in fact, that she'd spent the better part of the afternoon digging holes in the south gardens—until one of the gardeners had found her out and sent her to confess to her mother. Evony's mother, Queen Charmaine, had merely laughed with amusement and instructed her eldest daughter to wash her hands well with warm water and soap. But it had taken hours for Patrice to recover from the incident. In fact, she'd experienced nightmares of earthworms for several days following the event.

Yet try as she might to convince herself it was only Patrice's physical similarity to Evony that drew Stavos to her, Evony knew it was not true. Patrice enchanted anyone who made her acquaintance. She was truly that lovely and sweet.

With Stavos's return to Patrice's company yet again, Evony felt as if she could endure no more. She could not bear another two hours of standing in the frigid night air, peering in through the window only to see Patrice and the other women of the Midnight Masquerade savoring the handsome smile and warm touch of Prince Stavos

Voronin. Furthermore, in less than four hours, she would need to report to Agnes Teche's seamstress shop again. The thought made the acidic contents of her stomach well in her throat. Yet it had to be—at least for a time.

For a moment, Evony wished she had accepted Stavos's offer to be his "kept woman"—but only for a moment, for such lurid, scandalous ideas were not at all proper to ponder. Yet goose pimples broke over her arms at the thought of being Stavos's all the same. She tried to attribute her prickling flesh to the cold of winter's night and not to the idea of being kept by the handsomest man in all the world.

And so, feeling far less hopeful and far more discouraged than she had upon first peering through the tiny window of the inn, Evony turned toward the dark forest to make her way home. She would leave Stavos at her back—try not to worry in constant about what was transpiring between him and the women trapped at the Midnight Masquerade—try not to think of what was transpiring between Stavos and her cousin, the lovely princess Patrice.

Dawn arrived all too early. As Evony rinsed her face and tied her hair in a tight knot at the crown of her head, she wondered how she would manage the pretense of nothing having changed since last she saw Agnes Teche. If she seemed too distracted while stitching, Mrs. Teche would rap the back of her legs with a willow wand. Evony had learned that slow stitching led to red and painful welts, and she'd learned it the first day she'd worked for Agnes Teche. Yet if the hope she was feeling in her heart were to be visible at all in her countenance, Mrs. Teche might become suspicious somehow.

Yet Evony knew things would not go as badly that day for Evony as they no doubt would for the two other girls who sewed for the old crone—and they were Agnes Teche's very own daughters. Evony winced as she thought of the way the cruel woman whipped her daughters with a willow switch whenever she was in a foul mood, even if the girls had done nothing wrong or stitched as quickly as their boney fingers allowed. The woman did not deserve to be called "Mother."

Still, if Stavos did manage to champion every member of Evony's family so miserably trapped in anguish and danger, she vowed then and there that she would beg the Teche girls to join her in Elawyth as her personal seamstresses—whisk them away from their merciless matron. Agnes Teche did not merit such sweet daughters as were Lillian and Camille, and each was old enough to escape her mother's cruelty, if the means of escape would simply present itself. Evony was determined that if all were well in the end, she would provide the means of escape for Lillian and Camille herself.

But a wave of trepidation, fear, and anxiety traveled over her in that moment. Her mind leapt to Stavos. Was he well? What information did he glean? Had he spent the remainder of the Midnight Masquerade with Patrice in his arms? The not knowing was nearly as wretched as what she feared the answers might be. Yet what could be done but wait? She would go to Mrs. Teche, work her needles and threads until the tips of her fingers were numb with labor, and then she would pray that Stavos did not forget who had set him on his path in the first of it and that he would return to report that evening.

No sooner had Evony thought of Stavos, however, than there was a quiet knock on the door. As her heart leapt with sheer gladness, Evony hurried to the door, for she knew it was he; Stavos had come to her. Quietly she raised the latch, for Mikol and Tressa still slept.

Stavos did not pause—not for an instant—but rather stepped into the room, closing the door behind him.

Evony smiled as he took her shoulders in his hands and, with great excitement in both his voice and expression, whispered, "Evony…the things I have learned this night will boggle you!"

His hands at her shoulders—just his touch—sent a warmth flowing through her, a warmth she'd only ever felt in all her life in his presence.

"Truly?" she managed to ask, though she was more delighted simply by the sight of him than any information he might now own.

"Oh, so truly," he chuckled quietly. "I cannot wait to reveal all to you…now…here…this moment!"

"And I cannot wait to hear it," she admitted. "But I must away to Mrs. Teche's shop and—"

"Pff!" Stavos puffed, frowning. "Mrs. Teche and her shop, indeed. I cannot let you go," he stated. "I cannot allow that woman to hold any power over you whatsoever. I am certain all will be well soon, Evony. And even it if is not to be, I cannot endure the thought of you laboring for that ugly old crone."

By the firm expression on his face, Evony knew he was in earnest. He did not intend to let her leave.

Her heart was aflame with delight and gratitude, yet she reminded, "I must not raise suspicion or attention whilst you are endeavoring to work this all out. You yourself agreed with me on that yesterday. I must go, or she'll come to find me and—"

"And find you have charmed a nobleman and that he intends to keep you and yours well and cared for," he interrupted, still frowning.

"But she is in league with Ewan Happer, and should he see us together…" She paused, tempted by his willingness to care for her and her siblings—by the thought of never having to face Agnes Teche again. "You know I must go," she told him. Then she sighed with the pleasure of knowing he was helping her—helping them all—and added, "But I am more grateful than you know that you are willing to keep me from her." When he still continued to frown, she said, "You know I am right. You're obviously very tired from an evening of decadence. But once you've had your rest, you'll be in agreement with me once more concerning dear Agnes."

"Decadence?" Stavos questioned, however. "What decadence? I attended the Midnight Masquerade, danced with many a young woman for whose welfare I am greatly concerned, spoke with Ewan Happer and several of his men—what decadence was there?"

Evony shrugged. "Well, none that I observed, I suppose...though I did wonder for what reason you were lacing Ewan Happer's hand with coins when—"

She stopped speaking when she felt his hands tighten at her shoulders. "You followed me," he stated.

"Well...yes," she admitted. "I couldn't just sit here near the fire wondering all the while what was going on and worrying about your welfare."

His frown deepened as he growled, "What if you had been seen? What if Happer had become aware that a girl from town knew of his activities? You might have been killed, Evony."

Evony turned her face from his—humiliated, hurt, discomfited by his scolding. But when Stavos released his grip on her shoulders to take hold of her chin with one hand in forcing her to look at him, she could do nothing but bow to his will.

"You cannot go to the inn again, Evony...never," he told her. "I will help you. I will help your cousins, your mother, whomever is entrapped in this contemptible affair. But you must trust in my word that I will do so...and that I am able. I cannot have you harmed, nor can I be found out because of you. Do you understand?"

"Before you came to Abawyth, all this was on my shoulders," she reminded him as tears of frustration and anxiety filled her eyes. "You cannot expect me to simply give it all over to you...to simply step back and do nothing."

He paused a moment, exhaling a heavy sigh. As his frown relaxed, he nodded and said, "You're right. I can see how difficult it is for you." Now cupping her face between warm, strong hands, he added, "But you cannot come to the inn again. It is far too dangerous. You know that. Keep your focus on Agnes Teche. If she's supplying dresses to Happer for the women to wear at the Midnight Masquerade, then she knows far more than it might appear at first glance. Keep your pretty little ears fixed on conversations she has with anyone who comes into her shop, yes?"

Evony nodded, trying not to melt into a puddle at Stavos's feet as one of his thumbs caressively traveled over her lower lip.

"So…so no more argument from you about my going to the shop and laboring for Mrs. Teche then?" she asked.

Stavos sighed again, his beautiful blue eyes suddenly narrowing with fatigue and forfeit. "No, I expect not. Sew for the old hag then. I suppose you must." Releasing her face then, he wagged an index finger at her, adding, "But do nothing to provoke her suspicion."

"Or her temper," Evony mumbled.

"What's that?" Stavos asked.

But Evony shook her head. "Nothing. Nothing at all."

"Stavos?" Tressa yawned then as she appeared at Evony's side, rubbing the sleep from her eyes. "Have you come to breakfast with us?"

Stavos smiled at Tressa. "Not today, I'm afraid, love," he answered. "I must return to the inn and steal a few hours of sleep before tonight."

"You're going to be late, Evony!" Miss Lovie exclaimed, suddenly bursting through the door that adjoined her rooms with Evony's. "Mrs. Teche will hang you up by your thumbs if you're tardy. It's well you know that."

"Yes, it is," Evony sighed, recalling the one instance when she arrived at the seamstress's shop several moments past her due time. The backs of her legs could still feel the sting of the willow wand Agnes had wielded as punishment.

"Oh, the rumpus you women make in the morning," Mikol grumbled from his place in bed.

Evony smiled, bent, and kissed Tressa on the forehead, placed a quick kiss of affection and gratitude on Miss Lovie's sweet, wrinkled cheek, and then stepped aside to move past Stavos.

"What's this?" Stavos asked, however.

"What's what?" Evony asked in unawareness.

"The child, even the sweet, elderly lady receive of your affections…but you have nothing to offer your champion?" he asked, feigning sincerity.

Evony could not help but smile at him, for he was a charming flirt, if nothing else.

"My champion?" she teased in return. "What champion is this before me? One who spends all the night long in flirtations with my cousins while I stand cold and miserable in the elements?"

"That was not my fault, princess…and well you know it," Stavos reminded with a sly wink.

"Oh, for pity's sake, give him a kiss, Evony!" Tressa exclaimed. "Else you'll be tardy and old Mrs. Teche will give you the willow wand again."

"Hush, Tressa," Miss Lovie shushed the girl.

"Yes," Stavos said. "Give him a kiss, or you'll be tardy, and that old crone will give you…" He looked to Tressa, asking, "What was that again, Tressa?"

"The willow wand," Tressa answered. "It's a stick that Mrs. Teche uses to—"

"Oh, for the love of Christmas pudding," Evony mumbled. "Give us your cheek then, sir champion," she said to Stavos. "I swear you're worse than Mikol at letting me out the door."

Stavos grinned a handsome, triumphant grin and bent toward Evony that she may kiss his cheek. However, an instant before she would've pressed her lips to his face, he took her chin in one hand, pressing his lips to hers in a tender, warm, oh-so-warm kiss.

Despite the fact that the kiss lasted no more than a moment, it left Evony entirely breathless—stunned and speechless as well.

"Kisses on the cheek are for brothers and grandfathers, my pretty little gem," Stavos mumbled, winking at Evony as he lifted the latch of the door and opened it for her. When Evony paused—still paralyzed with delicious astonishment—Stavos nodded toward the village and said, "Now, off with you, pet. Let's not keep that old crone waiting. Hmm?"

Not even the sound yet soft pat he gave to her backside as she stepped over the threshold astonished her as much as his kiss had. She heard the door latch behind her, gasped for the breath that had been eluding her since Stavos's lips had pressed hers, and began to hurry toward Agnes Teche's shop.

In fact, resplendence lingered in her heart yet as she entered the shop and found Mrs. Teche waiting within—willow switch in hand. "You're late, girl," Agnes growled.

"F-forgive me, Mrs. Teche," Evony stammered—for she was, at last, ripped from the euphoria of Stavos's kiss and to the fact Mrs. Teche was angry.

"And before you ever think of pulling such a prank as having some nobleman carry you into my shop and beg me for a day of rest for you...lift your skirt to your knees," Mrs. Teche ordered.

Evony glanced to Lillian and Camille. Both already had tears welling in their eyes, empathy and compassion for what they each knew Evony was about to endure.

Evony thought of turning and running—running out of the shop and back to the safety of Stavos and her little hovel in the village. But at once an image of her mother flittered through her mind, and she was calmed—resolved to what she must endure if she were ever to find out what had happened to her mother and her aunt—if Stavos were ever to solve the mystery of the twelve sleepy princesses.

And so, gritting her teeth against the pain she knew would come next, Evony lifted her skirt to her knees. She heard the fling of the willow wand cut the air before she felt the excruciating sting on the back of her legs just below her knees—at least the first time she heard it. Thereafter, the sound seemed simultaneous with the pain.

Evony closed her eyes tightly shut, envisioning her mother's face in her mind's eye as Agnes Teche whipped—relishing the lingering sensation of Stavos's warm kiss on her lips.

CHAPTER SIX

The wind was so cold. It cut through Evony's thin shawl with little effort, chilling her to her core as she made her way home.

The sun was already setting. Still, she hoped to rest a bit before making her

to the inn in the woods again to watch Stavos interact with Ewan Happer and the women of the Midnight Masquerade. That morning, Stavos had demanded she not go to the inn again. Still, she could not stay away—that she knew for certain.

Oh, how Evony wished she hadn't had to go to Mrs. Teche's shop for the day—that she could've stayed and heard all that Stavos had discovered during his first infiltration of Ewan Happer's secret world. The wondering of what Stavos had learned the night before had nearly driven her mad as she'd sat stitching and stitching and stitching all the day long. Yet the kiss—the kiss Stavos had stolen just before she'd left for the seamstress's shop—it had carried her through, even distracted her from the pain of the red welts throbbing on the backs of her legs. What a magnificent kiss it had been!

Even for the bitter cold, Evony smiled at the memory of it, her insides feeling warmer than they had the moment before. Of course, several young men had stolen kisses from her over the years—princes or young noblemen who were playful, if not arrogant enough to risk such a thing as kissing a princess. And handsome and charming though each one was, no kiss had ever affected Evony the way Stavos Voronin's had!

Over and over throughout the day, Evony had let her thoughts nest on the memory of Stavos's kiss. She wondered for an instant how many other young ladies he'd kissed in like manner—then determined to make believe there had been no others.

She could see the light in the window of home then. It spurred her on, quickened her pace even for the soreness in her ankle and the still throbbing pain at the back of her legs. Lovie would have made ham for their supper, and Mikol and Tressa would be waiting with warm hugs and kisses. For a moment, Evony wished that Stavos would be there too, but she knew he would be at the inn, resting and preparing for the night to come.

Evony knocked softly on the door, smiling as she heard Tressa exclaim, "It's Evony! She's home!" as she pulled the door open to let her elder sister in. "Evony!" Tressa cried, throwing her arms around Evony's neck in a loving greeting. "We've missed you so! All day we've missed you! And it's so very cold out tonight. I was worried you would freeze walking home to us."

"Oh, but I am fine and well," Evony said, returning Tressa's embrace. "And, oh, so happy to be home with you and Mikol."

"And Miss Lovie," Tressa added.

"Yes," Evony giggled. "And of course, our dear Miss Lovie."

"And Stavos too?" Tressa asked. She drew her arms from around Evony's neck, took her hand, and turned her to see that, indeed, Stavos himself was sitting in a chair just behind the door.

"Good evening, Evony," Stavos greeted, smiling with amusement as Evony immediately began to neaten her hair.

"Good evening," she greeted in response, blushing to the tips of her toes at the memory of his kiss.

"And how did your day with Agnes Teche fare?" he asked, rising and striding to stand in front of her.

Tressa quickly drew the latch across the door, hurrying back to where Mikol was helping Miss Lovie to set the table.

"Stavos has come to sup with us, Evony," Mikol called, smiling. "And he's brought pastries for our desserts."

Evony nodded to Mikol and then continued to smooth her mussed hair as she answered Stavos. "Much the same way it always does. Only…I did listen to the things she went about today with a little more adherence than usual."

"I've brought the hairbrush, Evony," Tressa announced, suddenly appearing behind Evony in possession of the hairbrush she used each evening to brush Evony's hair.

"Oh…oh, thank you, Tressa," Evony stammered as Stavos simply stood smiling at her. "But I think we should wait until after supper to—"

"But I always brush your hair for you after a day at Mrs. Teche's," Tressa interrupted. "You say it's your solace."

"Then by all means, Tressa," Stavos said. "You must brush your sister's hair for her. I can talk with her just as well with her hair being brushed as without it."

"Then come along, Stavos," Tressa said, taking Evony's hand and leading her to sit on the bed. "Bring your chair, and you can talk while I brush."

"Yes, little princess," Stavos chuckled.

Evony had not expected Stavos to be there when she returned home—dreamt of it, yes, but not expected the dream to come true. Yet now there she sat—a sad, tattered, tired mess on the edge of her bed, with the very fresh and rested-looking Prince Stavos seated on a chair before her.

Evony gasped when she felt Tressa begin to tug the pins from her hair in order to release it from its hold. It was certainly one thing to appear before Stavos in such a disheveled state—but to have her hair down in front of him was entirely improper!

"Hush, Evony," Tressa scolded, having misunderstood the reason for Evony's slight gasp. "You are such a baby sometimes. I will be careful with the knotted strands, silly goose."

"Forgive me, but she does not know the improprieties here, my prince," Evony began to apologize to Stavos.

Stavos simply grinned, studied Evony from head to foot, and shook his head. "What did you learn today in Agnes Teche's shop?" he asked.

What he would not give to be the one to loose her hair one day, Stavos thought as he watched Evony's chestnut hair cascade down about her shoulders and neck. What was it about a woman's hair that always lent such softness, such defenselessness to her appearance? he wondered. Evony Elorietta was a changed woman without her hair pulled into such a spinsterly knot at the back of her head. Of course, she was a tasty little morsel indeed, no matter what she wore or how her hair was coiffed. But this vision before him now—she was temptingly vulnerable in appearance, soft and alluring.

Stavos's attraction to her only escalated the more her discomfort increased, in fact. The way the fire from the hearth reflected in her jade-green eyes mesmerized him—drew him in like some bewitchment. He could not stop his thoughts and gaze from lingering on her mouth—the petal-soft lips he'd kissed so briefly that very morning. He thought how confectionary a deepened kiss would taste with her, and the idea caused him to involuntarily moisten his lips.

"She...Mrs. Teche was quite impatient that we finish two new dresses today," came Evony's first answer. "They were very elaborate, and she said she would deliver them to the patron herself...this evening."

"And you think she means them for Ewan Happer?" Stavos asked.

"Who is Ewan Happer?" Mikol asked. Stavos was startled to find the boy standing right beside him, for he had neither seen nor heard him approach.

"Mikol, you mustn't worry about anything," Evony answered. "Stavos and I are both working very hard to—"

"Of course I must worry, Evony!" Mikol exclaimed unexpectedly. "I am to be king one day! Elawyth and its people are already suffering, and it is my responsibility to see that they do not suffer a day longer!"

Stavos looked to see Evony's expression of astonishment. "Hush, Mikol," Evony soothed in a whisper. "You must speak quietly. No one must know that you are—"

"I cannot sit idle by, Evony!" Mikol continued, however. "I cannot sit by and watch you labor for that crone of a seamstress, or let some other man do that which is my responsibility to do!" Gesturing to Stavos, Mikol added, "Though I am grateful, and eternally indebted, to you, Prince Stavos...for your service to us all."

"Mikol, listen to me—" Evony began.

But Stavos understood the young prince's concern, pride, and worry. "No, he is right," he therefore stated. "You are right, Mikol. I was wrong to take on this challenge without your help in the first of it. And now...I think you must know all that we know, Evony and I."

"Really?" Mikol asked, obviously astonished by Stavos's support.

"Of course," Stavos answered. "You are to be king of Elawyth one day, and the missing Queen Charmaine is your own mother—not to mention that Evony is your sister and therefore also your responsibility. In fact, I would maintain that even the twelve princesses of Abawyth may fall under your responsibility of protection. Therefore, I will tell you, Mikol. I will tell you all that I know. And I hope Evony will do the same."

"He is too young for such worries, Stavos!" Evony cried out as tears filled her eyes. The thought of such burdens being settled on her small brother's shoulders caused her heart to ache for him. He was a child and should not have such burdensome worries. "He should be in the street playing with the other boys in the village...building snowmen and hurtling rocks at wagon wheels. He should not have the worries of all of this."

"And yet is it fair to keep him in ignorance, Evony?" Stavos asked. "When so much is at stake?"

"But he is my little brother!" she cried. "He is mine to protect and…ow!"

In her emotional state, Evony had leapt from her seat on the bed to standing and, in doing so, had scraped the sore welts on the backs of her legs against the bed's frame.

"Whatever is the matter, love?" Miss Lovie asked, hurrying to Evony's side. "Is it your ankle?"

"No…no, 'tis nothing," Evony lied, even for the renewed pain of the welts Mrs. Teche's willow wand had left.

"Evony!" Tressa exclaimed then. "You're bleeding! Your legs are bleeding!"

Mikol leaned down to investigate Evony's legs, and Stavos rose from his seat, frowning with concern.

"She gave you the wand, didn't she?" Mikol asked. "For being tardy this morning."

"Not exactly," Evony whispered.

And before she knew what was happening, Stavos had taken her arm, turning her away from him and hunkering down himself to investigate her legs.

"What goes on here?" he growled.

Tressa, wiping tears from her cheeks, explained, "That old Mrs. Teche uses a willow switch to beat her daughters when they make her unhappy…or to beat Evony when she is tardy."

"What?" Stavos nearly roared. "On this bed, girl…now!" he ordered.

Evony could not make to move before he had lifted her and laid her on her stomach on the bed. She could feel Stavos and Miss Lovie removing her shoes and then her stockings. She was humiliated—far beyond humiliated.

Evony felt Miss Lovie's cold fingers on the backs of her legs—felt Stavos's warm ones as well. And then he growled, "Five on each leg is my count. She switched you five times on each leg?"

Frantically, Evony rolled over to her back and tried to sit. "But I learned so much today, Stavos. If only you'll listen to what I have to—"

"She beat you with a willow wand, Evony!" he interrupted. He was furious, the anger so apparent that his narrow eyes fairly blazed with it. Shaking his head, he gritted his teeth and said, "I will not allow this to go unheeded…nor unpunished."

He turned on his heel, and Evony knew what he meant to do.

"Stop him, Mikol! He means to call out Mrs. Teche!" Evony cried. "We cannot let her know what we are doing! Mother's life may depend on it!"

"Mother's life?" Mikol gasped. Quickly Mikol barred Stavos's way to the door. "You cannot leave, Prince Stavos. I cannot let you leave without first telling me all you know."

But Stavos was yet enraged. Pointing to Evony, he growled, "The woman has beaten your sister, Mikol! Drawn blood! It cannot go without condemnation!"

"Only wait, sire," Miss Lovie ventured. "Think clearly for a moment."

"Do not try to stop me," Stavos threatened, however.

It was then that desperation clutched Evony. Stavos could not leave; he could not call out Agnes Teche, or all would be lost! Yet who would stop him? Miss Lovie—an old woman? Mikol and Tressa—two children? No! Evony knew that only she had the chance to stay Stavos—to keep him from revealing all in his anger.

Therefore, rising to stand on her feet on her bed, she leapt onto Stavos's back, wrapping her arms tightly around his neck as she wrapped her legs around his middle.

"You cannot leave in this temper!" she told him. "You risk everyone's safety! Everyone's!"

And Evony's efforts seemed to work. Stavos was caught not only surprised but also off balance. Stumbling backward, he fell into a heap with Evony on the bed.

"Release me, woman!" he demanded.

"Not until you settle your temper!" Evony demanded in return.

Stavos was silent for several long moments—though his broad chest rose and fell with the labored breathing of fury.

At last, however, as Miss Lovie stood clutching Tressa and Mikol at her sides, Stavos spoke. "If you want to take me to your bed, Evony Elorietta…you only need ask. Such lengths of restraint and forcefulness are not necessary, I assure you."

Mortified with embarrassment, Evony instantly released him, sliding back across the bed and away from him. Stavos sat straight, rubbing at his neck as though Evony had caused him discomfort.

"Forgive me, please…each of you," he sighed, rising to his feet. "But I cannot stand idle by when a woman has been abused. I…I do not excuse the anger that came over me, Evony. I only admit to it." He turned to look at her, and the warm smolder in his blue eyes rendered her breathless and unable to move. How could any woman not forgive him his burst of temper—not forgive him of anything, for that matter?

Tressa sniffled, and Stavos stretched his arms out to her. She was in them in an instant, held warm and safe in his embrace. "I will keep your sister safe, Tressa…I promise. No more beatings. And I will give her one more day under Agnes Teche's employ, but I swear if she tries to return after that, I will tie her up and sit on her to keep her here. All right?"

Tressa sniffled once more and nodded, clinging to Stavos for comfort.

"Now, I know your sister is weary and worn from an obviously miserable day with that old crone," Stavos began. "So what's say you and Miss Lovie snatch two of the extra pastries I brought tonight and enjoy a little treat before supper—just this once—while I talk with Evony and Mikol a moment, all right?"

"All right," Tressa agreed.

"Come along, darling," Miss Lovie said, taking Tressa's hand. "We'll have our pastry in my rooms."

Tressa smiled as Miss Lovie retrieved two of the pastries from the plate at the center of the table. As Miss Lovie led the child toward the door, Tressa looked back to Stavos and asked, "You won't take long?"

"Not long at all, dumpling," he answered with a reassuring smile and wink.

The moment Miss Lovie had closed the door behind her and Tressa, Stavos turned, placing both powerful fists on the bed as he leaned toward Evony.

"You should not have endured the switching, Evony," he grumbled, frowning at her. "You should have walked away before letting that old hag harm you." He wasn't shouting—not really. Still, Evony heard the residual anger in his voice.

"Yes, Evony," Mikol agreed. "You should not have allowed it."

But Evony retorted, "Perhaps not. But I had to be certain that Mrs. Teche did, in fact, have some sort of knowledge of Ewan Happer's escapades...and now I do. If she means to deliver the dresses to him in person, she has to know that at least something is afoot. These are expensive dresses...not the sort a common innkeeper could afford to commission."

Stavos nodded and exhaled a sigh of compliance. Taking his seat on the chair before the bed once more, he retrieved the hairbrush that Tressa had abandoned.

"Here," he said, offering the brush to Evony. "You'll feel better if you brush your hair as we talk." As Evony accepted the brush with one trembling hand, Stavos looked to Mikol and said, "Pull over a chair, Mikol. There is much to discuss."

Mikol smiled and nodded with the pleasure of being included in the conversation. He hurried to retrieve a chair from near the table and placed it just beside Stavos.

Running her fingers back through her hair, Evony then began to brush the long mane of chestnut she'd inherited from her mother. Brushing her hair always settled her nerves.

"So Agnes Teche is in league with Ewan Happer," Mikol began. "But I have questions. Who is Ewan Happer? And why do you think Mother is alive, Evony?"

"If I may, Mikol," Stavos began. "I have much to discuss with Evony. Yet I must also away very soon...and you will understand why once Evony tells the whole of the tale to you. Might I ask that you listen as I speak with your sister, even if you do not understand all? Otherwise I may be late getting back to the inn and raise suspicion."

"Of course," Mikol agreed.

Stavos looked to Evony, momentarily distracted by the manner in which she was brushing her hair. She'd brushed the long mane of silk to one side and over one shoulder. It gave her the look of a calm beauty—of allure and, again, vulnerability. But Stavos knew his time was short. If he did not return to the inn in time for supper but suddenly appeared for the Midnight Masquerade, Ewan Happer might well wonder what could keep a patron more entertained than his diabolical efforts.

Thus, trying to ignore his powerful attraction to the princess settled so trustingly on the bed before him, he began to tell Evony of what he had learned the night before.

"First, I have determined which of the women at the Midnight Masquerade are your cousins, Evony," he offered.

"Our cousins?" Mikol gasped.

"In due time, Mikol…remember?" Evony soothed her brother.

"I hope it gives you a small measure of comfort to know that they do seem well enough…considering," Stavos added.

"Yes," Evony agreed. "Especially Patrice, I noticed."

Stavos frowned. "What do you mean?"

"Patrice," Evony repeated. "I saw that you favored her over any other woman last night."

"Patrice?" Mikol asked. But when Stavos looked to him, the boy clamped a hand over his mouth in a gesture he would not interrupt again.

"Yes, Mikol," Evony said, however. "It seems Prince Stavos favors our cousin Patrice. I have no doubt that when he has solved it all, Patrice will be his choice of wife."

Stavos could not keep an understanding grin from spreading over his face. Evony was jealous! It was there in the envious expression in her lovely eyes; in fact, their jade green fairly flashed with it. Stavos felt a warm and delicious satisfaction settle in his chest at the knowledge.

"And how do you come by such a bold assumption?" he baited her.

"You danced with Patrice three times to every other girl's once last night," she answered without pause. "At least for the hours I was present." She waved a hand in a gesture of dismissal, however, and said, "But that is no matter. So you have sorted the princesses from the other unfortunate maidens caught up in Ewan Happer's activities. What else?"

Trying not to broaden his smile of amusement and pleasure in Evony's obvious jealousy, Stavos answered, "There is a man there, employed by Happer for some purpose. He appeared several times throughout the night, and each time Happer was unsettled for a moment. Then, at one time, I heard him say to the man, 'Then give them more water and food! Keep them quiet is all. Give them whatever they require to settle down for the night.'"

"And what do you think it means?" Evony asked, her eyes wide with intrigue.

"I don't know," Stavos admitted. "But there's something else."

"And what's that?" Mikol asked before again clamping a hand over his mouth.

Stavos smiled at Mikol, reached out, and tousled his hair with understanding. He knew it was difficult for Mikol to listen without knowing what Evony and Stavos already knew. Evony smiled, in admiration at Stavos's patience and understanding with her brother.

"The dimensions of the inn," Stavos began to answer. "There is no sense to them."

"What do you mean?" Evony inquired as she twisted her hair into a long, loose braid and tossed it to her back.

"I walked the perimeter several times yesterday morning," he said, "while Happer was still unconscious with intoxication from the night before. Then last night, during the dancing, I walked the perimeter of the inside of the ballroom and then the inn itself. It is obvious there is more to the structure than is easily visible…even if one is aware of the secret ballroom."

Evony frowned. "What would that mean?" she asked.

"Well, to my way of thinking, as well as experience in the building of structures, it would seem to me that the ballroom is not the only room or rooms of the inn that are well hidden." Stavos chuckled a moment. "In fact, one has to admire whomever built it…for when you approach or are a resident of one of the rooms, you are well aware of the rooms for visitors, the pub, and dining areas. But because the trees are so thick round about the sides and back of the structure—coupled with the fact that the outer walls are somehow deceiving in their depth—any person would not think the inn is any larger than the obvious rooms observed by patrons. I wager even a local man might not find anything suspicious in its perimeter…unless it is measured from within and without. Then it is apparent, mathematically, that there is more to the inn than meets the eye."

"How is that relevant…the fact that there is more space that is unseen than just the ballroom?" Evony inquired.

But Stavos shrugged broad shoulders and answered, "I do not know. Perhaps the space is simply used for storage. Or perhaps it is where some of the ladies of the Midnight Masquerade who are not royals reside during the day." Stavos glanced to Mikol then as if deciding whether to continue. "Or even it may be a space used for…for goings-on of ill repute between strangers…men and women."

Evony gasped, horrified at the thought Stavos had suggested. "Stavos! Surely not!"

But Stavos shrugged once more. "If Happer is using princesses to attract men and line his pockets with gold and silver, it stands to reason that the girls who are not princesses may find themselves in much more dire circumstances than even your cousins, Evony."

Evony's stomach churned with nausea. Could it all be so much more horrid than she'd even thought before? And worse, how could one man, even Prince Stavos Voronin of Ethiarien, combat it? How could he possibly thwart Ewan Happer, King Standwood, and everyone else who might be involved, all alone?

"It seems hopeless," Evony whispered her thoughts aloud.

"No...only challenging," Stavos said, taking her hand in his and raising it to his lips to kiss the back of it in reassurance. "We simply have to bide our time...work more and more of it out for ourselves before we act. Therefore, I will attend the Midnight Masquerade again tonight. I will discover more and more, Evony...and I will ruse Happer into taking me into his confidence. The more I discover, the more power we have, very well?"

"But—" she began to argue.

"And I will go alone this time, Evony," he reminded her. "I will not have you put yourself in further danger by spying on me at the inn. I'm a big boy, and I can fend for myself."

"Well, I think—" she began again.

"And I'm giving you one more day in Agnes Teche's company," he interrupted, however. "You did accomplish all to this point, entirely on your own. And now it is time for you to allow me to champion you, your brother, your sister, and whomever else I may serve. Therefore, glean what you can from Agnes tomorrow, for the day after that...you become mine. I will keep you and yours well and fed here, including Miss Lovie. Until this is all at an end, you will be in my care beginning tomorrow night."

It was not a request but an informing. At first, Evony's pride manifested in her countenance, she knew. But he was right. The fact was that Stavos's appearance in the street of Abawyth—his carrying her to Agnes Teche's shop—had already given rise to Agnes's temper and suspicion of Evony.

"But what will I tell her is my reason for leaving her employ?" Evony asked. There must be a reason—a reason that would be believed by Agnes Teche.

"Tell her the truth of it," Stavos answered, "of the nobleman whose horse nearly trampled you...that you have agreed to be his mistress and that he will care for you and yours, so you no longer require another means of earning wages."

"And the old crone will easily believe that, Evony," Mikol interjected. "She knows you are beautiful and that a man such as Stavos would want to keep you."

"Mikol!" Evony exclaimed, blushing through and through. "You should not even be privy to such ideas."

But Mikol rolled his eyes with exasperation. "It's not as if Stavos truly intends to bed you, Evony. It's only pretense, after all."

Evony gasped with being mortified that her little brother had knowledge of such things. But Stavos only chuckled and tousled Mikol's hair once more.

"A future king must be informed of all the ways of the world, Evony," Stavos explained, "even the loathsome things."

Mikol smiled and nodded with affirmation.

"But he's only a child!" Evony whimpered, sickened in realizing that Mikol's innocence was tainted.

"He's a prince and a future king, as am I," Stavos reminded her. "It would be a disservice to us and our people if we were not prepared to face any situation or truth." He smiled at Mikol once more and added, "Is it not true, my brother prince?"

"It is, my brother prince," Mikol answered.

"Now, I must away to the inn, lest Happer wonders what I am about," Stavos said, rising from his chair. "Let Tressa know I am sorry I could not stay to sup with you, Mikol, please," he said to Mikol. "And you," he said, turning his attention to Evony. He smiled, reached out, and tugged at her braid. "You remain here and rest. Tomorrow is your last day with Agnes Teche, and you must glean all that you can." His smile turned to a frown as he added, "And place some cool, moist cloths on those injuries on your legs. They will soothe you. Then after tomorrow, you are Edith no more...simply Evony Elorietta, Princess of Elawyth, understood?"

"Yes, your highness," Evony responded tersely.

But Stavos smiled, patted her cheek as if she were only Tressa's age, and then turned to leave. "Keep her in, Mikol. It is I can already read her thoughts through her eyes, and she means to entirely disobey me. So tie her to the bed if you must…but do not let her wander to the woods tonight."

"Yes, sir," Mikol agreed, smiling at Stavos's insight.

Stavos was gone then, and Mikol drew the bolt across the door before turning to Evony and saying, "Tell me all of it, Evony. Everything you and Stavos know."

"Yes," Evony said, nodding. "Stavos is right. You should know."

Smiling at her little brother—her little brother who was far too young to carry such burdens as he already did—Evony began to reveal all that she knew about the twelve sleeping princesses and the two sister queens who had disappeared, all the while silently plotting how she would evade Mikol's guard in the dark hours of midnight to make her way to the little window to watch Stavos at the Midnight Masquerade.

"It is even thicker than I thought…this muddy mess of mystery," Stavos told his companion as they sat supping in the dining room of the inn.

"That is growing more and more apparent," the man sharing the meal with Stavos affirmed. "So what would you have me do? How should I act?"

"Well, my fear is that you and I alone will not be enough when it comes to facing Standwood…which it will come to, I am certain," Stavos answered. "But as I have not unraveled it all yet, I say send William with a message, for we will need more men, I am sure. Whether or not the queens are found alive, whether or not their lives are in truth what Happer holds over the Abawythian princesses, you and I alone—though a formidable force indeed—will not be enough."

The man nodded. "I agree." He paused a moment and then added, "I will send William tonight."

"Thank you, Andrew," Stavos said, "though I still do not understand why you chose to accompany me on the quest to prove my capability to Father."

Andrew laughed and in a lowered voice answered, "Because if you fail, then the rule of Ethiarien will one day fall to me…and I do not want to be king. Therefore, I will help to ensure that you will!"

"You're so very kind, brother," Stavos grumbled.

"Come now, Stavos," Andrew encouraged. "Solve this mystery of Abawyth, and you will have her princess of your choice as bride…and the sure inheritance of the rule of Ethiarien!"

"Fail in solving the mystery or marrying a princess of Abawyth and it will be King Andrew instead of King Stavos who rules Ethiarien one day," Stavos reminded himself aloud. "But fear not, little brother, for I *will* have what I want. That I vow. But I cannot promise the same for you."

Andrew chuckled. "I can make my own way, brother. You worry about your quest for Father, and let me worry about mine."

"Done," Stavos said, smiling. "Now send William with the message, for I sense that time is not our ally in this matter."

"I'll send him tonight, brother," Andrew said. Then smiling, he added, "Whilst you are in the arms of your preferred damsel in misery at the Midnight Masquerade, William will be on his way."

Stavos smiled. "She was jealous, you know."

"Who?" Andrew asked. "The princess Evony?"

"Yes. She was quite perturbed that I appeared to prefer her cousin Patrice over the other young ladies at the dance."

"And that pleases you, doesn't it?" Andrew asked with a knowing expression.

"It does," Stavos admitted.

"And will it be the princess Patrice you choose once you've thwarted Happer and his Midnight Masquerade? Once you've thwarted Standwood?" Andrew asked. "I have heard she is lovely…in feature, figure, and character."

Stavos smiled. "I have heard that as well."

"Then you have already chosen your prize?" Andrew asked. "Though all the princesses are masked at the dance…though you've never seen their faces?"

"There's more to a woman than her face, Andrew," Stavos teased.

"Well, of course there is, brother. But I would think you would want to at least see all the princesses unmasked before making your choice."

But Stavos shrugged. "Some choices are more easily made than others, little brother. Sometimes the obvious is obvious and undeniable," Stavos answered. "And I will have what I want…all of what I want. You will see."

CHAPTER SEVEN

Evony was grateful that this night was not as cold as the previous had been. Her feet were not quite as numb as they had been the night before. As she stood peering through the small window of the inn's ballroom, she knew she would be able to remain at the window for a longer period of time—though she was uncertain as to whether to be grateful, considering that Stavos had already owned three dances with Patrice.

The man Stavos had mentioned seeing several times the night previous suddenly entered the ballroom, and all thoughts of cold were lost to Evony. Indeed, she watched as the homely man approached Ewan Happer and seemed to mumble something quietly to him. Happer frowned, exhaled a visible sigh, and responded. Then the terribly unattractive man nodded and left by way of a small door behind the musicians.

Happer did not look pleased. In fact, he drew a pipe from his pocket and began stuffing it with tobacco. Evony frowned, wondering what the homely man had said to Happer to provoke his temper.

Patrice danced past the window then, held firmly in the arms of Stavos, of course, and Evony's attention was drawn from Happer to Stavos and her cousin. Oh, how her temper flared as she watched them together, smiling at one another just as if they were old friends—or lovers.

"Some of the rest of us might like to enjoy a dance with him now and again, Patrice," Evony mumbled to herself. Yet she knew it was not Patrice's fault that Stavos was smitten by her. In fact, it was not even a fault in Stavos. He was, after all, planning to choose a bride from amongst her twelve cousins in the end of it. And why not Patrice? She was more than worthy of Stavos.

But no matter how she tried to convince herself otherwise, Evony could not let go of the deep-rooted envy that had taken hold of her heart. Over and over, since the very day she'd met Stavos— nearly been trampled by his horse—Evony had endeavored to let go of dreaming of the handsome prince of Ethiarien. He wasn't for her, after all, but for one of her cousins—and at his father's bidding. Furthermore, no prince questioned his king father, no matter the circumstances. Therefore, Evony knew that if she continued to be naive and foolish enough to dream of Stavos choosing her over a princess of Abawyth, he would never disappoint or disobey his father.

Evony closed her eyes and shook her head. She was being ridiculous, and she knew it. Two kingdoms were at stake, and who knew how many lives, including her mother's and her aunt's. Why wasn't her attention on solving the problem before her, rather than being frustrated over circumstances that did not matter?

The filthy hand that suddenly clamped over mouth from behind, mingled with the strong arm wrapped around her waist from the same direction, caused Evony to begin struggling at once.

"And what have we here?" a deep, raspy voice asked in her ear. "Who sent you, girl? And what are you doing at this window?"

Again Evony tried to struggle, but the man's hold was too tight.

"Settle yourself, girl," another voice said. Evony glanced up to see that none other than Ewan Happer himself was standing before her, puffing his pipe. The burning embers of tobacco in the pipe glowed in the darkness, lighting Happer's face and causing him to look like the devil himself.

"Now, if I have Cedric here uncover your mouth, do you promise not to scream?" Happer asked. "'Cause if you do, I'll have him slit your gullet. Do you hear me, girl?"

Trying not to panic, or faint from fear, Evony nodded. She inhaled a long, gasping breath through her mouth once the filthy hand had retreated.

"Now what are you doing at that window?" Happer inquired.

"W-watching the dance, sir," Evony answered in a whisper.

Happer and Cedric both chuckled. "Well, that much I gathered, deary," Happer said. "But why were you watching?"

Evony knew that in that moment her life was in peril. Ewan Happer and his henchman, Cedric, would kill her before they would let the secret of the Midnight Masquerade escape. Oh, why hadn't she stayed home the way Stavos had instructed?

Grateful that her wits returned promptly, Evony answered, "I-I was seeking a way of earning w-wages, sir."

"Were you now?" Happer asked. "And just what led you to the inn—or, rather, to this side of the inn—and at such an hour as this?"

"I-I overhead a conversation today," Evony stammered. "I heard something happened here…something that could earn a woman better money than sewing does earn me now."

"And where did you hear this conversation?" Happer asked, moving closer to her.

But Evony shook her head. "I cannot tell you, sir…else I risk a far worse punishment than I already endured this day."

Happer frowned. "Punishment? What sort of punishment?"

"If I tell you, sir…she might kill me this time!" Evony sobbed.

"Who?" Happer asked. He nodded to Cedric, and Evony felt his dirty hand encircle her throat. "Tell me who, or I'll have Cedric choke the life from you."

There was no other course open to her but to tell him. "I-I sew for Agnes Teche, sir. In f-fact, the dresses she delivered today to you…I stitched them. They are my work. I followed her here and waited until she left. Then I saw the light in the window, through the tear in the curtain and…and…"

Much to her surprise, Ewan Happer began to chuckle. "That old biddy!" he laughed. "She has been holding out on me, it seems, for you're far more lovely than any of the other girls she has sent to work for me here…even her own daughters. It would be like Agnes to sacrifice her own children before giving over a pretty little seamstress like you to me. She's made loads of coin off me with them dresses you've stitched, my pretty. But no more! Right? Nope, ol' Agnes will have to find some other young thing to torture…because you'll be working for me now, girl, dancing the night away. And no worries…for I'll pay you twice what old Agnes Teche did."

Evony gasped as Happer bent and lifted her skirt. He pulled down one of her stockings and studied the welts on her legs.

"And there won't be none of this, neither," he laughed. "Yep, I can spot old Agnes's girls easy enough." Happer shook his head. "That woman's a devil with a willow switch."

"S-so…you'll hire me to…to dance with those men in there?" Evony ventured. "And pay me well for doing so?"

Ewan Happer smiled, puffed on his pipe, and answered, "That I will. But on one condition."

"Yes?" Evony urged.

"If you tell anyone about what you've seen here or what you're doing for me for work or about any of the men you spend your time with under my roof…I'll have Cedric here slit your throat before you can blink an eye. Do we have an understanding?"

"Yes, sir." Evony answered. "We do. And…and I do understand the importance of secrecy."

"Good," Happer sighed. "Then Cedric will take you to the closet where we keep those gowns you and Mrs. Teche worked so hard to make. Choose a gown and a mask, and get dressed. You'll start this evening, I think." He started to go but paused. "Oh, and one thing more. You are never to give any man your real name, got it? In fact, let's call you…hmmm…let's call you Lynet and leave it at that. Furthermore, you're never to inquire of any of the gentlemen as to their name or from whence they have traveled. If you do…"

"Y-you'll have Cedric slit my throat?" Evony whimpered.

"Why, yes, I will, love," Ewan chuckled. "You're a smart girl, you are." He studied her from head to toe a moment, adding, "And with an ample bosom. Yes, you and I…we'll make plenty of money in each other's company."

"Come along, Lynet," Cedric said, taking hold of her arm. "It's time we got you ready for the Midnight Masquerade."

As Cedric began to lead Evony away, Ewan Happer called, "Oh, and Lynet…"

"Yes, sir?" Evony asked.

"Try that green gown old Agnes delivered today," he instructed. "I think it might look right nice with those green eyes of yours."

"He can see that my eyes are green? Even for the darkness?" Evony asked Cedric as he pulled her along.

"Yes, miss," Cedric confirmed. "Old Ewan…he can see a lot of things even for the darkness. Some folks say it's because he's the devil's own brother."

"I wouldn't doubt it for a moment," Evony mumbled.

"It's well you shouldn't, miss. It's well you shouldn't."

Stavos watched as Ewan Happer finally reappeared by way of the door behind the musicians. Where had he been? And where was the sinister-looking fellow who was always reporting to him about something? Stavos deduced the malevolent-looking man who was ever scurrying to Ewan Happer's side and whispering information to him most likely served as Happer's guard dog and henchman. No doubt Happer sent him out to patrol the grounds in case any would-be curiosity-seekers might happen upon his secretive, immoral enterprises. Stavos surmised that the man probably saw to anything Happer ordered him to see to. He knew the type; it was not Stavos's first step into the world of secrecy and evil design.

Though Happer had returned to the ballroom, his guard dog had not. Stavos wondered what the man was about. He worried in that moment that perhaps Mikol had not been able to keep Evony from following him into the woods in order to spy on the Midnight Masquerade. What if she had followed and Happer's henchman found her lurking about?

Still, he calmed himself with remembering that even if Evony had ignored his pleas that she stay at home, she had been somehow circumventing Happer and his man for some time before Stavos had arrived in Abawyth. So what reason was there to think she would not yet be able to avoid him?

The henchman. Yes, Stavos would need to find out more about Happer's trusted man. If anyone knew the details of Happer's endeavors, it would be he.

"You seem distracted, sir," the princess with whom Stavos was dancing commented.

Stavos looked down into the beautiful green eyes of the woman he knew to be the princess Patrice. Smiling, he said, "Not at all, my lady. I suppose I'm merely not used to keeping such late hours as this."

"Nor was I before..." the princess Patrice began.

"Before what, dove?" Stavos pressed.

But Patrice's lovely smile had vanished. "Oh, oh...before I was allowed to keep such hours."

"Ah. I see," Stavos offered in an effort to soothe her nerves. Yet she had stiffened in his arms and would not be soothed for the moment. Stavos knew Patrice had almost revealed too much. It was obvious the near slip had frightened her. Thus, he changed the venue of their conversation. "So tell, me, Rosemaria," he began, addressing her by the name she had given him when first they'd danced the night before, "of all the men in attendance tonight, of all the partners you've shared dances with, who is your preferred partner?"

Even for the lovely white mask covering most of her face, Stavos knew she had blushed.

"Why...why, you, of course, sir," she answered.

Stavos chuckled. "What a wise and flattering response, my dear."

"But it's the truth," she told him. "For one, you are the only man who has not attempted to take unsolicited familiarities with me."

"You mean, as of yet," he teased.

She giggled. "Yes. As of yet."

"And?" he prodded.

"You are not the most accomplished dancer of all the men here," she complimented.

Stavos laughed. "An insult? My rather unrefined dancing finds me in your favor? How so?"

Patrice smiled up at him. "I find it attractive…very masculine, in truth."

"Well, thank you, dear Rosemaria. I am quite flattered, in truth," Stavos said.

"I hope so, sire…for I am being sincere," she told him.

The music ended, and Stavos bowed to Patrice as he released her from his arms. "Thank you for the dance, Rosemaria," he told her. "And if I may return the compliment and say…that you are my favored partner thus far as well."

"Thank you, sir," Patrice giggled, dropping a perfectly graceful curtsy. "Might I favor you with another dance, sir?" she asked.

Even though Stavos had fully intended to send her on her way— for it would draw too much attention from Happer and anyone else in the room were he to dance a third selection in a row with the same woman—it was Happer's voice interrupted him first.

"Here now," Happer said, "Rosemaria, you go off now. Leave this gentleman to me, and let some of the others enjoy your charms a while."

Stavos turned to look at Happer, forcing a friendly smile to his face as he studied the ugly man before him.

"Are you enjoying yourself this evening as well, sir?" Happer asked.

"Blissfully," Stavos answered, feigning delight. "These young ladies are truly pleasurable company." Grinning slyly and lowering his voice, he added, "My one regret is that we men are only allowed to dance with them, yes? There are one or two that I fancy I wouldn't mind finding myself in seclusion with…if you follow my inference?"

At that, Ewan Happer's face lit up like the morning sun in summer.

"Why, isn't that a bit of a coincidence, sir?" Ewan asked. "For I was just on my way to introduce you to a new young lady that has joined our Midnight Masquerade this very evening." Happer lowered his voice, adding, "And for the right price, I might be persuaded to allow you a few minutes of seclusion with her…if she strikes your fancy well enough, that is."

"Really?" Stavos asked, smiling yet fighting the urge to take hold of the man's throat and crush it between his hands. Forcing women to dance with strange men for money was one thing, but to force them into…

"And here she is now, sir," Happer said, interrupting Stavos's vision of beating him. "Might I introduce you to our newest young lady of the Midnight Masquerade…Lynet."

Stavos turned to look in the direction Happer indicated. There, standing just a few feet from him, was a very pleasantly compiled young woman dressed in a gown of emerald green. Like all the other women, she wore a white mask that covered most of her face, thus hiding her identity. Yet her eyes sparkled from behind the mask as bright as two polished gems of jade.

All at once then, Stavos inhaled a deep breath to calm himself, for full recognition washed over him like a summer monsoon storm. Evony! It was Evony behind the mask! He could never mistake the opalescent green of her eyes; anywhere he would recognize them! And her lips—the soft pink lips he'd dared to kiss as she left for Agnes Teche's—and the figure—the perfect curve to her hips, the small waist, and the attractive bosom that rose and fell with the quick breathing of anxiety.

"Why, what a pleasure to meet you…Lynet, is it?" Stavos asked, taking Evony's hand and gripping it far more tightly than he should have. Yet he wanted her to know that he perceived her—that he knew she had somehow found herself in peril by joining the Midnight Masquerade.

"Yes, sir," Evony said. "And it *is* Lynet, sir."

Immediately Stavos pulled Evony into his arms as the music began once more. "Well, Lynet, I have it in mind that you and I will…shall we say…fit perfectly as dance partners. Wouldn't you agree, Happer?"

"Absolutely, sir," Ewan Happer chuckled. "I knew it the moment I saw you two in the same room together."

Stepping up beside Evony, Stavos heard Ewan Happer whisper to her, "You be good to this gentleman, girl. His pockets are deep and filled with coins. So no matter where his hands roam, you let them, do you hear me?"

"Yes, sir," Evony answered, nodding.

"Then enjoy your dance, sir," Happer said to Stavos.

"Oh, I intend to, Happer," Stavos assured him as he walked away. "I truly intend to."

Stavos Voronin was furious! Evony knew it by not only the tight grip he held her in—the way his body was pressed flush with hers as they danced—but also the flame of wrath evident in his eyes.

"What are you doing here?" he growled low in his throat.

"Please do not be angry with me," Evony whispered, inwardly begging the tears gathering in her eyes not to spill over her cheeks and give her away to Ewan Happer. "I-I was just outside watching, and…and his man—Cedric is his name—this man found me. I could think of nothing to say but that I was seeking wages and had heard of—"

"You are fortunate to have been brought here rather than to have found your throat cut and your body tossed in the river," Stavos rumbled.

"I know it," Evony whimpered. "How full well I know it, you cannot fathom."

"Smile at me," he ordered, pasting a false smile on his own face. "You must appear as if you're doing the job for which you were hired. Then give me a moment to think on this…on how to extract you from this…this mayhem you've stepped in."

"Stavos, listen," Evony whispered. "Agnes Teche is far more vile than I thought. She has sent her own to daughters here to work for Ewan Happer. I cannot believe a woman would…" Evony gasped, startled when she felt Stavos's hand at her waist move rather caressively down over the left curve of her backside.

"Quit talking at me and smile," he growled. "I need quiet in order to puzzle this out…to think of a way to…to revise my original plans now that you've walked into the hornets' nest."

Evony did smile, though her entire body began to tremble with fear and trepidation. Stavos was right: she'd compromised not only her own well-being but Stavos's—perhaps Mikol's, Tressa's, Miss Lovie's, her mother's, and...

"Listen carefully," Stavos said then. Bending to place his cheek to hers, he whispered, "Time is no longer our ally...if it ever was. We must learn as much as we are able this very evening. In truth, *I* must learn as much as I am able. You, however, must endure the remainder of the night being passed from one man to another. Otherwise Happer's suspicions may thwart us both. Do you understand?"

"Yes," she breathed. Even for the danger she was in—for the peril she had placed Stavos in were they to be discovered—even for the threat of death, she was rendered weak in his arms, her blood heated by the feel of his whiskery face against hers. A desire she could not escape caused moisture to gather in her mouth, and her arms and legs were alive with goose pimples breaking over them.

The music ended, and Stavos released her. Stepping back from her, he bowed and said, "Thank you for the dance, Lynet. I assure you that I enjoyed it immensely."

"May I, my lady?" an older man with a large belly and graying hair asked, offering his hand to Evony.

"O-of course, sir," Evony said, smiling at him. She glanced to Stavos one last time to see his lips sealed tightly with restrained anger—his beautiful eyes still burning like two flames rather than two beautiful pools behind his mask.

For more than an hour Stavos had endured it—endured watching man after man take Evony in his arms and parade her past him like a temptress he could not touch. His temper was piqued and his patience spent. Therefore, with powerful resolve and determination, he strode toward the place where Ewan Happer sat drinking ale at a table in one corner of the room.

Upon reaching Happer, he took a seat in the opposing chair at the table and said, "I know the rules as you explained them to me, Happer," Stavos began. He allowed his eyes to narrow and a wicked grin to spread across his face. "But I'm wondering if you could not bend them just a bit for me tonight, eh?"

Producing a gold coin from his vest pocket, Stavos began toying with it on the tabletop. His smile broadened as he found that Ewan's greedy eyes did, indeed, become fixated on the coin.

"And what kind of bending of the rules did you have in mind, sire?" Happer asked, still staring at the coin.

Stavos chuckled and answered, "Oh, just a wee bend, my man. Just a wee bend, a bend the like you implied earlier—such as my owning the undivided attentions of one particular lady in your employ here this evening…the newest addition to your harem of lovely women, in fact."

"Undivided attentions, you say?" Ewan repeated.

Settling the coin on the table, Stavos drew its twin from his vest pocket and placed it before Ewan as well.

"Yes. Just twenty minutes or so…alone with that tasty little tart there in the green dress," he said, nodding toward the place where Evony danced with a masked man.

"Twenty minutes?" Ewan asked. Then smiling, the miscreant snatched the two gold coins from the tabletop and said, "For two pieces of gold, you can have your way with her for thirty minutes, sire." Ewan chuckled as he pocketed the coins. Then gesturing toward Evony, he said, "I'll tell her I give her my permission to accompany you outside for a short…stroll in the moonlight. Then you may do what you will, but only out of sight of the others, mind you. Only out of sight of the others."

"Agreed," Stavos said, forcing a pleased smile.

"But make certain you bring her back as unruffled as possible. She's still got two more hours to work once you've finished with her," Ewan answered, wagging an arrogant index finger at Stavos.

Though he nodded his agreement to Ewan's terms, Stavos barely managed to keep from taking hold of the man's finger and snapping it off—had to fight to restrain himself from reaching across the table and pounding the innkeeper's face into meal.

Evony gasped when she felt someone take her arm as she stepped away from the man she'd been dancing with.

"You," Ewan Happer grunted, "you're going for a walk, love. A moonlight stroll with this gentleman here."

Evony exhaled a quiet breath of relief as she turned to see Stavos standing nearby. "But we aren't supposed to…to consort with the men…only dance with them," Evony managed to remind the fulsome innkeeper. "Cedric's instructions were very specific and—"

"I've made an exception here," Ewan said. His breath smelled like the rotted remains of uncooked fish, and Evony held her breath to keep from gagging. "You be a nice little lamb to him, you hear me?"

"Yes, sir," Evony whispered.

Stavos smiled as he approached. "Come with me, miss," he said, taking her arm. "The moon and stars are ripe for lovers tonight." Yet as he led her toward the door—as they moved far enough away from Ewan and anyone else so as not to be heard—Stavos grumbled, "I should take you out and turn you over my knee for a good spanking!"

"What are you doing?" Evony asked Stavos as they exited the inn. She could feel he was still angry with her. It was painfully obvious by his tight grip on her arm and the way he was rather marching her toward a thick cropping of trees.

The night air was cold, and frost clung to everything in sight, offering the mystical illusion that the forest was dusted in tiny diamonds—for the moonlight caressed the frost, causing each tiny crystal to sparkle with pleasure in return. The soothing scent of pine hung heavy on the air, made strong by Stavos's and Evony's footsteps on the pine needles littered on the ground.

Once they were somewhat hidden by the darkness and trees, Stavos whirled her around to face him, taking her shoulders firmly in hand. Glaring at her, he growled, "What are *you* doing, Evony? What have you done? Are you mad? You were to stay at home and allow me to discover what I might. We had a plan, for me to infiltrate…and has it not been going well? But I endure this damnable abomination tonight to find *you* arriving? Do you want to tip Happer's hand to us? Standwood's or even your cousins? What of finding your mother and her sister? But even more important, what about your own safety? This is no place for any woman, but especially you!"

"It was not my intention to join the Midnight Masquerade!" Evony cried quietly. "I-I was caught! I told you I was! Happer's man caught me peering through the window, and all I could think to explain myself was that I had heard there was work at the inn...that I needed work and was willing to...to do what was necessary."

"Peering through the window? Why were you even here?" He still held her shoulders in his firm grip. "This was my part of it! You are to remain hidden at home! Or had you forgotten that part of the strategy?"

"I couldn't help myself!" she confessed. "This is such an abominable condition, Stavos! I would have gone mad just sitting at home—waiting, wondering...waiting to see if you would return...wondering if you were learning anything! I could not endure it! And so I came. I had to see what progress you were making, which princesses you were dancing with, and I was caught. And I was quick-witted enough to save my own life...without your help or anyone else's!" As Stavos shook his head with obvious frustration, she whispered, "I am so very sorry. I did not mean to stir the pot like this."

Stavos exhaled a long breath in an attempt to settle his temper, even as he continued to glare at her. "Evony," he said through clenched teeth, "for the mere price of two gold pieces, Ewan Happer gave you over to me for half the hour," he continued. "He knows nothing about me, knows nothing of my character or morality, and he cares not what kind of man I am. He gave you over to me at my request...to do what I will. Now, what if some other man had offered payment for you, hmm? What then?"

Fear—understanding—gripped Evony then—gripped her much more tightly than Stavos's hands gripped her shoulders. She trembled as he continued to chide her.

"What if it were not I standing here alone with you, Evony Elorietta?"

"H-he agreed that I would but dance with his patrons," Evony whispered. "He promised. He promised that he would never ask more of me than to dance with those who paid."

"And you took him at his word? A man who uses your cousins as slaves?" he gently reminded.

"I-I saw no other recourse before me," she admitted.

Releasing his tight hold on her tender shoulders, Stavos straightened—inhaled a deep breath. The moment his hands left her shoulders, however, Evony's fearful trembling was joined by the discomfort of a thoroughgoing shiver for the sake of the cool night air.

Exhaling the deep breath he'd inhaled a moment before, Stavos said, "You are headstrong and selfless—indeed, qualities to be admired, but often treacherous to one's own well-being when united in a common cause involving loved ones."

"But I saw no other path before me," Evony said, gazing up at him. "What would you have done…were you me instead of you?"

She watched as an all-too-telling grin spread across Stavos's handsome face. Evony could not keep her heart from leaping in her bosom with renewed and sudden felicity as she gazed into his bluest of blue eyes, so perfectly framed and beautifully accented by the black mask he wore. Quickly she studied every visible aspect of his face—his high-set and prominent cheekbones, the slight cleft at his chin that served to emphasize his square jaw, the perfect shape of his upper lip and the light crease in the middle of his lower lip that caused her mouth to warm and water when she looked it.

"Well," he began, sighing as he studied her a moment, "any man would be a liar if he did not admit how intriguingly beautiful you are in that mask." He reached out to tug at one long strand of her hair hanging at her shoulder.

Evony smiled. "So you've chosen to flatter me rather than admit that you would have acted as I have were the circumstances reversed, is that it?"

Stavos's smile broadened as, in complete avoidance of admission, he said, "My mother does not allow masks at the balls she and my father hold. She says that masks encourage deviant behavior."

Evony smiled, relieved he no longer seemed vexed with her. "Deviant behavior?" she asked. "How does a simple mask such as mine or yours encourage deviant behavior?" She paused as she realized that her cousins were embroiled in a trade of deviant behavior and that the masks were what kept them slaves to it.

Stavos chuckled. "I see by your faded smile that you've already thought of one exemplar," he said, "that Ewan Happer would not be able to hold your cousins in such condition were it not for the masks he forces them to wear."

Evony nodded. "You are right," she admitted. "Yet to disallow them altogether?" She studied him a moment as he gazed at her—her heart leaping with pleasure once more. "Surely not all mask-wearing leads to deviant behavior."

A sudden shiver overwhelmed her then, and her teeth began to chatter.

"Here," Stavos said as he reached out and gathered her against him. "You will catch your death out here if we are not mindful."

As he wrapped powerful arms around her—as he held her tightly against the strong contours of his warm body—Evony could not resist melting to him. He was so warm—so very, very, very warm—and he smelled of woodsmoke and horsehair and all things comforting.

"I have kept you in the cold too long," he mumbled into her hair.

"No," she argued in a whisper, fisting the fabric of his shirt in her hands as she clung to him for warmth—as she clung to him simply for the fact that she wanted to linger against him, to linger in his embrace. "I know more safety here exposed to the elements as I am than I will when I return to the dance."

Evony heard the rumble of a chuckle in his chest as her head remained pressed against it. "You seem quite certain about that, Evony."

"I am certain," she sighed.

"Hmm," he said. "Naively so, perhaps…for it seems you have entirely disregarded my mother's opinions of masks…of their leading to deviant behavior."

Evony smiled, amused by his teasing manner, grateful that he was no longer angry and scolding her.

"Oh…so your mask has turned you into some malicious fiend, has it?" she taunted.

"More likely it has given me the impish boldness of a rogue," he answered in a lowered voice.

Evony smiled, asking, "How so?"

She felt his hand cup her chin as he tipped her head back so that she looked up at him. His eyes were narrowed behind his mask, and Evony felt her heart's beating increase in its rhythm.

"And after all, I did give the miscreant two gold pieces for the reserve of your attentions," Stavos mumbled.

"And you have them in reserve," she whispered. She was, of a sudden, utterly intoxicated by his appearance. As she stared up into his handsome face, she watched him moisten his lips with his tongue—and the gesture caused her stomach to leap inside her and more goose pimples to race over her arms and legs.

"You're in danger here. You know that," he mumbled.

"I know. But what else was I to do when that vile man happened upon me?" she asked him.

"I wasn't speaking of your being in danger from Happer or his guard dog, Evony," Stavos said.

As his thumb softly caressed her lips, Evony began to quiver. Something in her mind whispered that Stavos intended to kiss her. Oddly, her thoughts leapt to one afternoon when she was but fourteen—when she had arrived at the stables to find a stableman and a milkmaid wrapped in one another's arms, their mouths so blended in an impassioned exchange that, for a moment, Evony had been certain they would devour one another. She had thought the scene to be fairly scandalous at the time, yet more than a little intriguing. And for all the years since, Evony had wondered if a man would someday endeavor to devour her with such a kiss—and whether she would enjoy it.

Stavos's head descended toward hers, and Evony's eyes involuntarily closed, her heart beating so ferociously within her bosom she was sure he could hear it drumming. In that instant, all her wondering was gone. In that instant, she knew that if she were about to be devoured by Prince Stavos Voronin of Ethiarien, her soul would soar to the very blisses of heaven.

Stavos kissed her almost cautiously at first—gently pressing his lips to hers with an unhurried, tender conduct, a tentative manner that she sensed was meant to encourage her rather than overwhelm her inexperience. Several times in succession he kissed her thus, until Evony perceived her tentativeness abandoning her in the wake of the swiftly flourishing pleasure she savored in returning his affection.

It was then—after long, bliss-filled moments of bathing in the incomprehensibly affecting exchange—that Evony startled, quietly gasped when, having only just found her confidence in meeting and returning Stavos's kiss, she felt his lips part when next he kissed her—felt the warm, moist sensation of his tongue softly touching her upper lip. His hand still at her chin, he directed her head to tip to one side as his slightly open mouth tenderly claimed hers.

In an instant, Evony's instincts were wholly ripened. A wild and wonderful breathlessness began to consume her. She was rapturous with a sudden awareness of how consummately her mouth fit to his, as if it had been formed for that singular purpose—not for speaking or eating or any other necessity, but only to kiss Stavos.

Of a sudden, Evony began to shiver in slight, even for the fact that she was no longer cold but rather euphorically warm. At the perception of her trembling, Stavos's arms banded around her, pulling her body taut against his. Evony's hands slid up over the solid contours of his chest, across the breadth of his shoulders, to the back of his neck, to at last be lost in the soft dark of his hair.

She was warm—oh, so very blissfully warm—warmer than she had ever been in all her life long! Her arms, legs, and every part of her was warm. Even her mind lingered in balmy visions—fair images of a cloudless, sun-inspired sky, of green grass ever so soothing when lain upon. It was as if her mind were swimming in the tender velvet of pink and violet flowers—of yellows and lavenders and greens— and all served to somehow free her mind and body. Even as Stavos's kiss increased in eager coaxing of reciprocation from her, Evony bathed in growing warmth—warmth and rapidly heightening desire.

Unexpectedly, however, he broke the seal of their lips, his mouth traveling from her chin, caressively down over her neck, as he placed slow, moist kisses there. She could feel his breath on her sensitive flesh as his kiss tarried at the hollow of her throat a moment—quivered with fascination as his embrace of her ended so that his hands could take her face between them as he kissed her throat—as he seemed to draw some sort of enlivening elixir from her skin.

Every thread, every essence, of Evony's being was alive with delirium, so that when Stavos's hands directed her face so that their mouths were meet once more, it was like the powerful crashing of ocean waves against rock! All the pinks and lavenders and greens that had been swirling in Evony's mind only moments before suddenly burst into flaming reds and golds. And as Stavos once more bound her in his arms and against the warm, protective power of his body, Evony received his kiss with a desire she'd never known—or even imagined! Moreover, she answered his kiss—answered it as full confidently and with as much skill as if she'd been kissing him forever, and not merely a few minutes.

"Enough!" Stavos breathed, breaking not only the impassioned seal of their mouths but their embrace as well. "My point is made," he said, his breathing still labored from the intensity of their exchange. "Ewan Happer can sell your affections to any man at the Midnight Masquerade. It is not safe for you to attend beyond tonight."

Evony blushed, suddenly uncomfortable under his gaze. "Surely you do not think I would allow any man to…"

"I'm not worried about you *allowing* anything, Evony," he growled. "Any one of the men in presence here tonight would simply take from you whatever he wanted, and you would be powerless to stop him."

"I am not so weak as you perhaps think," she defended herself.

"You're not?" Stavos asked, his eyes narrowing.

"No. I am able to defend myself when the need arises, and I wish you would have a little more faith in me," she told him.

"My faith in you is not lacking, Evony," he said. "But neither is my understanding of men." Before Evony could make to evade him,

Stavos had captured her wrists. "Fight me," he ordered. "Fight me as if you did not know me…as if I were one of those degenerates at the Midnight Masquerade."

"Let me go," Evony demanded. She did not feel comfortable being restrained in that moment.

"No," Stavos growled. Maneuvering very quickly and with dominant physical strength, Evony found that he easily forced her arms behind her, holding her wrists tightly in one hand as he took her chin with his other. "Fight me off. Defend yourself from my advances if you are so capable."

But as he crushed his body against hers, pinning her back hard against a tree—as Evony found she could neither wrench her wrists from his hold or her chin from his grasp, nor drop to her knees or move her body in any way to evade him—she frowned and admitted, "Your point is proven, Stavos. Now let me go."

She felt the full power of him relax a bit, yet he did not release her. "And still, I have another point to prove, do I not?"

"And what would that be?" Evony asked. "You've rendered me flightless, established that I can be trapped. What more do you have to demonstrate?"

He grinned at her, his blue eyes softening to a warm, inviting smolder. "That my mother was right…as it seems she always is. Masks do, indeed, seem to encourage people toward deviant behavior."

He kissed her again then. Still holding her hands at her back, still cradling her chin, Stavos applied such a kiss of physical and emotional pleasure that Evony literally felt her knees buckle. Had Stavos not held her pressed so tightly between his body and the tree at her back, she would have collapsed at his feet—exhausted of all physical stamina because of the hot, moist supremacy of his kiss.

She was ambrosial—purely ambrosial, from the scent of her flesh in his nostrils to the sense of her skin beneath his palms. Evony Elorietta's kiss—the flavor of her warm, velvet-soft mouth—was nearly his ruination! It was then Stavos understood that he must break from Evony in that moment—release her from his hold, leave her mouth for further savoring another night—or she might prove her own virtuous undoing, and his!

Thus, at the prompting of his honorable character and moral soul, Stavos let go of Evony's wrists and chin, stepping back from a temptation the like he'd never known. He studied her a moment. The emerald green of her gown caught and held the moonlight like a water sprite's wings. Her dark hair was not so perfectly coifed and piled as it had been before his passionate attentions, yet from behind her mask, her eyes shimmered with a near tangible quality of unequaled satisfaction. Her lips were so wine-red and full from the affectionate exchanges and caused him to take a cautionary step back from her, lest he weaken and drink of their petal softness and nectared indulgence again.

"We will return now," Stavos told Evony. "And I will watch over you as best I can for the remainder of the Midnight Masquerade. But then…then you must go home and remain there until I come to you. And I must glean what information I can, for you cannot attend another night. I will glean what I can, and then in two days' time, I will approach King Standwood and offer myself as a champion to solve the mystery of the twelve sleeping princesses of Abawyth."

"Stavos…I am sorry. You know that, don't you?" Evony asked. For all the kisses and passion that had passed between, she still feared he would despise her for the mistake she had made in being caught by Cedric.

He nodded and then seemed to force a grin. "I know…and so am I," he said. "I should never have expected you to simply give over everything you've worked and suffered so hard to discover…to simply give it over to me, a complete stranger, to trust me emphatically as if you'd known me all your life. For that I apologize."

Stavos chuckled then, pulled Evony against him once more, and captured her mouth in one last, deep, heated, and driven kiss. "But for *that*, my dear Lynet…I do not apologize."

Evony blushed with delirium as Stavos took her hand and began leading her back to the dance. She knew he could not fathom the feelings he had provoked in her, the rapturous euphoria in her heart, the sweet burn still lingering on her lips. Even in that moment, her legs and arms were weak and numb. She wondered how she would dance for the remainder of the night when every part of her had turned to soft pastry frosting the moment Stavos Voronin had kissed her.

CHAPTER EIGHT

Stavos poured the contents of another bottle of rum into Ewan Happer's tankard.

"My, my! You are a generous lad, sir," a drunken Happer chuckled.

"Hmmm," Stavos chuckled in return. "Well, why wouldn't I be generous, Happer, especially to you? These past two nights have been wildly entertaining, to say the least of it. I'm grateful to you for making my stay in Abawyth far more enjoyable than I ever imagined it would be."

The intoxicated miscreant laughed. "I do what I am able, sir. I do what I am able."

Stavos fought the urge to grimace with disgust as Happer downed the entire tankard of rum in several large gulps. Once more, Stavos poured the contents of his tankard into the spittoon he'd placed next to his chair when first he'd seated himself at the table with Happer. His intent was to get Happer so intoxicated that his mind would be too drowned in spirits to keep secrets. It was how Stavos planned to glean information from the idiot.

Dawn was quickly approaching, and Stavos was weary, not only from the anxiety of wondering whether Evony had returned home safely once the Midnight Masquerade had ended but also from sitting for near to three hours watching Ewan Happer consume bottle after bottle of rum.

Yet the man's speech was so slurred, his eyes so red and watery, and by the way he kept swaying in his chair, Stavos decided that the moment of chance had finally presented itself.

"So, Happer," he began, "where did you find so many ravishing young ladies willing to dance through the night with masked strangers...all for the want of coins?"

Ewan Happer laughed, rum spilling from the corners of his mouth as he slumped back in his chair.

"Well, that, my good man, is a mystery indeed, isn't it?" Happer slurred.

"Indeed, it would seem so," Stavos said. "And yet my curiosity is piqued as to why some of the women seem far more proper and polite than the others. I'd almost swear one or two of them were noblewoman...if I didn't know better."

Happer grinned, leaned forward, and attempted to whisper. "Well, just between you and me, sir—and no one else can ever hear of this..."

"Your secrets are all safe with me, Happer," Stavos urged, offering a conspiratorial smile.

"Some of them are noblewomen," Happer laughed. "Princesses, in fact!"

"No!" Stavos gasped, feigning surprise. "But how?"

Happer nodded, drunken with wine and pride in his own cleverness.

"Well, you see, friend...weeks and weeks ago—perhaps months even, for I forget now—King Standwood, the very king of Abawyth, came to me late one night, asking me for a favor."

"A favor?" Stavos urged. "A favor asked from the king? My! You must be a wise man indeed to earn the confidence of the king!"

"I am that, sir. That I am," Happer said, nodding. "So King Standwood, he comes to me for a favor...wants me to work out a manner in which to snatch his wife, the queen—wants me to kill her, get rid of her, so to speak, so that he can take the throne. Not only that...he wants her twin sister, the queen of Abawyth's sister kingdom, Elawyth. Do you know Elawyth?"

"I have heard of it," Stavos answered, trying to appear intrigued and admiring rather than enraged and sickened. He could not tip Happer off to his true purpose.

"Standwood wanted me to abduct and dispose of both queens…Queen Raina of Abawyth and Queen Charmaine of Elawyth," Happer confessed in a drooling whisper. "He said he would make me a wealthy man…shower me with more gold than I could ever dream up." The man chuckled. "But I can dream up a lot of gold, sir…that I assure you."

"I can well imagine…especially with a cleverness like yours," Stavos complimented. The act caused the contents of his stomach to churn.

"So I tell Standwood…sure! For the amount of gold he was willing to pay, I'd make the queens disappear," Happer said. He laughed, lowering his voice even more. "But I never agreed to kill them, you see. I just said I'd make them disappear. And that's what I did. I worked it out…managed to have my men take both the queens without anyone the wiser. But I didn't kill them, you see. No, sir, I did not. I'm much smarter than that."

"Indeed. So what did you do with them, these two queens you managed to, shall we say, spirit away?" Stavos asked. His heart was hammering inside his chest like a thunderstorm. They were alive! The sister queens of Abawyth and Elawyth were alive. Evony's mother was alive!

Ewan Happer laughed. It was prideful, self-confident, diabolical laughter. "They're right here, sir! Right here in the inn!"

"What?" Stavos asked, stunned beyond any other speech in the moment.

Ewan nodded his dirty, greasy, drunken head. "Yes…right here. I've kept them here the whole time, you see. And it's why some of the ladies you've danced with at my Midnight Masquerade seem so noble to you—for they are noble…royal, in fact." Happer's foul smile broadened. "Twelve of them women at the Midnight Masquerade…they're the twelve princesses of Abawyth. They work for me, Ewan Happer, selling themselves to dance with strange men…all because I was wise and smart enough not to kill their mother once I captured her. Abawyth's princesses—they know I have their mum. I told them, and I told them I'd slit her throat if they didn't do exactly as I say."

Stavos exhaled a sigh of feigned admiration. "Ewan Happer," he began, smiling as if he thought Happer the most intelligent man on the earth, "what a great mind you have inside your head."

"Don't I already know it, sir?" Happer slurred.

"Not to mention you've the bravery of a knight," Stavos added. "I've never met a man brave enough…never met a man with the kind of courage it would take to fool a king, let alone keep two queens captive and manipulate twelve princesses. You are a man to be admired."

"Oh, I know that too, sir," Happer agreed proudly.

"In fact," Stavos said, reaching for the final bottle of rum sitting on the table, "I think we should drink to your smarts and success…don't you?"

"That I do, sir!"

Stavos filled Happer's tankard one last time. Then as Happer began gulping again, Stavos stood, strode to stand behind Happer, drew the dagger from its sheath at his thigh, and hit Happer hard over the back of the head, rendering him still living but entirely unconscious.

Quickly, Stavos cleared the table of the empty bottles of rum and both tankards. He dumped the spittoon full of rum that he had only been pretending to consume in a chamber pot he found in one corner of the room. Then, dragging Happer out of his chair, he lifted the drunken fool over one shoulder and carried him out of the inn and into the woods.

Grateful that no one was up and about at such an early hour, Stavos dumped the intoxicated miscreant in the woods a ways away from the inn. He silently prayed that Ewan Happer awoke with no memory of all that he had revealed to Stavos.

As he hurried to the inn, Stavos knew what he must do—and he knew what he must ask his brother to do. Andrew must ride to

Ethiarien himself. Their father must be told all that Stavos had learned about the queens of Abawyth and its princesses. It was two days' ride to Ethiarien, and even though William would reach the kingdom first and inform Stavos's father, the king—and even though Stavos knew his father would respond by sending troops to assist Abawyth at once—Andrew must inform their father of all that had been revealed, especially of King Standwood's having initiated the malevolence.

He would speak to Andrew first and send him to intersect their father on his way to Abawyth. There was not time to wait in pursuing rescue of the queens in that moment—not when all who labored at the inn during daylight hours would be up and about soon. Stavos would find the queens' captive place later. He would find them and spirit them away once more—and he would need Evony's help to do so.

As Stavos hurried up the inn stairs toward the room Andrew had procured, he grimaced in knowing that Evony would have to endure one more night of the Midnight Masquerade. There was no alternative. Though he suspected where in the inn the queens were being kept captive, he could not be certain, nor remove them, without some sort of distraction to Ewan Happer and Cedric—short of killing Happer, which Stavos knew might draw King Standwood's attention to the inn. Thus he would have to allow Evony to return to the Midnight Masquerade that coming evening. He saw no other recourse. The queens must be taken before anything else malicious unfolded; they must be made safe in the very first of it.

"Well, you look unusually fresh and bright this morning," Miss Lovie chirped as she entered the room. Evony was already at the task of making breakfast for everyone.

Evony could not help but smile and blush, for the reason for her bright appearance instantly leapt to the forefront of her mind's eye—Stavos.

"And especially after having disobeyed Stavos last night, Evony," Mikol scolded. "You realize that it was *I* responsible to keep you here. Now Stavos will never trust me again."

Evony shook her head, kissed her little brother on his frowning forehead, and assured, "Stavos trusts you implicitly, Mikol. He knows that it was my own doing, leaving the house against his will. But he is not my father...so I hardly disobeyed him."

"Either way, you are very smiley this morning, Evony," Tressa noted. As Evony blushed, Tressa added, "And your cheeks pink up so very much now and again, I wonder if you are not fevered."

"Not at all," Evony consoled her little sister. "I'm just...well, I don't know...I just feel rather...rather different for some reason."

"Is that so?" Miss Lovie asked, smiling with suspicion. Through narrowed eyes, Miss Lovie studied Evony very closely for several long moments. At last she said, "Hmmm. If I didn't know better, I might think that last night, something happened to make you—"

The sudden heavy pounding on the door startled everyone in the room. But when Stavos's voice ordered, "Let me in!" from the other side, Evony found she could not rush to open it fast enough.

"Evony!" Stavos breathed, bursting through the door and fairly slamming it behind him. Taking her by the shoulders, he said, "Evony...it's true! The queens—both of them—they're alive, and they're right here in Abawyth!"

"What?" she exclaimed. She was somewhat disconcerted by his appearance. He looked overly tired, overly excitable, and overly handsome—as ever. "What do you mean? Do you mean you have proof of them being here...my mother and my Aunt Raina?"

Stavos smiled. "Yes. Some, at least...enough to make me think we will have your mother and aunt back here with you in mere hours," he answered, "if all goes as I have planned."

"Mother?" Tressa cried, erupting into tears. "You've found Mother, Stavos?"

"There is much to explain...and *all* is not yet clear," Stavos began, "but there is more hope than ever before. However, some risks will have to be taken, Evony." He looked to Miss Lovie. "And there are risks for you as well, Mrs. Wiggin." Nodding to Tressa and Mikol, he added, "And even for you two."

"Any risk," Mikol stated, puffing out his chest with courage. "I would do anything to help my mother…to have her back with us." Inhaling a deep breath of brave excitement, he asked, "What must we do?"

Stavos strode to a chair and sat down, raking his strong fingers through his hair. No doubt he was weary. He looked as if he had not taken any respite after the Midnight Masquerade had ended, and Evony worried for him.

"I was able to coax information from Happer," he began. "Not all of it, for he was so drunk with rum that, in truth, his words were hard to understand at times. However, he did confess to having both queens as his captives…to having used his leverage as their captor to manipulate the twelve princesses of Abawyth into doing his bidding, thus participating in the Midnight Masquerade."

"What's the Midnight Masquerade, Stavos?" Tressa asked. "And who is Happer? And why does he have our mother?"

"Hush a moment, Tressa," Evony said, gathering her sister into her arms to soothe her. "I will explain it all later. But please allow Stavos to tell what he must, all right?"

With a sigh of disappointment, Tressa nodded.

"He likewise gave me proof of your suspicions, Evony," Stavos continued. He smiled at Tressa and spread his arms in coaxing her to sit on his lap. Tressa giggled and gladly accepted his offer.

Evony was delighted with how Stavos—even for his great fatigue and the profound desperation of the situation—still managed to spoil Tressa a bit.

"What do you mean? What suspicion did Evony have?" Mikol asked.

"That King Standwood is the puppet master of all things evil," Lovie mumbled. "Isn't that right, sire?"

Stavos nodded. "As you know, it was Standwood who set Lord Rothvern as steward over Elawyth," he said to Mikol. "Your cousins told Evony as much. But what they did not tell her—for they did not know it—is that King Standwood himself plotted to kill Queen Raina…and your mother, Mikol."

"And then me," Mikol added.

"Yes. And then you," Stavos affirmed. "Standwood knew of Ewan Happer's character…or rather lack of it. He approached Happer himself, paid him well to abduct and then murder both the queen of Abawyth and her sister, the queen of Elawyth. But fortunately, Happer thinks himself smarter than any man, even a wicked king. So he did abduct your mother and your aunt, Evony."

As Stavos looked up to her, Evony's heart swelled with gladness in knowing her mother was truly alive, with joy in the hope that she could be saved, and with elation that Stavos was wholly the champion she had sensed he would be.

"But he held them for…for ransom, so to speak," Evony offered.

Stavos nodded. "Yes. He held them captive, using his knowledge of their whereabouts and captivity to force your cousins to dance at the Midnight Masquerade. Thus, all twelve are profoundly fatigued during the day…for they've danced all through the night."

Evony grinned as understanding washed over her. "So with his ignorance to what Happer had truly done with my mother and aunt, it was King Standwood himself who beckoned you here with the promise of accolades and a princess of Abawyth as bride. King Standwood lured my champion here only to thwart himself in the end."

Stavos smiled, his eyes narrowing with amused pleasure. "Your champion?" he teased.

Instantly, Evony's face flushed crimson. "I-I mean, he lured you here to champion the princesses…Mikol, Tressa, and me…all of us, I mean."

"But what now, Stavos?" Mikol asked. "How do we retrieve Mother and Aunt Raina with this Ewan Happer always about and King Standwood at the helm of such a plot?"

Stavos chuckled. "Oh, I've worked that all out already," he answered. "We simply do this. Evony will go to Mrs. Teche this morning and quit her as we had planned." He looked to Evony and expounded, "Tell her you've found a wealthy lover, and you would rather remain in his bed all the rest of your life than sew one more stitch for her," he instructed.

"Stavos!" Evony scolded, blushing three shades deeper of crimson. When Mikol snickered, she turned to him and gently reprimanded, "Such things are not the subject of amusement, Mikol."

"I don't think it would be much fun at all...staying in bed for the rest of one's entire life," Tressa said, a quizzical expression on her sweet face.

Stavos laughed again a moment and then cleared his throat and continued, "Evony will quit Mrs. Teche, and then she will attend the Midnight Masquerade again tonight."

"You mean she will watch the Midnight Masquerade from the safety of the woods through the little window—" Miss Lovie began.

"Oh, but no, Mrs. Wiggin," Stavos interrupted. "Did Evony not confess to you this morning?"

"Confess what?" Miss Lovie asked, looking to Evony with worry apparent on her lovely, wrinkled face.

"That she was caught in the woods last night by Happer's henchman...and forced to dance at the Midnight Masquerade with the other poor girls there," Stavos tattled.

Miss Lovie gasped. "Evony! You might have been—"

"But I wasn't...and I simply joined the dance," Evony interjected, looking from Mikol to Tressa and back.

"What is the Midnight Masquerade? Why won't anyone tell me?" Tressa pouted.

"In a moment, love," Stavos said, kissing the top of her head.

"Continue, please, Stavos," Mikol requested. "I want to know your strategy to retrieve Mother...all of it."

"Of course," Stavos said with a nod. "Evony will quit Mrs. Teche in favor of her new, wealthy lover." He paused, winking at Evony as her face lit up red once more. "Then she and I will attend the Midnight Masquerade, where I will pay Ewan Happer another gold coin or two for another thirty minutes of her affections."

"Awww! So that's it!" Miss Lovie breathed in a giggle. "That's what finds you so lively this morning, Evony."

"Please go on, Stavos," Evony instructed, attempting to avert his attention from her now flaming blush.

Stavos smiled, winked at her, and said, "While we are sharing our paid-for affections, I will take Evony to the place where I have reasoned the queens are being held."

"Where?" Evony, Mikol, Tressa, and Lovie exclaimed in unison.

Stavos's smile widened. "Remember, Evony, how I told you that the size of the inn does not make sense to me? The outside is larger than the inside?"

"Yes," Evony said, nodding.

"Ewan Happer and his ugly guard dog, Cedric…each disappears through a door behind the musicians' stand in the ballroom. Several times a night Cedric comes and goes through that door. But I looked today. Inside the inn's pub, where that door should open in the back of the pub room, there is nothing but a wall. Therefore, I think the space that I cannot account for is between that musicians' stand in the ballroom and the pub. And I think that can be the only space large enough to keep two women captive."

"What about another room in the inn?" Mikol asked.

"I checked them, each one, during the day while patrons were away," Stavos explained. "There is nothing amiss in any of them…either in their proportions or patrons. No, I am certain they are being kept in that space between the ballroom and pub. And you and I, Evony…we are going to bring them home in the morning."

Evony's arms raced with goose pimples. Her mother! Stavos would find her mother! All would be well. She and Mikol and Tressa—they would reunite with their mother! And her cousins, they would have their mother returned as well. Abawyth would have her queen, and so would Elawyth. And King Standwood would be—but no! Evony realized then that Standwood could still command the castle guard to…

"I see it in your eyes, Evony," Stavos said, drawing her attention back to the moment at hand. "Fear not, pretty princess, for

Standwood *will* fall. The king of Ethiarien is already on his way with soldiers. Standwood will fall, and all will be well. I promise that to you, pretty Evony."

Evony smiled at him, her whole heart swelling with admiration, desire, and—and yes—love! She loved him! Evony knew she'd loved Stavos from the moment he'd gathered her from the muddy street of the village and into the protection of his powerful arms.

"And you, Stavos, you will have solved the mystery of the twelve sleepy princesses and will win your choice of them as your bride," Tressa exclaimed with excitement. "Who will you choose, Stavos? Who will you choose? For my part, Patrice is my favorite of the cousins. Then Laura. What about you, Mikol? Whom do you think Stavos should choose for his bride?"

An overwhelming sense of pain and loss—stronger even than she'd felt the day her mother had disappeared—began to consume Evony's mind and body. She trembled and tried to hide it from the others.

"H-how do you know your father is on his way to assist you, Stavos?" Evony stammered, attempting to appear unaffected by being forced to remember that Stavos would marry an Abawythian princess as his prize when all ended well.

"Simple enough," Stavos answered, smiling at her. "I sent my brother to fetch him."

"Your brother, Andrew!" Mikol exclaimed. "I had forgotten there were two princes of Ethiarien." Mikol looked to Evony proudly, explaining, "There are two princes of Ethiarien, you see, Evony. Stavos is the elder…and Andrew the younger." He looked to Stavos, asking, "Correct?"

"Correct," Stavos affirmed. "Well done, Mikol. You do have quite an exemplary knowledge of royal families."

"I know it," Mikol boasted.

"But how far away is your father?" Lovie asked. "If you plan to rescue the queens tomorrow morning…will they be here in time?"

Stavos's smile faded somewhat. "No. They will not."

"Then…then how do we take the queens from Ewan Happer, alleviate our cousins of their horrible Midnight Masquerading, and swoop away King Standwood…all by ourselves?" Mikol asked.

"We stall," Stavos answered. "Tomorrow morning, Evony and I will bring the queens here, before daylight and dressed as villagers so that they are not recognized. Then, once it is done, I will go to Abawyth Castle and present myself as a candidate to King Standwood."

"A candidate?" Lovie asked.

Evony sighed with a disappointment that was so thoroughgoing she knew it could never, never be soothed. She understood—completely. After all, it was what Ethiarien's king had sent his eldest son and heir to do: to solve the mystery surrounding the twelve sleepy princesses of Abawyth, as Tressa had only just reminded them all. It was his charge. His charge from the beginning had been to solve the riddle of the strange fatigue that plagued the Abawythian princesses and then choose a bride from amongst them.

Though her heart felt as if it were tearing into pieces, what had she expected Stavos to do? Fall in love with her in the space of only a few days and nights? Certainly she could not deny that she had fallen in love with him in such a short span of time. She knew that if circumstances were different—were she and he not royals but villagers allowed to choose their own ways and court one another for months instead of knowing each other for only hours—she would feel the same. Were circumstances different and Evony herself were an Abawythian princess—and if a miracle occurred and she were the princess Stavos chose from among the twelve candidates—she would love him all the more with every passing moment of every passing day.

But it was not what his father had sent him to do. Stavos had been sent to champion Abawyth and her princesses. So why shouldn't he present himself to King Standwood as a candidate for the challenge? Why didn't he deserve to choose the princess of Abawyth he most favored? And Evony had no right to resent whomever he chose, for in the end, he would be Elawyth's champion as well—and hers. Stavos deserved no less than to return to his kingdom of Ethiarien with accolades and his champion's prize, an Abawythian princess as his bride.

"He means to present himself as a candidate—a would-be champion of Abawyth," Evony heard herself respond to Lovie's question. "He means to do what he came here to do: to solve the mystery of the twelve sleepy princesses…as his father sent him to do."

"I do," Stavos confirmed. "And in doing this, we will purchase ourselves a measure of time…time enough for my father, brother, and their soldiers to arrive—that Abawyth's and Elawyth's queens will be not only protected but assisted in reclaiming the throne from the devil who aspired to steal them."

"Yay!" Tressa and Mikol exclaimed together.

Miss Lovie smiled and exhaled a heavy sigh of relief and hope. She nodded to Evony as if to say, *He was the one, and you were right to trust him.*

Still, even with the knowledge that her mother and aunt would be safe by the time the sun rose next, a great hurt and longing—a sense of loss, regret, disappointment, and despair—began to settle in Evony's heart and mind. She thought of the way Patrice had gazed up at Stavos whenever he had danced with her at the Midnight Masquerade—of how Stavos had smiled at Patrice. Patrice would be queen of Ethiarien one day. For that, Evony did not envy her cousin. But for the fact that she would be Stavos's wife, friend, confidant, and lover, that she did envy—more than envy. That made Evony's entire body ache with sickness of body and misery of mind. Yet such was the life of royals; rarely did royals choose their own spouses or way. Rarely did a royal know true happiness once reaching the age of maturity and responsibility. Few royals were ever as happy as Evony's mother had been in the blessing of being married to the one man who had truly owned her heart. Few royals were as happy as her Aunt Raina had been when her Uncle Albert had been alive. In fact, her Aunt Raina's choice to marry King Standwood, a husband of royal connection—instead of finding another man to love her and to love in return—had nearly wrought ruination upon her and her subjects, as well as upon Evony's mother and Elawyth.

Yet monarchy was what it was. And what choice did Evony have? Should she throw herself at Stavos's feet and beg him to love her? Should she suggest he defy his father's charge, abandon Abawyth in its hour of need (and Elawyth too), abdicate his future throne, and run away with her to live in hiding, fear, and poverty all his life? Oh, but she would love him even then! Such a love he could not imagine; of that she was certain.

"Evony?"

Stavos's voice interrupted her wretched ponderings.

"Yes?" she responded in a whisper.

"Shouldn't you be trotting along about now?" he asked, smiling at her.

"Where?" she asked in return, still too drowned in misery to think clearly.

Stavos chuckled. "To tell that old crone Mrs. Teche that you've taken a rich nobleman as your lover and will no longer be in her employ," he answered.

"Oh yes. I-I suppose I should," she stammered.

Stavos frowned and guided Tressa from her seat on his knee as he stood. "Are you well, Evony?" he asked, taking her shoulders between his hands. "You've gone pale as a ghost suddenly."

"Have I?" she breathed, gazing up into the astonishing comeliness of his face. "I-I'm just tired," she managed at last.

He grinned a little and released her. "All will be well, Evony," he told her. "Haven't I promised you that all along the way?"

"Yes, Stavos," she affirmed. "You have." Tears were welling in her eyes, and she did not want to appear weak before him—or the others. "I'll go speak with Mrs. Teche now. You should return to the inn and rest," she told him as she turned from him, pulled the door open, and dashed out in desperate escape.

Even facing Agnes Teche did not frighten Evony—not anymore—not since realizing that in gaining her mother's return, she would lose the one man she had always dreamt of, the man she'd fallen in love with. And in losing him—even in losing the hope of him, for now she knew he truly existed and would be wed to someone else—Evony would lose herself, her heart, her soul. But what did it matter, after all? She was a royal, and wasn't what villagers said always true of their royals? That they had no hearts or souls?

CHAPTER NINE

"Two gold pieces for the same little chit I owned last night for half the hour," Stavos said, reaching into his vest pocket and withdrawing two gold coins. "What do you say, Happer?"

Ewan Happer laughed, displaying his rotting yellow teeth as if the sight of them were something someone would want to see.

"I'll make you a better contract, sire," Happer answered. "Double the gold, and I'll double your time with her…and toss in the use of one of my empty rooms in the inn to offer you some privacy, if you like."

Stavos smiled. "Agreed, innkeeper!" he said, though the realization of how far beyond any propriety Ewan Happer would eventually force the girls trapped at the Midnight Masquerade, if he were allowed to continue his diabolical business, caused every muscle in Stavos's body to tense with restrained rage.

Handing Happer the two gold coins he'd offered and then producing two more and dropping them into his filthy upturned hand, Stavos chuckled, asking, "And what room might be available, sir?"

"Third floor, second door on your left, sire," Happer answered. "But let no one see you, sire…not a soul."

"All the guests are tucked in tight for the night, I assume?" Stavos prodded.

"Snug as ticks on a horse's hindquarters, sire."

"Lovely," Stavos said, forcing an expression of being amused by superior wit.

"Enjoy your hour, sire," Happer called as Stavos strode from him and toward Evony.

"Oh, I will," Stavos mumbled, still attempting to control his rage.

As he reached Evony, again bedecked in the lovely emerald gown and white masquerade mask, he took hold of her arm none too gently and growled, "Come with me. We have one hour."

"An hour?" Evony whispered in surprise. "Whatever did he expect you to do with me for an entire hour?"

Stavos felt his eyes narrow as he glared down at her for a moment. Was she truly so innocent? The quiet gasp she made, the way her beautiful eyes widened in horrified astonishment—her soft whisper of, "Oh!"—told him that she was indeed.

"Happer will not stop with this damnable dancing, Evony," Stavos growled as he fairly dragged her over the ballroom threshold and out into the gold night. "He will push those girls he's managed to enslave to participation in far more indecent goings-on. He has to be stopped. Even if your mother, aunt, and cousins were not in jeopardy here…Ewan Happer has to be stopped. There are other innocent girls involved."

"Yes, I know," Evony agreed, thinking of Mrs. Teche's poor daughters, Lillian and Camille.

"But for tonight, we will find the queens and spirit them away before dawn," Stavos said. Evony sensed he was talking to himself more than to her in that moment. "Then we will worry about Ewan Happer and the others."

"How do we proceed?" Evony asked. Clouds partially covered the moon, and it was not as easy to discern the landscape around them. "However do we go through the door behind the musicians if Happer or Cedric is always watching?"

"We don't," Stavos mumbled. Taking her hand again, he led her to one side of the inn. "It cannot be the only entrance. There must be another way in and out, for the only way Cedric ever leaves the ballroom is through the door at the musicians' backs…but yet he routinely prowls the outer perimeter of the inn."

"But…there's no other door," Evony reminded him.

Stavos dropped her hand and began pressing on boards on the outer wall of the inn. "The hidden room has to be right here," he said. "To the right is the ballroom, to the left the pub. It has to be here, and there has to be a door."

Evony glanced to the left of where Stavos was pushing on the outer wall. There she noticed an outcropping of brush. "Look here," she said.

"Where?" Stavos asked.

"Just there…behind the brush," she instructed, pointing to the area. "The entrance to the tunnel from the castle is hidden by brush and trees. Any passersby would never notice it, for even the door itself is covered in vines that further secret it. If I were Ewan Happer, the door to the hidden room would be there…even if it does make it more awkward to come and go."

Stavos grinned at her. "Of course you would," he said. Then, going to the space Evony had indicated, Stavos began to push on the outer wall. She knew he had to feel his way, for the clouds covering the moon meant that they were searching in near pitch-blackness.

Evony watched as Stavos hunkered down and pressed the wall behind the brush. "Ah ha!" he exclaimed in a hushed voice. "There's a latch hidden here…and I can feel the outline of a small, thin door."

"But large enough for a man to pass through?" she asked as her heart began to beat with anxious anticipation.

"Yes," Stavos assured her.

He stood then, taking her chilled shoulders between his hands. "You must be prepared, Evony. Though my intuition tells me we will find your mother in there and your aunt…I-I cannot fathom in what condition we may find them. Furthermore, the danger I have put you in by bringing you here…" Stavos's voice trailed off as he shook his head with disappointment in himself.

"It is I who have put you in danger, Stavos," Evony reminded him. "I-I had no right, no claim, no good reason to involve you in all of this, and I—"

"I involved myself, Evony," he interrupted, however. In the dim light of the stars, Evony could see him gazing at her—an expression akin to that of regret owning his handsome face. "You forget…I came here to unravel whatever it was that was plaguing Abawyth's princesses. I brought myself here, willing to face any menace. I just did not expect to find an enchanted angel at hand to point my way."

Evony wanted to throw her arms around him—kiss him—cling to him eternally! All through the day, as she tried to rest and cache her strength in knowing what her last night with Stavos would bring, she had silently told herself that she would simply accept things the way they were. Over and over and over she reminded herself that Stavos had not come for her—that though his appearance and courage and strength may in the end save her, her siblings, her mother, and even her kingdom, he had come for her cousins, to champion the twelve sleepy princesses of Abawyth and to take one for his bride.

After quitting Mrs. Teche's employ—and finding secret, thorough satisfaction at the enraged, dumbfounded look on Agnes's face as she did—Evony had spent the remainder of the day lamenting her impending loss of Stavos. All through the long day, she'd thought of nothing else, sometimes whispering aloud to herself of what was and what would be—and what could not be. Even Tressa was concerned for Evony, asking why she kept mumbling to herself and would all be well. And after hour upon hour upon hour, Evony had finally managed to find a place in her mind where she could exist without the constant threat of tears rising to her eyes or her heart crumbling with pain.

Yet now—now as Stavos stood before her, as they both stood, together, on the very brink of saving her mother, her aunt, her beloved cousins, and the sister kingdoms of Abawyth and Elawyth— in that moment all the resolve she had cached, the determination to be steadfast and strong, all of it was gone. All she wanted in all the world was Stavos—his heart, his love, him.

Clasping her hands tightly together in an effort to keep from throwing herself against him and begging him to be hers—to defy his father's charge—Evony gazed at Stavos and said, "Th-thank you,

Prince Stavos. Thank you for helping me. With all that is before you, I hope that you will know my gratitude."

"There is much before both of us, Evony," he reminded her. "We are far from finished with our adventure, eh?"

He was trying to encourage her, for he thought she was merely fearful of what condition she might find her mother and aunt in once they entered the hidden room of the inn. Again, it was a manifestation of his kindness and compassion. But Evony's heart had begun to break once more; the pain of knowing that Stavos Voronin would belong to another began to overwhelm her.

"Let us go in then," she said, pulling herself from his grasp and lunging toward the secret door.

"No, wait!" he called in a whisper.

But it was too late. Evony had opened the door to find that there was indeed a secret room hidden there—just as Stavos had predicted.

Instantly, she called, "Mother? Mother? Are you here?"

"Evony!" Stavos said, clamping one strong hand over her mouth. "Are you mad?" he asked, glaring down at her. "Cedric may well be here, as well!"

"Evony? Evony, darling! Is that you?"

Pushing Stavos's hand from her mouth, Evony cried, "It's my mother!" as tears began spilling from her eyes. "You have found her, Stavos! You've truly found her!"

"Evony, wait!" Stavos growled.

"No! I'll not come this close, only to give you up and not have my mother as well!" she sobbed. Turning from him, Evony evaded his reach and hurried toward the direction from whence her mother's voice had come.

"Mother?" she called.

And then Evony stopped abruptly—for the sight that met her was horrifying, in the very least! There, trapped behind a wall of iron bars as perfectly secure as any prison cell, knelt her mother and aunt. They were dirty, their once lovely dark hair matted and wild. They each wore only a long chemise, also dirty, and no shoes. There was a pile of straw to one side of the cell and a low fire burning in a tiny hearth to one side of the room outside the cell.

"Evony! My darling!" Queen Charmaine cried, desperately reaching through the bars in an effort to clasp Evony's hand. "What are you doing here? How came you to find us?" Almost instantly, just as Evony took her mother's hand, clinging to it with sheer desperation, her mother's countenance altered. "You must go! Run! There is a terrible man here, and he—"

"Why are you masked, my darling?" Queen Raina asked, taking Evony's free hand and placing a quick kiss to the back of it. "Oh, my dear! Do not tell me that Ewan Happer has trapped you in that heinous Midnight Masquerade, as well?"

"Run, darling!" Evony's mother insisted. "Run as fast as you can! Cedric will return and—"

"Your majesties," Stavos said then. Dropping to one knee, he quickly explained, "I am Stavos Voronin of Ethiarien, and we have a strategy to not only free both of you and the twelve princesses but also render King Standwood your prisoner, Queen Raina. But we must act quickly, and you must not let this dog Cedric or his master Happer suspect anything. Do you understand?"

"No…but we will adhere," Queen Raina said.

"Thank you," Stavos said, exhaling a sigh of relief at their compliance. "First—and I know you have questions, and I promise that all will be revealed to you later—but first, does the man Cedric…does he carry a key to this cell on his person?"

"Always," Queen Charmaine assured him.

"Good. Now, Evony and I…there is only but a moment, so please listen well—"

They were identical in appearance. It was somewhat unnerving to Stavos at first—the fact that he could not have discerned one queen from the other if it had not been for Evony's mother's attention to her daughter. Yet there was no time to linger. Evony was in danger. The longer she lingered, the more treacherous their mission became.

Thus Stavos hurried his explanation. "We will come for you, just before dawn, Evony and I," he told them. "Then we will see you safely to a tiny home where Evony has been residing with her brother, her sister, and a kindly old woman."

"What? Tressa and Mikol are here?" Queen Charmaine exclaimed as tears streamed down her beautiful but very dirty face.

"There you will wait with Evony and the others, while I distract Standwood long enough for my father, brother, and a legion of Ethiarien soldiers to reach Abawyth so that Standwood may be overthrown." He paused a moment, looking to Queen Raina and asking, "You are aware that it is your husband, King Standwood Warde, who has been the puppet master in all of this?"

"Yes," Queen Raina answered. "Ewan Happer, for all his imbecilic pride, has told us everything. He knows it tortures me to know that my sister, my daughters, and my kingdom are suffering because of my ill choice in a husband."

"You will be rid of him soon, majesty," Stavos assured Queen Raina. "Ethiarien will answer the call for assistance and—"

"But wait. The palace guards are loyal to me, my prince," Queen Raina said, weeping. "If you can somehow get word to the captain of my guard, Dillon Thoringil, you will find no resistance when the time comes to take Standwood captive. My guard, my soldieries...they will champion me over Standwood's threats. I know this."

"First we will liberate you both and then see you safely hidden," Stavos said. "Only after that will we make further plans to overthrow Standwood."

"We understand," the queens responded with simultaneous voices and nodding.

"And now, I must take Evony, my queen," Stavos told Queen Charmaine, "for you know she is in great danger if she lingers."

"I do know it," Queen Charmaine said, though tears of fear and despair cascaded over her face.

"Remember, you may expect us just before dawn," Stavos encouraged. "Come with me, Evony."

"We can't leave them, Stavos!" Evony wept, however. "How can we leave them like this?"

"Take her forcibly, Prince Stavos," Queen Charmaine ordered. "Make her go...however you can. She will not leave me of her own will now."

At once, Stavos bound Evony in his arms, lifting her off her feet and turning her toward the secret door. They must leave at once, lest they be found out and all hope lost.

"Let me go! Let me go, Stavos! We cannot leave them!" Evony cried as they reached the door leading from the secret room to the woods beyond the inn.

"Hush, Evony," Stavos scolded as he pushed her through the small door and out into the cold. "Keep your wits about you! Would you come so close to saving your mother, only to let panic foil our plot?"

He was right—and Evony's sense began to return to her.

"No," Evony sobbed, shaking her head. "No...no." Trembling, she inhaled a deep breath to calm her tears and emotions. "No. I-I will be fine, Stavos. I promise. It's just the cold, and I'm so very tired...and...and I so badly want all this to be over so that I may attempt to heal the wounds to my own soul as well as..." Her words were lost, for she felt more sobbing threaten to erupt if she continued.

"You are a brave woman, Evony Elorietta," Stavos told her, his voice low and soothing. "Strong and brave...unlike any other woman I have ever had acquaintance with."

Evony forced an accepting nod of appreciation at his well-meant compliment. Yet it was not what she wanted most to hear from him. She did not want him to think her strong and brave; she wanted him to think her vulnerable and worthy of his protection—worthy of his love.

"Come along," he said then. "You need a brief respite, and I would not mind one myself."

Taking her arm, he began to lead her toward the front door of the inn. Evony paused when he led her up the stairs and across the threshold into the public part of the inn, however.

"We cannot be seen!" she reminded him in a whisper.

Stavos smiled. "We won't be. I'm sure Happer made certain of it." Putting a strong arm around her shoulders, he tucked her safely against him and said, "And after all, I did pay four gold coins for an hour of your time, love, now didn't I? So what's say we use it to gather our wits, eh?"

Evony sighed with the anticipation of even a few more minutes away from the lurid Midnight Masquerade—a few more minutes alone in Stavos's company.

"Third floor, second door on the left," Stavos mumbled as they reached the hallway at the top of the stairs. "Ah…here it is."

Opening the door, he let them into the room and then closed the heavy door behind them and turned the key in the lock until it latched with a loud clunk.

Stavos shook his head with disgust as he looked around the room. "The filthy scoundrel already had a fire laid and lit in here," he said. "He planned on you earning four gold pieces for his pocket tonight all along, no doubt."

"At least we can warm ourselves," Evony sighed, going to stand before the fire. Rubbing her hands together before its warmth, she closed her eyes a moment. Her mother was alive! And her Aunt Raina! She offered a silent prayer of thanks and then continued to warm her hands.

"I'm so weary of being cold and tired all the time," she said aloud.

"You mean of late?" Stavos asked from behind her. "Since coming to Abawyth in early winter?"

But Evony shook her head. "No. I mean always…at least the cold part, anyway," she explained. "I haven't always been tired. That did come with Abawyth and Agnes Teche…and then this Midnight Masquerade. But the cold—I don't know if I can remember the last time I was truly warm, for Elawyth is a mountainous region, just as Abawyth is at the foothills of mountains. It's never truly, truly warm, not even in summer—not warm the way I dream of being warm. Not warm the way I feel when you…not warm the way I imagine other places to be."

"Then you would like Ethiarien," Stavos said. He was standing just behind her; she could feel his breath on her hair, feel his stirring presence even though he was not touching her. "It's warm there most of the year," he began to explain, "late summer through

147

midautumn. We have winter and spring, and harvest of course. Each season is ripe in its own time. But it is warm there…especially in summer."

Evony smiled. "It makes me happy to know you will be warm again soon, Stavos," she mumbled. "I've…I've grown quite fond of you, and I wish you all the happiness you deserve."

She heard him chuckle. "I've grown quite *fond* of you too, Evony." Evony's body tensed with the overpowering sensation of bliss Stavos inflicted upon her when he took her shoulders between his hands, placing a warm kiss on her neck just below her right ear. "Quite fond, indeed."

Though she tried to resist him—tried to resist surrendering to her own desires to own his affections during what she knew would be their last moments alone together—she could not. As Stavos kissed her neck again, she felt her body nearly collapse back against his. Instantly, the warmth of him caused goose pimples to erupt over her arms and legs. She should flee—she knew she should—for he could not be hers and would soon belong to one of her cousins as husband. Yet the selfish part of her heart whispered that he was not Patrice's husband yet.

"Your mother is a wise woman, Prince Stavos," she breathed as he continued to place alluring kisses along her neck and the bareness of her shoulder revealed by her ball gown's bodice. "For that mask you wear…it does seem to inspire you to behavior you would not normally…"

Evony gasped as Stavos unexpectedly turned her to face him.

"Oh, but, Evony," he mumbled as his smoldering eyes looked at her, "as you can see…I'm not wearing a mask." And it was true! Whilst Evony had been warming herself before the fire—lost in dismal thoughts of never seeing Stavos again—he had indeed removed his mask. "Thus now you know…that my deviant behavior in this moment is simply due to the fact that I am so *fond* of you." Reaching to the back of her head, Stavos untied the ribbon that held Evony's mask in place, sweeping it aside and tossing it to the floor as he gathered her in his arms. "I am so very, very, very fond of you, Evony. And if time and circumstance would allow for it—"

Evony pressed her fingers to his lips to quiet him. "Don't say anything more, please," she said, tears welling in her eyes. "Y-you don't understand that I'm…I'm very…I'm very attached to you, Stavos. More than I dare express when you will soon be choosing from among my cousins…when you will choose which of my cousins to take as your—"

It was Stavos's hand covering her mouth that silenced Evony. He pushed her hand from his lips, removed his from hers, and said, "I don't care about what the next few hours will bring, Evony…not now, not in this moment. I chose long ago…in fact I was taught by my father and mother to live each day, each hour, as if it were my last. To never own regret—or at least, attempt to never own it." He tenderly brushed a stray strand of her hair from her forehead. "And I intend to continue to do that. And on this day, in this night, in this hour…I fully intend to live as if this moment were my very last. And if it were my very last hour, Evony…do you know what I would do?"

"No," Evony breathed, entirely bewitched by his words, his touch—by him.

A mischievous grin curved the corners of his delicious mouth as he said, "This."

The gasp that caught in Evony's throat as Stavos pulled her body to his was stifled when his mouth seized hers in a moist, impassioned kiss, smoldering with the heat of a summer sun. Instantly, tears trickled from the corners of Evony's eyes—tears of longing, love, and desire—tears of heartbreak. Yet she would not deny herself one last taste of Stavos's kiss—one last rapture of being held in his arms. She would do just as he said he would: she would live the moment as if it were to be her last of life, and she would not diminish its supremacy by avoiding the pain she knew would come once the moment had passed.

Desperately she clung to him, weaving her hands through the dark velvet of his hair, relishing the euphoric state of mind and body his kiss and his embrace wove about her. Eagerly, as if famished, starving for his kiss—for his mouth worked its exhilarating emotion over her—Evony kissed Stavos, met each driven kiss he offered with full as much intensity and hunger.

Only once did she break the seal of their kiss long enough to gasp a breath, for it seemed her body would rather perish—smother from lack of life-giving air—than to give up his mouth for a moment. Yet the pause was just long enough for Stavos to capture Evony's face between his hands, and he stared into her eyes for a long while—studied her face as his eyes narrowed with an intensity that should have frightened her but didn't.

Mere days he'd known her—days! Not years, not months, not even weeks! And yet Stavos sensed he knew Evony Elorietta's soul better than he would know any other soul in all his life—perhaps even better than he knew his own. It was what his heart felt for her—and what his body felt for her he dare not entertain.

He searched her eyes—her lovely eyes, so like polished jade—and in searching them, he read her thoughts, and her thoughts were his own. She wanted him; as fully as he wanted her, Evony wanted him. Yet she knew of his father's charge—she'd known it from the beginning—and still she wanted him, loved him as wholly as he loved her.

Yet who would believe it? Two royals in love? It was rare to be sure. And coupled with having only known one another a length of time that could easily be measured in hours, who would believe it? But Stavos believed it. He knew it: he loved Evony Elorietta.

But what if he failed her? What if her mother or aunt or one of her cousins were injured or killed in the battle to not only retrieve the queens but thwart Standwood Warde and his diabolic greed? Would her eyes still gaze up at him with longing, with love? He wondered whether she could forgive him if part of the strategy he had built failed and one of her family were lost.

"Stavos?" she breathed, her hands suddenly fisting the fabric of his shirt with a desperation that made his heart hammer even more violently within his chest. "The clock is striking the hour. When will Ewan Happer expect our return?"

"Fifteen minutes," Stavos mumbled. "And for fourteen of those minutes, I shall keep you here...for my own selfish purposes."

"Promise?" she asked in a whisper.

He was undone then, taking her mouth with his in such a kiss of unbridled, fiery passion that he feared for a moment it would harm her somehow. Yet when she clung to him with even more desperation than before—when she kissed him full as heartily as he kissed her—he was reassured of her welfare.

Stavos would release her soon; the ticking of the mantel clock was her assurance. He would not risk failing in his quest—not simply for a passing fancy he may have felt for her. He would release her and return her to the Midnight Masquerade, and then his plan would play out, and he would rescue her mother and her aunt. He would somehow dethrone her wicked step-uncle Standwood and choose from among her twelve cousins a bride to return with him to his kingdom.

Not caring if she ever drew another breath of life, Evony threw her arms around Stavos's neck, kissing him hard and with a near panicked desperation she herself did not understand. Something changed in Stavos in that moment, for he took hold of her wrists, maneuvering her backward and pushing her against the wall of the inn room. His hands held her waist as his mouth wandered to her neck, to her shoulder, and back to her mouth. The kiss he rained upon her in that moment was pure desire—a powerful yearning she felt in return, felt unable to satisfy. His hands were at her neck, encircling it caressively. His hands were next at her shoulders, his thumbs resting on the protuberance of her clavicle bones as he kissed her neck and then her shoulder. Stavos's hands pushed the sleeves of her dress, stitched to linger just off her shoulders. Yet she soon realized he endeavored to move them further down her arms, revealing the full roundness of her shoulder. He kissed the curve of one exposed shoulder and then the other. Again his hands encircled her neck as his mouth lingered at the hollow of her throat.

For all that she thought their passion could not advance, it was indeed advancing! But he was a prince—an honorable one. And she was a princess—a virtuous one. And almost simultaneously he drew back from her, and she stepped aside from him, barely catching herself from collapsing by bracing one hand on the nearby bed.

Evony found that her entire body was quivering, wildly trembling with barely restrained desire and crushing emotion. She looked up to see Stavos raking both hands through his hair repeatedly as he attempted to control his labored breathing. His massive chest rose and fell with the residual exhilaration he had also experienced.

"R-regret avoided…yes?" he breathed, stretching his hand toward her in a gesture that they should take their leave.

Evony nodded, though in truth her own regret had merely multiplied one thousandfold. Still, she determined she would forever savor the moment she had lived life as fully as she could have—that for all her life, whenever she heard accolades of Stavos Voronin, Prince of Ethiarien—or when the time came, as it inevitably would, that she heard tales of the handsome King Stavos and his lovely queen, Patrice—Evony promised herself to remember that she had lived that near hour in the secluded room in the Hungry Horse Inn to the fullest that it could have been lived—and that once upon a time Stavos Voronin had valued her enough to live that hour to its fullest with her.

CHAPTER TEN

"He has only just gone in through the door behind the musicians' stand," Stavos whispered. "The time has come, Evony…and I know you must be weary."

Evony was cold, having waited in the forest, exposed to the elements, while Stavos watched Ewan Happer and Cedric. Happer had retired a full fifteen minutes before, but Cedric had lingered in the pub in devouring his breakfast.

Still, the anticipation of her mother and aunt's rescue had kept her from giving into the cold and freezing. And now Stavos had returned, and her mother would soon be free.

Could it really be? she wondered. Would her mother and aunt soon be home with her, Tressa, Mikol, and Miss Lovie? Would they be safe? It seemed surreal, after all the misery and fear the Elorietta children had endured—after all the sacrifice and danger their champion, Stavos, had faced. Part of Evony—the tired and cold part—wondered if perhaps she were dreaming or the possibility of everything going as Stavos planned were fated to be thwarted. But another part of her—the hopeful part, the part that knew Stavos Voronin was the only man who could have come this far—knew he would succeed.

"I'll enter first, Evony," Stavos told her. He frowned. "I know it would be pointless to ask you to wait for me here."

"Quite pointless," she assured him with a teasing but tired smile.

He grinned and shook his head. "Well then, stay at my back at least. There's bound to be a confrontation with Happer's guard dog, Cedric."

Evony nodded, inhaled a deep breath of courage, and watched as Stavos opened the hidden door on the outer wall of the inn.

She had forgotten how wretched and closed in the room smelled—like dust and dirt and rotting food. Her heart ached for her mother and aunt. What misery they had endured for these past months. The realization humbled Evony at once. To think she had been silently complaining about her own lot only moments ago, when it was nothing compared with what the twin queens had endured, and for a much greater length of time.

Evony saw Stavos straighten his posture—saw his hand move to the sheath at his right thigh that held a dagger. He had not brought his sword, explaining to Evony that it was far too cumbersome for the small space in which he expected to confront Cedric. He was right, for there would hardly have been room for Stavos to draw his sword, let alone wield it well.

Rising on her tiptoes, Evony looked over Stavos's shoulder. There—standing with his back to them—was Cedric. He was mumbling to her mother and aunt, and from the angry expressions on their faces, Evony surmised he was somehow taunting them.

"Cedric," Stavos said then.

Ewan Happer's heinous henchman whirled on his heel. "Aye! What are you doing here?"

"I've come to barter with you, Cedric," Stavos answered.

"Barter with me? What could you have that I would want?" Cedric asked. "Now I'll have to kill you, for coming in here and seeing—"

"Oh, but I have your life in my hand, man," Stavos interrupted.

Cedric sneered and puffed a breath of arrogant disbelief. "My life, you say? How so? I need only snap your neck, nobleman, and it would be your life in my hands." He chuckled. "Rather, it would be your corpse in my hands."

"I'm offering this one opportunity to you, Cedric," Stavos began to explain, entirely unaffected by the man's threats. "I will give you more gold than you could ever imagine owning…and all you have to do is to release the queens into my care and leave Abawyth for good. But if you choose to face me in defense of your ignoramus of an employer—if you choose to attack me instead of accepting my offer—I will kill you, and it will be *your* corpse in *my* hands. I warn you—do not doubt it for a moment. The choice is yours…but you must make it now."

"Hmmm," Cedric sighed. "Riches…or you bleeding out at my feet. That seems a simple enough choice for me."

Evony gasped as Cedric moved quickly, retrieving a small ax he'd had tucked in his belt at his waist. Laughing, he nodded to Stavos and said, "I'll have your guts for my supper tonight, you arrogant fool."

"Do not attempt to cross me, man. It will mean your life," Stavos warned.

Again Cedric laughed, however. "What? You're going to throw that little needle at your leg there and scratch me?"

"No," Stavos answered.

Evony watched as Stavos simply strode directly toward Cedric— and without drawing his dagger. In one swift movement, his fist met with Cedric's nose with such force that she was certain she actually heard the ugly little facial appendage break. The blow sent Cedric stumbling backward, but he regained his footing, glaring at Stavos and still wielding his ax.

"One more chance, Cedric," Stavos told him. "Comply with my demands, or die."

"I've killed many men," Cedric growled, "men more powerful than you." He lunged at Stavos then, swinging his ax at his throat.

But Stavos was astonishingly agile for all his height, broad shoulders, and sculpted musculature, and he easily avoided the ax blade.

Cedric rebounded well too, however. "I even killed a prince—the first fool to try and solve the so-called mystery of the twelve sleepy princesses of Abawyth. The idiot thought he could face me, and he ended up with his throat cut and floating down the river to hell!"

Again Cedric moved to strike Stavos. Yet Stavos was more than merely capable in battle—that was evident in the way he caught Cedric's ax-wielding arm with his left hand as his right simultaneously drew the dagger at his thigh, burying it deep in Cedric's chest.

"I warned you, Cedric…you murdering mongrel," Stavos growled as Ewan Happer's guard dog gasped his last breath. "And you've made your choice," he added, shoving the dagger deeper into the man's body until its hilt was the only thing stopping it from plunging further.

Evony stood in horrified shock at what had only just played out before her eyes. In mere seconds, Stavos had rendered the obstacle between them and her mother and aunt entirely nullified. She watched, still motionless with astonishment, as Stavos removed his dagger from Cedric's dead body and pushed his corpse to the ground. Hurriedly then, he began to search for the key to the cell.

Looking up, she saw that both her mother and aunt stood in their cell, clinging to the iron bars that imprisoned them and staring, mouths agape, at Stavos.

"Evony," Stavos said as he drew a ring of large keys from Cedric's trouser pocket, "where are the cloaks?"

"J-just outside the door…hidden in the brush," she answered, still attempting to comprehend how quickly and efficiently Stavos had vanquished Cedric.

"Be wary," he instructed, rising and handing her the keys he'd obtained. "We should've brought them in with us, but I was thoughtless for some reason. I will retrieve the cloaks for the queens, and you try the keys. One of them has to fit the lock of the cell."

"O-of course," she stammered, her hands trembling as she accepted the keys he offered. "Yes…of course."

"Hurry," Stavos told her. "I do not know how long it will take Happer to notice his man is missing."

Evony nodded and hurried toward the cell. Fumbling with the keys, she began to weep, for her mother and aunt were weeping as well—with renewed hope.

"I-I'm so sorry, Mother," Evony gasped through her tears. "I'm so overwhelmed. I can't seem to find…"

"Here," Stavos said from behind her. Gently taking the keys from Evony, he smiled at her with understanding. "Do not melt away yet, princess," he kindly instructed. "We still have far to go before sunrise, yes?"

Evony nodded and whispered, "Yes," in agreement.

And then—all at once, it seemed—Stavos freed her mother and her aunt! As he inserted a large key into the heavy iron lock, there came upon the stifling, stale air a large clanking sound. And in the next instant, he pulled their prison cell door open, and Evony was in her mother's arms for the first time in months.

"Mother!" she sobbed against her mother's dirty chemise. "Oh, Mother!"

"My darling! My darling!" Charmaine Elorietta cried, trembling with disbelief and joy as she embraced her eldest daughter.

"Aunt Raina!" Evony cried then, releasing her mother and falling into her aunt's desperate embrace. "Oh, I'm so happy you are well!"

"Forgive me, my majesties," Stavos said in a calming voice. "I am sorry to hurry you, and I do not mean to seem insensitive, but you are still in danger. We cannot linger any longer here."

"Of course," Queen Raina agreed.

Evony saw her mother nod as well.

"Evony, help your mother on with a cloak," Stavos directed. He offered Evony a dark woolen cloak, and she accepted it.

Her hands were numb with cold, and she was shivering so badly herself that she had a difficult time in assisting her mother in putting on the cloak. Her mother was weak as well, malnourished and spent of vigor from the ordeal she and her sister had endured.

"All will be well, my queen," Stavos said to Queen Raina as he pulled the cowl of the hooded cloak down over her face in order to hide her identity. "Come along, ladies," he said then. "We must make our way to Abawyth village and safety before we are found out by Happer…or seen by anyone else."

Stavos reached over, pulling Evony's hood up over her head as well. Then taking Queen Raina's hand, he led them out of the hidden room—led them out of the dank prison—and into the fresh, crisp air of Abawyth's winter woods.

Silently, they made their way through the woods and toward the village. Evony stumbled several times, wondering if her mother's feet and her aunt's were as numb as her own, for indeed they wore only light slippers. Yet each seemed more stable on her feet than Evony felt she was. Her fingers were numb as well, and her teeth chattered so violently that she was afraid their loud knocking together would wake the entire village when they entered.

All was quiet in Abawyth when they reached the outskirts. Yet there was warm light glowing in many of the shop windows already and in homes. Thus, Stavos hurried all three women, dropping behind them and nodding to Evony that she should lead the way.

She nodded her response and that she understood. Yet as she worked to hurry toward home, she felt as though her legs would not carry her much longer. She was cold—cold to the core—and truly wondered if she would make it home to see Mikol's and Tressa's resplendent expressions when they saw their mother enter.

But soon she was at the door of their beloved hovel. Using her numb knuckles to rap on the door, she stepped aside when Miss Lovie opened it so that her mother and aunt could precede her into the room.

"Mother? Oh, Mother! Is it really you?" Tressa cried, throwing her arms around her mother's waist and erupting into sobbing.

"It is, my angel!" Charmaine wept, collapsing to her knees on the floor as she drew Mikol to her as well, hugging her two youngest children in wondrous desperation as they all wept.

"Your majesty," Miss Lovie greeted Queen Raina with a proper curtsy, "it is solace to my heart and soul to see you are alive and well and once again with us."

"Thank you, ma'am," Raina said.

Her voice drew Mikol and Tressa's attention then, and they released their mother, exclaiming in unison, "Auntie Raina!" as they ran to her—she gathering them in her arms with loving delight.

"Oh, my darlings!" Raina cried. "How we have missed you all! Our wee babies!"

Even the wondrous, magical beauty of reunion unfolding before her did nothing to warm Evony's cold body or tired and cold brain. She stood watching as if she were merely a passerby who knew nothing intimate of the players before her.

"Evony?" Stavos said then. "Are you well?" Pushing back the hood of her cape, she saw his frown deepen—heard a growl of deep discontent rumble in his throat.

"Miss Lovie," he began.

"Yes, sire?" Miss Lovie answered.

"Have you prepared your rooms as I instructed…with baths and warm bedding for the queens?"

"Of course, Stavos," Lovie assured him.

"Then, everyone, all of you go with Miss Lovie…at once," Stavos ordered. There was no teasing in his manner. In fact, he was firm when next he spoke in a somewhat raised voice. "Go now. See to their majesties' welfare, Miss Lovie. Mikol and Tressa will help you."

Evony stared at him, her mind feeling not only cold but confused as she watched him remove his cloak, his vest, and then his boots.

"I said go!" he roared at the others.

"Oh, Evony!" Evony heard her mother cry out.

"Evony! Your lips…they are pure blue!" Tressa gasped.

"Out! Out now! I will see to Evony," Stavos again growled.

"Yes, sire," Evony heard Miss Lovie respond. "Come along, Tressa…Mikol. Prince Stavos is best prepared to help your sister. Your majesties…please follow me."

But Evony saw her mother pause, staring at Stavos a moment as he stripped off his stockings and began to unfasten his trousers. "You *will* save her, won't you?"

"S-save me?" Evony felt her mouth whisper.

"I will, my queen," Stavos said, pulling off his trousers to stand in front of Evony dressed only in his undertrousers and shirt. "I will, my queen, but you and your sister are yourselves still in danger from exposure, so please go…and trust me. I have protected her thus far, and I will protect her from this as well."

Evony's mother nodded and then followed the others through the door that led to Miss Lovie's rooms.

Evony was confused. She could not seem to form a solid thought. All she could comprehend was that she was bitterly cold, that Stavos had sent everyone from the room, and that he now stood before her in only his undertrousers and shirt.

Striding to her, he untied the cloak's bow at her neck, tossing the thing aside. She tried to raise her hands to stop him as he then began to pull at her shirtwaist and skirt, but she could not raise her frozen arms more than a few inches. She was helpless! Frozen! It was only when Stavos had stripped her of all her clothing, save her pantalets and short chemise, that she realized she was freezing to death!

"Stavos!" she cried through her cold and frozen lips.

"Hush now," he mumbled, stripping off his shirt and putting it on her. "This is warm. It will help." The body-warmed fabric of his shirt as he slipped it over her arms and head sent a painful sting of heat pulsing over her skin.

"I-I just need to warm my hands and feet a bit," Evony managed to gasp through her shivering. "I will sit before the fire until I am warmed."

"No," Stavos growled. "Your core must be warmed first."

Hurriedly he pushed back the coverings on Evony's bed with one bootless, stockingless foot. It was only then that true understanding began to seep into her mind. Save his undertrousers, Stavos had stripped his body of his own clothing. He meant to warm her body with his own.

"Oh n-no…please n-no," she whispered. "You can't p-possibly mean to—"

"I mean to save your life, yes," he grumbled as he swept her up into his arms and then laid her on the bed.

Evony's eyes widened as she watched Stavos's body settle next to hers.

"We must warm you, and quickly," he explained as he gathered her frigid, shivering body against his.

The warmth of his body against hers was nearly as excruciating as was her shivering—yet simultaneously blissful.

"Try to breathe slowly…to remain calm," he said into her hair as he maneuvered them so that her face was flush with his shoulder and neck. "Damn, girl!" he grumbled as he wrapped the protection and warmth of his powerful arms around her body—held her tight against his. "Why didn't you tell me you'd grown so cold?"

"I-I don't think I knew I had," she admitted. "And there were mother and Aunt Raina to worry over…and I…I…"

"Of course. Of course," he said.

The warmth of his breath in her hair felt like a knife cutting into her skin. And she wondered, *How did I manage to grow so cold?*

"Just relax, Evony," Stavos mumbled. "Try not to panic or be afraid. Just let the warmth slowly consume you. Think of it…the warmth. Just keep whispering to yourself that you are getting warmer."

But Evony Elorietta was not only freezing to death; a great fatigue was also beginning to devour her body and mind. She found that her thoughts were becoming more and more disjointed and that she was having difficulty keeping her eyes open—staying conscious.

"I'm so tired of being cold," she mumbled through still chattering teeth. "Sometimes it seems that I've never been warm…that I've been cold all my life…always chilled…as if some sort of blessed, thoroughgoing heat was just out of my reach. I just want to be warm." Tears began to moisten the warm, soft skin of Stavos's chest against which she lay.

"I know, Evony," he said in a calm, soothing voice. "You told me last night at the inn, remember? Remember our time together in the inn room? That was warm, wasn't it? Think of it again, Evony…for you were in my arms then, just as you are now…and I will keep you warm."

"You will?" she asked in a whisper.

"I'm trying my best," he mumbled against her ear as he tightened his embrace around her.

"I don't mean that," she whimpered as her mind began to struggle to keep dreams separate from actuality. "Can you not find a way to make my mind feel warmer...my thoughts...everything inside me?"

"Have you ever visited my kingdom, Ethiarien?" he asked, pulling her more tightly against him as she shivered with the lingering chill.

"No," Evony breathed.

"It is warm most seasons of the year," he said. "In summer, there are so many flowers to be seen...so many trees with cool green leaves and fragrant, brown bark. Farmers are in the fields caring for their crops. And my brother and I, and oft times my father, are with them, for a kingdom is only as strong as what she can provide for her people. Nights are balmy, and the air is scented with the perfume of growing vegetation, flowers, and hedgerows.

"But autumn and harvest are warmer yet—not in temperature but in the colors nature brings," he continued. "Yellows and browns, crimson and orange. All of Ethiarien is rich with apples and fruit, ripe vegetables, and smokehouses brimming with port and beef. And though the air is crisp and cool in the mornings, the noonday sun warms the earth with a golden sun that hangs heavy and bold in the sky."

Evony had ceased in her trembling. And now she lay asleep in his arms, her breathing a healthy regulation as it should be. It had been an hour since she had fallen asleep during his accolades of Ethiarien—since her body had begun to warm and return to its normal temperature. Yet Stavos had not left her there in her bed but lingered.

Stavos had felt her hands beginning to warm where they lay pressed against his chest, and even her legs were not so cold anymore. She would be well—he knew it—and he sighed with thanksgiving. Winter had nearly taken her, and he'd been so consumed with rescuing the queens that he had not noticed the grip the cold had on her until the moment they had entered the hovel. It was then he looked to see her lips were blue instead of their berry pink—that she was shaking, trembling so violently that he was surprised she had managed to keep her footing.

Yet the imp that sat upon his shoulder at times reminded him that Evony's near succumbing to the cold was exactly what had blessed him with one more moment of intimacy with her. Because of the cold, he had been gifted the opportunity to hold her again—breathe in the sweet fragrance that clung to her skin.

He brushed a long strand of hair from her cheek—studied the smooth slope of her neck as she slept. Yet Stavos found that tracing the lines of Evony's face, chin, and neck with simply his gaze—of visually admiring her soft, round shoulder that had somehow escaped the confines of his shirt she wore—only intensified his desire to touch her, to caress her, to feel the tenderness of her velvet skin beneath his fingers and against his palms. And even as his resolve not to touch her weakened and then vanished—even as the flush of the tender flesh of her shoulder caused the palm of his hand to burn with a fascinating pleasure when he touched her, a consuming euphoria that caused every muscle in his body to tense and twist with desire—Stavos knew that even touching her would not satisfy him.

Before he could convince himself to do otherwise, Stavos felt his own hand slowly slip beneath Evony's neck. The moisture of anticipation and desire flooded his mouth as he pressed his parted lips to the soft, alluring curve of her throat, leisurely savoring the ambrosial taste of her sweet flesh.

Stavos held his breath a moment as Evony stirred in her sleep. He watched her face—grinned when he saw that she smiled as she slept—and when in the next moment, she sighed with perceptible approval, he felt a measure of confidence begin to grow within him that the kiss had not offended her.

Again he pressed a lingering, moist kiss to her throat—pressed another to the side of her neck just below her ear. She did not wake—not fully at least—but her smile broadened nonetheless.

Stavos bent, caressing the bareness of her discreetly exposed shoulder with his unshaven chin a moment before kissing her there as well. He heard her exhale another sigh, and as she turned her face toward him—as he watched her tired, beautiful eyes flutter open and look at him—he kissed the side of her neck that he had neglected before—kissed her there over and over, encouraged when she did not push him away but rather raised one weak hand to rest at the back of his head, gently weaving her fingers through his hair.

In an instant, Stavos found himself conquered by desire! Gathering Evony into his arms, he increased the intimate nature of the kisses that he now trailed over her neck, tasting her at his leisure, indulging himself in the feel of her skin against his mouth, and relishing the manner in which she clung to him. Yet he knew he must give her up, that he must release her—let her go before weakness caused of great fatigue found him dishonorable and her ravaged.

Therefore, he forced his mouth from her cheek and gazed into her narrowly open eyes. Evony smiled at him—reached up with one small finger and began trailing it around the perimeter of his lips. Several times she did this—slowly tracing his mouth with her index finger as if endeavoring to memorize every contour.

"Sire," she began in a whisper, still smiling up at him, "are you, perchance, endeavoring to take advantage of my fevered and pitifully vulnerable state?"

"Perhaps," Stavos mumbled in return.

"Well then, if perhaps you are endeavoring to corrupt me, sire," she whispered, "I do wish you would neglect my neck for a moment or two...in favor of my mouth."

Stavos smiled—entirely enraptured, lured, and provoked by her words. "As you wish, princess," he said.

What a dream it was! What a perfect, rapturous, delicious dream! As Stavos's mouth claimed Evony's in a heated, impassioned kiss, she clung to him—clung to him with the same desperation with which she always clung to him in her dreams. In those moments, she was glad she had nearly frozen—that Stavos had endeavored to save her and had inspired her to such warm and beautiful dreaming. Oh, she was ever so warm—so very, very warm! Evony had never known such warmth—such comfort—not in all her life. It seemed every essence of Stavos Voronin summoned warmth—radiated warmth. His kiss was warm, of course—his mouth hot, moist, and ravenous as he kissed her. Yet it was more than that. *He* was warm—his very being—his body—his soul.

As Evony's dream continued—as she and Stavos continued to kiss, as he rained an otherworldly sort of bliss over her—Evony allowed her hands to caress the strong breadth of his shoulders, the firm, sculpted muscles of his upper arms as he held her. His skin was so smooth and hot that it caused her palms to tingle with a sort of wild, thrilling sensation she had never known before—never—not even in her dreams.

It was in that moment, as Stavos ground a particularly ravenous kiss to her mouth, that Evony was at last fully aware—aware that she was awake, not dreaming. Breaking the seal of their kiss and pushing at his shoulders to distance herself from him a bit, she felt tears fill her eyes—tears of embarrassment.

"I'm awake?" she breathed as she felt her cheeks blush crimson.

"You are," he affirmed. "And you have driven off Winter's killing hold on you."

"You mean to say that *you* have driven it off. And now…now that your business of saving me is finished," she whispered, shyly glancing away from him, "now that you have assured my survival, it is no longer necessary nor appropriate for us to…to remain in such…in such circumstances."

"And yet," he said, smiling at her, "having lingered in your bed for near an hour…what difference would one more minute make, eh?" he teased.

"Y-you mean even though I'm awake?" she asked in quiet disbelief.

The low chuckle of amusement that rumbled in his chest and throat further warmed her—just as everything about him warmed her. "You have been awake this past while when I was kissing you," he reminded her. His smile broadened as he added, "Whether you were fully aware of it or not."

"Stavos," Evony began. She must tell him! She must confess her love for him, no matter what pain the future promised to bring. "Stavos, I—"

"Is she well?"

Her mother's voice startled her so that Evony thought for a moment her heart had stopped.

Glancing over, she saw her mother and her aunt, both bathed, hair washed and combed, and wearing fresh chemises, standing in the room studying Stavos expectantly.

"She is," Stavos answered.

Evony felt her cheeks blush vermilion, wondering how long her mother and aunt had been witness to the intimacy of words and affections that had passed between her and Stavos.

Still, Stavos seemed unaffected. He simply raised himself and exited the bed.

"She will need to stay in bed…stay warm for the rest of the day," he told the queens as he pulled on his trousers.

"What? No! I am well enough," she argued, even though the simple action of sitting up caused such a dizziness in her head as to force her to lie back down.

"Forgive me, your majesties," Stavos countered, however. "But Evony has not had sleep in days. And having been gripped by the cold the way she was, she needs rest and plenty to drink."

"But there is so much to do, Stavos," Evony mumbled from her place. "Mother and Aunt Raina…there is so much…"

"What would you have us do, Prince Stavos?" Queen Raina asked.

"Stay hidden," he answered as he pulled on his stockings and boots. "I will go to King Standwood this evening and present myself as a candidate for the challenge of solving the sleepy princesses' enigma." He chuckled a moment, paused, and looked to Evony. "Fool," he said, shaking his head. "His ridiculous call for champions for his stepdaughters is exactly what thwarted him. Pride goeth before the fall, it is said, yes?"

Evony nodded.

"Prince Stavos," Queen Raina began, approaching Stavos, "while you were tending to Evony, Mikol and Miss Lovie explained your plans to us. You are clearly a brilliant strategist as well as a capable man. That is why I entrust you with this."

Evony watched as her aunt offered a folded and sealed parchment to Stavos.

"I have written instructions to the captain of my guard, Dillon Thoringil," she explained as Stavos accepted the communication. "He will make certain that all is ready when you are presented to the king to report your findings—when you reveal that Charmaine and I are no longer captive and that he has been found out."

Stavos nodded. "I am honored, my queen, to be trusted with such a charge as this."

Evony blushed as her mother and aunt giggled in unison. One would have thought them no more than girls, for their own cheeks pinked up as Charmaine said, "You have been trusted with far more important charges and proven yourself capable as well as honorable, our prince." She glanced at Evony, smiling with understanding.

Stavos smiled as well. "Thank you, your majesties," he said with a polite and respectful bow.

"Please, Stavos," Raina said, taking one of Stavos's hands in a pleading fashion, "find a way to get this into the hands of Dillon. Please. It is more important to me than you even imagine."

"I will find a way, my queen," Stavos promised her.

"Oh, Evony!" Tressa exclaimed as she bounded into the room like a loosed puppy. "You are well! Oh, you are well!"

Evony managed to sit up in her bed and returned her sister's exuberant embrace. "I am well, sweet darling. I am well. And soon we will all be safe and back home again."

Tressa released her then, pulling back a bit and studying Evony for a moment.

Her soft, sweet brow wrinkled with a puzzled frown, and she said, "Evony, you look just like that Greek woman Mother read us the story of—the one with all the snakes in her hair," Tressa commented.

"Do you mean Medusa?" Evony squeaked in horror.

"Yes! That's her name!" Tressa giggled. "You look just like I imagined Medusa would look."

Evony was mortified with embarrassment when Stavos chuckled, reached out, and tousled her hair as if she were only a child.

"She does look rather rumpled, doesn't she?" he said to Tressa, though winking and smiling at Evony.

"I'll get the brush, Evony!" Tressa giggled. "We can't have you looking like such a damp dishcloth in front of our handsome Prince Stavos, now can we?"

"Indeed not," Charmaine teased Evony, understandingly.

"I feel there is too much merriment afoot, considering all the danger that has been endured and that which still must come," Mikol said from behind his mother. He was frowning, his arms folded across his chest with obvious disapproval.

"Ah, but, Mikol," Miss Lovie said, appearing in the doorway and placing a loving arm around his shoulders, "it is what gets us all through the trials and tribulations of life. Sad times…frightening times…all of them are better endured if mirth and laughter are our tonic."

"Well said, Miss Lovie," Queen Raina complimented. "I admire not only your strength, kindness, compassion, and charity but also your wisdom. Would be that my own daughters would have had you at their sides during Standwood's wickedness."

"Keep her warm," Stavos grumbled as he fastened his trousers and then angrily tugged a heavy boot onto each foot. "Feed her broth and see that she rests."

"Yes, sire," Lovie agreed as the man opened the door in making to leave.

"But you wear no shirt, Stavos," Tressa informed him.

Frowning, Stavos inhaled a deep breath, snatched up his fur cloak from the chair, and grumbled, "I've no need of it," before closing the door behind him.

"But it's so very cold out!" Tressa cried, looking to Lovie for reassurance. "And Stavos...out in the snow with no shirt and only his cloak for warmth."

Lovie smiled, stroking Tressa's hair with comfort. "He will be well enough, darling," she said. Then looking to Evony but still speaking to Tressa, she added, "He has been well warmed tonight, and it will see him safely to his own shelter."

"Then wish me well, ladies and fellow prince," Stavos said, "for I am off to the Hungry Horse Inn to portray the appearance of ignorance to Cedric's demise and the queens that have vanished from their prison. I will rest and present myself to Standwood this very evening, as a candidate to solve the mystery surrounding your daughters, my queen." He nodded to Queen Raina. "And if all goes well, tomorrow night I will spend the night in the castle...and the next day King Standwood will be vanquished from the throne by Ethiarien and our good queen's own castle guard."

Yet Evony's tired mind had a fleeting thought in that moment. "But only wait, Stavos!" she exclaimed. "The prince that Cedric confessed to killing...my cousin Kathleen...and the tunnel...there is something I must tell you before you go to the king. There are things I've only just now realized and—"

But the debilitating fatigue that had been threatening to conquer Evony all through the night was winning the battle at last.

Collapsing back onto the bed, she whispered, "I must tell you of Kathleen...of my suspicions...of...of the..."

"I will return to you once more, Evony...this evening, after the king accepts my candidacy," Stavos soothed her, brushing a hair from her cheek. "I promise. I will come speak with you once more before I begin the last battle we must fight in this. Very well?"

He had given his promise, and Evony knew that Prince Stavos Voronin of Ethiarien ever kept any promise he made. She knew it with all her heart, for she had seen it proven.

"All right," she breathed. "I will wait for you to come to me."

"Good. Now rest," he said. "It is not at an end yet. We must all be steadfast…and strong. Feed them all well, Miss Lovie," he instructed as he retrieved his own cloak, donning it over a bare and magnificently sculpted torso. "We must be at our best and at the ready when my father and brother arrive. There may be a battle yet…for we do not know how thoroughgoing Standwood's wickedness is."

It was then that unconsciousness consumed Evony, at last. She could fight it no more. In knowing her mother and aunt were safe and that Stavos would return to speak with her one last time— perhaps to bless her with one last, blissful kiss—her mind surrendered to the darkness of cruel, crushing exhaustion.

CHAPTER ELEVEN

It seemed an eternity, the long day during which Evony waited for Stavos to return. Exhaustion tossed her between sleep and wakefulness. She slept, yes, but no more than an hour at one stretch, for strange nightmares and feelings of anxiety and loss kept her from resting well—from falling into the deep sleep her body and mind desperately needed.

So many haunting questions pricked at her thoughts. Would Stavos succeed in thwarting King Standwood? And if he did, would her Aunt Raina honor the promise Standwood had made—that the man who solved the mystery of the twelve sleepy princesses would have the Abawythian princess of his choice as wife? Yet Evony already knew her aunt would reward Stavos with his choice of wife; in the very least she would give him that. Thus, would he choose her cousin Patrice to wed? Would King Standwood even accept his candidacy as a champion for the tortured princesses? Would Stavos truly return to Evony that night as he had promised? Would she see him one last time before he became bound to another woman? Would she have the chance to tell him of her suspicions of Kathleen's alchemy, to warn him of the profound secrets the hidden tunnel beneath the castle held? Would he kiss her again?

In fact, Evony's mind was so plagued with questions, worries, and despair that when at last her mother suggested she rise from her bed, freshen, and join them all for supper, Evony did not hesitate. She could not find sleep any longer, and lying in bed vainly chasing it only kept her mind inundated by concern and puzzlements. Perhaps company—loving conversation with her mother, her aunt, her siblings, and Miss Lovie—would ease her restlessness. After all, Evony had owned hardly a moment in savoring her mother's safe return, and her aunt's. The horror of the last months, the misery and fear that found her and her little brother and sister homeless and seeking sanctuary with Miss Lovie in Abawyth, the horrid Midnight Masquerade, and the vile Ewan Happer and Cedric—all of it had worn her so thoroughly to the core that she had not even realized and rejoiced in all that was good since Stavos arrived. Stavos—every thought led back to Stavos.

Evony wondered whether King Standwood had accepted him as a candidate for champion. She wondered whether he had supped with the king, with her cousins—with Patrice. And as her thoughts again returned to haunting, anxious questions, Evony fairly leapt from her bed, for she feared distraction was all that could save her sanity. She would embrace her mother and her aunt, kiss their lovely cheeks, relish their return and the fact that they were alive and well— for the moment.

In truth, Stavos had rarely experienced such a lavish feast. It was obvious that King Standwood had not hesitated in taking all the Abawythian throne had to offer—now that he supposed his queen wife to be dead. He was an arrogant man, proud and haughty. There was not one thread of humility about him, and he sickened Stavos. Such men were the worst kinds of kings—men who cared not for their people or even their own families, men who more often than not were the ruination of kingdoms. Yet Stavos had endured Standwood's boastings of wealth and accomplishments.

As Stavos and King Standwood had supped together, the twelve princesses of Abawyth were quite markedly absent. When Stavos inquired as to why they did not attend the evening meal with their stepfather, Standwood replied that until they were cured of whatever infection had found them so awash in lethargy, Standwood felt it his duty to keep his distance from his stepdaughters. After all, since the queen's disappearance, he was the ruler of Abawyth and could not risk *his* kingdom losing its king if the strange lethargy were to overtake him somehow.

In all, it was an appalling acquaintance—a miserable, infuriating circumstance to endure—supping with *King* Standwood. But it was necessary, and in the end, Stavos managed to be accommodating and charming enough toward the villain Standwood to secure the opportunity to solve the mystery of the twelve sleepy princesses. He would begin the very next evening, spending the whole of the night in the princesses' bedchambers, standing guard over them, watching for whatever or whoever was causing their lethargy and unhappiness—their plaguing despair.

King Standwood himself decided that Stavos should meet Abawyth's princesses that night, however. Standwood suggested that familiarizing himself with each princess might somehow assist him on his quest.

Naturally, the king warned Stavos of the strange stupor that overtook each man who had tried before him—even caused the first prince to attempt the quest to disappear altogether. But Stavos smiled at the king, thanked him for his concern, and assured him that the stupor would not overcome Stavos of Ethiarien.

Hence King Standwood welcomed Stavos as a would-be champion of the twelve princesses. He then instructed his personal herald to present the princesses to their new advocate.

Thus it was that Stavos found himself led to the grand hallway of Abawyth Castle, located just outside the princesses' personal chambers. There, standing regal and beautiful against one portrait-lined wall, stood the twelve. They nodded their greeting, in unison, as the herald approached.

"Prince Stavos of Ethiarien," the needle-nosed, ink-eyed herald began. Bowing and gesturing toward the princess at the head of the line, he proceeded, "The princess Kathleen Lardosean of Abawyth."

Stavos had recognized Princess Kathleen at once, from Evony's description and because Stavos himself had danced with her at the Midnight Masquerade. Tall, slender, and as graceful as an angel, the eldest of the twelve princesses of Abawyth was just as lovely as the men in the pub at the Hungry Horse Inn had claimed. Her long raven hair and sable-brown eyes echoed a character steeped in mystery and allure. Stavos smiled, for the princess Kathleen's eyes simmered, as if she carefully cached some great, expressively taxing secret within the very depths of her beautiful soul.

"Welcome to Abawyth Castle, Prince Stavos," the eldest princess said. Her voice was soft and soothing as Stavos remembered it had been at the dance—like the warm breath of a smoldering fire in the hearth on a cold winter's eve.

"Thank you, Princess Kathleen," Stavos responded.

Taking one step forward, the herald nodded to Prince Stavos, gestured to the second princess standing in the reception line, and said, "The princess Laura Lardosean of Abawyth."

At the sight of the princess Laura unmasked, Stavos felt his brows arch in astonishment. When first he and Evony had begun to conspire and she had told him of her cousins, she remarked that Laura was Kathleen's twin sister. Yet never had he seen two sisters of any sort who looked so dissimilar. He glanced back to the princess Kathleen, quickly studying her ebony hair and dark eyes.

"It is our pleasure to welcome you to Abawyth, Prince Stavos," Laura greeted, also offering her hand.

Still stunned at the dissimilarity between the princesses Laura and Kathleen, Stavos again looked from one to the other, even as he took Princess Laura's hand in his own.

"Oh, the pleasure is mine, to be sure, Princess Laura," he said as he studied her a moment—her slight yet well-formed figure, her lovely eyes of soft, enthralling azure, her fawn-colored hair, so flawlessly coifed in silken curls.

The tiny laughter of a lovely fairy tickled his ears. "We *are* twins, Prince Stavos, Kathleen and I. You've no need to doubt your own eyes," Princess Laura affirmed. "Simply we are not *identical* twins."

Stavos smiled, chuckled lowly, and said, "I did manage to eventually work that one out—though it did take me a moment or two, princess."

"The princess Abbitha Lardosean of Abawyth," the herald stated, continuing down the line.

The princess Abbitha was just as beautiful as her two elder sisters. Eyes wide and sparkling with excitement, Princess Abbitha offered her hand to Stavos, simultaneously greeting, "Welcome, Prince Stavos. My! You *are* a handsome one, are you not? And look at your shoulders—so broad and strong! I daresay we've not had any man the likes of you come to Abawyth...*ever!*"

"Well, I thank you for the complimentary greeting, Princess Abbitha," Stavos said, feeling the heat of awkwardness in being bathed in such flattery rise to his face.

She was a beauty, and again Stavos was struck by her individual appearance. While the princesses Kathleen and Laura boasted skin as flawless as fresh porcelain, the princess Abbitha owned the radiant glow of a more olive tone of skin. Her hair was the color of acorn hats, and her amber-bay eyes were wide and dazzling with curiosity as she stared at him with such a manner of dauntlessness that it indeed caused him mild discomfort.

Clearing his throat with obvious impatience, the herald stepped forward yet again. Gesturing, he announced, "The princess Karamelle Lardosean of Abawyth."

"Abbitha and I bear little resemblance as well, Prince Stavos," the attractive young woman offered as Stavos took her hand. She blushed for no apparent reason—simply blushed such a deep crimson that Stavos was near afraid to kiss her hand at first. Yet he did, only to rise and see that the deep shade of crimson bright upon her lovely cheeks had indeed deepened to a raging scarlet.

"It is my pleasure to meet you as well, Princess Karamelle," Stavos greeted. He was fairly certain that if he lingered any longer, her cheeks might catch fire.

"The pleasure is ours," Princess Karamelle managed all the same. This cousin of Evony Elorietta bore an even greater difference from the others than those he'd been introduced to before. Her hair was like fine-spun gold that had been laid out in the sun to render into cream butter, and her eyes were blue like priceless sapphires.

Stavos wondered how it was that one kingdom was so wildly blessed with such unequaled beauty in its royals. And yet he thought of Evony—Evony, who was, in his mind's eye and memory, more beautiful than any of her cousins thus far. And he knew that though there were more princesses to meet, none would trump the graceful, strong, brave, beautiful enchantress he'd left in the humble hovel in Abawyth's village.

"The princess Victoria Lardosean of Abawyth," the herald sighed as his exasperation noticeably grew. Stavos smiled, owning sympathy for the man. No doubt he had heralded the twelve princesses of Abawyth so many times that the task had grown quite tedious to him.

"Hello, Prince Stavos," the princess Victoria greeted. She offered a hand to him, and Stavos did not miss the wildly flirtatious expression in her blue eyes. And when he took her hand in his, noting the manner in which she rather caressed his as he did so, he instantly knew which princess of Abawyth was the playful coquette. Eyes as blue as the heavens themselves were Victoria's, eyes glittering with confidence and mischief, enhanced by long lashes—lashes that perfectly complemented her flaxen hair, hair more the color of platinum than gold. Indeed, Stavos had no doubt that the princess Victoria of Abawyth could win any man she set her mind to winning—any save Stavos Voronin, for she was not the first siren he had encountered and bested.

"Moving along, sire, if you please," the herald sighed. "The princess Patrice Lardosean of Abawyth, Prince Stavos," the herald nearly yawned.

"Good evening, Prince Stavos," the princess Patrice greeted, offering a graceful hand.

Unmasked, it was even more apparent that Patrice resembled Evony. But though lovely and beautiful in her own right, Patrice was not Evony Elorietta, no matter how similar the color of her chestnut hair. The princess Patrice also boasted green eyes. Yet Evony's eyes were the color of polished jade, jade that held the light of the sun and all things in life that were green and beautiful, and Patrice's were more emerald in hue. He recognized Patrice for her voice if nothing else, for he had danced with her at Happer's Midnight Masquerade far more often than he had any of her sisters. She was sweet in countenance—humble, like her cousin. Yes, she was very beautiful, this cousin of Evony's that owned a similar countenance and loveliness, but Stavos thought how much more striking was Evony in her own character and physical allure.

"The princesses Anne and Diana Lardosean of Abawyth," the herald announced then.

"And I see we have a set of twins identical, at last," he chuckled as the young, raven-haired, brown-eyed princesses curtsied in unison, "and proof that the princess Kathleen is indeed your blood sister."

"Yes!" one answered—though he was not sure whether it was Anne or Diana. "We could have been triplets, we two and Kathleen. Do you not agree, Prince Stavos?"

"Absolutely," he did indeed agree. "You are the visions of your elder sister."

Both girls giggled with delight, blushing as Stavos took their hands and kissed them.

"And the princesses Jewel and Opal Lardosean," the herald rushed.

"Also identical, I see," Stavos said, studying two very young princesses, both with green eyes and hair the color of autumn acorns.

Stavos kissed the backs of the princesses Jewel's and Opal's hands, just as the weary herald sighed, "And lastly, the princesses Elspeth and Isabella."

These last two princesses bore likeness to none of the others. Their hair was a deep auburn, their eyes such crystal blue they rendered Stavos rather unnerved at first, for it gave them a rather ethereal appearance—as if they were not truly humans but some sort of fairy folk or angels.

"You will perhaps be told that we are too young, Prince Stavos," one young woman stated.

"Too young to be considered as your prize and bride if you do unravel our secret," her twin said.

"But we are not," they said in unison.

"For we are seventeen at this very moment," the first said.

"And far old enough to wed," said the second.

Stavos bowed to them both, kissed the backs of their hands, and soothed, "Well old enough to wed, yes."

They smiled, exchanged delighted glances, and dropped unified curtsies.

"And there you have it, sire," the herald breathed. "The twelve princesses of Abawyth."

"Indeed," Stavos said. "Twelve beautiful princesses harboring in one castle alone. The kingdom of Abawyth is undeniably blessed."

Several of the princesses giggled with flattered pleasure. Yet Stavos's attention had been arrested by something else—by a portrait that hung on the wall high above and just behind Elspeth and Isabella.

"And who is this?" he asked, feigning ignorance. "She seems familiar to me."

"Oh, that is our cousin, Evony Elorietta of Elawyth," Abbitha offered. "It is said she resembles our own Patrice. Perhaps that is why you find her familiar."

"Perhaps," Stavos mumbled as he gazed at the painting. It was Evony as he had never seen her—dressed in a lavish gown of gold, her hair upswept and pristine. Her berry-red lips donned a hint of a smile, but only a hint. And as glorious as the painting was—as flawlessly as it captured Evony's beauty—Stavos thought to himself that he preferred his Evony dressed in a simple villager's dress and with a full, amused, and alluring smile on her lovely lips.

"D-do you think you can help us, Prince Stavos?" one of the princesses asked, drawing Stavos's attention back to the secretly anguished young woman before him.

Each princess was staring at him with dread evident in her lovely eyes. And there was something else in their eyes as well: doubt. They doubted him—doubted he could solve the mystery surrounding them, doubted they could ever be freed from Ewan Happer's malevolence and his villainous business.

But Stavos smiled, particularly at the princess Kathleen, for her expression displayed the most doubt of all—though Stavos could not fathom why.

Looking directly at each girl in turn for a moment, Stavos then said, "I know I can help you. In fact, I promise to free you from whatever or whomever holds prisoner your abilities to find peace and respite."

Several of the princesses gasped. Yet the princess Kathleen did not. Stavos studied her countenance as one of her lovely dark eyebrows arched in disbelief.

"Do I appear so incapable in your judgment, Princess Kathleen?" he asked, offering her a confident smile.

"Of course not, Prince Stavos," the princess Kathleen answered. "It is only…well, to be honest, many have come before you and made the same promise to us. So please forgive me for my wariness."

"I expect wariness is only wise…especially with that which you have endured, your highness," Stavos responded. "But I promise you, I will free you all, princess—for I have something the other candidates given your stepfather's challenge did not."

"And what might that be, my prince?" Princess Laura asked.

Stavos smiled. "Why, simply a deep, beloved, and very beautiful secret of my own."

CHAPTER TWELVE

At the sound of the knocking on the door, Evony's heart surged with exhilaration. He had come back to her! Just as he'd promised, Stavos had returned following his evening at Abawyth Castle. In that very instant, she did not care whether King Standwood had granted him the chance to solve the mystery surrounding her cousins; all she knew was that he had returned to her, and it bathed her in a joy she had never known.

It was that Mikol lifted the bolt and opened the latch to greet Stavos.

Queen Raina was the first to speak. "Were you able to give to Dillon…um, Captain Thoringil my message, Prince Stavos?" Raina asked.

"Of course, your majesty," Stavos assured—though Evony smiled when she noted his gaze lingered on Evony and not on her aunt. "I placed it in his hand myself, when he was presented to me as I was welcomed into the castle."

Evony heard her aunt sigh with a great relief, and still Stavos was looking at Evony, smiling at her, melting her heart with the light of pleasure shining in the blue of his eyes.

"And did Standwood accept your candidacy to champion the princesses?" Evony heard her mother inquire.

"He did indeed, your majesty," Stavos answered, his gaze never leaving Evony, even yet. "I met your cousins, Evony, the twelve lovely princesses of Abawyth," he said, striding toward her then.

Taking her hands in his, his smile broadened as he looked at her. "And we are going to end this vile reign of King Standwood. We are going to free your cousins, just as we have your mother and aunt. Standwood will be dethroned and punished, and all in Abawyth— and Elawyth too—will return to the wonder it was before. And it is because of *you*, Evony Elorietta. *You* have made this possible. *You* and only you trusted me enough to allow me to assist you in your quest. And for that honor, I thank you." He chuckled a moment and then added, "And to think when this all began mere days ago…you feared you would be in my debt. How strange life is, eh?"

"Yes…strange indeed," Evony managed. She wanted to cry—to burst into tears of not only joy but also agony! There he stood before her—the man of her very dreams, the man she loved even more than her own life. There he stood, thanking her, commending her in recognizing her part in it all, her sacrifices and strength. She should be elated by such recognition, obvious admiration, and respect, and she was. Yet all her heart could feel was that, in some regard, it was all for naught as far as she was concerned, for though her mother, aunt, cousins, and the two kingdoms would be saved, she would not have Stavos in the end.

Thus she chose to simply press forward—to reach the end of her journey with her beloved as quickly as it could be reached, that she might endeavor to recover from knowing him, from loving him, from losing him.

"When do you begin?" she asked. "When do you begin your quest to solve this abominable mystery that, unbeknownst to King Standwood, you have solved already?"

Stavos's smile broadened as he answered, "Tonight. Tonight I will stay with the princesses, attempt to avoid the strange stupor that has overwrought every other man who has endeavored to help them, and—as you said, unbeknownst to the devil Standwood—solve the mystery that you have already solved."

She could not keep from smiling at him, for he was far too handsome not to smile at, especially in that moment, when being on the brink of success shone so beautifully in his countenance.

"And so," he began, "being that your last words to me were of things you had riddled out for yourself that you needed to tell me...here I am, princess. So tell me."

Evony swallowed the lump of anxiety that had formed in her throat. Then, glancing about to her mother, her aunt, her brother, her sister, and Miss Lovie, she said, "I-I must speak with Stavos privately."

"Of course, darling," her mother said. Smiling with understanding at all her daughter was now enduring, Charmaine kissed her on the cheek and said, "He could not have come so far without you...nor you without him."

Evony nodded and watched her loved ones retire to Miss Lovie's rooms. Quickly, she called, however, "But wait—Miss Lovie?"

"Yes, dear?" Lovie Wiggin asked—her sweet, loving face alight with hope and happiness.

"In truth, you are the hero here," Evony told her. "Without you, Mikol, Tressa, and I...we may have perished and—"

"Please, my dear, princess," Miss Lovie interrupted, however, "please do not shower me with accolades. I am merely grateful that God put me in your path and gave a lingering purpose to my long life."

Evony nodded, understanding that the elderly angel did not wish to be praised. She sensed that to Lovie Wiggin, it would have somehow made her feel distressed.

Once the door to the adjoining rooms was closed and Evony was alone with Stavos, she looked up to him and began to gush, "I-I want to thank you for saving my life, Stavos. I did not realize how the cold had overcome...how close to being truly frozen I was. And I...I want to thank you for—"

"The danger of the cold, of becoming so cold that one's body literally freezes and dies, is something I am all too well acquainted with from my time as a soldier," he explained. "I have seen more men than I care to remember who have died of it." He chuckled, winked at her, and added, "Though never have I enjoyed saving a person from it as I enjoyed saving you, princess."

Evony blushed and shook her head in mirthful scolding at his flirtation.

"And now," he began then, "tell me what else you have riddled out." He paused, his smile broadening as he brushed a strand of hair from her cheek. "You have quite the talent for riddling out mysteries, after all."

His touch! It was as if the heat of it at her cheek branded her his own. How she would miss it. How she would miss the sight of him—his touch, his laughter, his strength, his kiss.

"I-I don't know why I neglected telling you this in the first of it, Stavos," she began. "Perhaps simply because my mind was weary, or perhaps because I did not think you would believe me if I had told you when first we began to talk of your saving us all."

"Then I hope that your willingness to tell me now means that I have earned your full trust at last…yes?" he inquired. He gestured toward the small table in the room, took her arm, and led her to a seat there.

"I feel foolish for not having told you this part of it before," she admitted as he took the seat next to her.

"What is it, Evony?" he prodded.

Inhaling a deep breath of courage, Evony trudged forth. "I think I know what the strange stupor is that overtakes every man who has previously been allowed to try and solve the enigma of what is ailing my cousins. And I think I know why it began in the first of it."

"Then tell, witty woman!" Stavos exclaimed with obvious relief. "For if the truth be told, whether or not you think me weak and cowardly because of it, I have been, admittedly, somewhat concerned about that—afraid that there truly is something in Abawyth Castle that might overtake me and thwart my efforts."

Evony smiled and admitted, "I did wonder why you had not seemed concerned about the stupor. I thought…well, I'm not sure what I thought because I believed all this time that I knew how to ensure that it would not overtake you."

"How?"

"My cousin Kathleen, she began to dabble in alchemy when were all just girls," Evony explained. "When we all visited Abawyth last summer, Kathleen demonstrated to Patrice, Laura, and I just how proficient she has become. I do not pause in claiming that my cousin Kathleen is a very gifted alchemist, for she concocted a tonic and put it in the watering dish of King Standwood's large black dog. Within minutes of the dog having drunk of the tonic, he fell into a deep sleep—a sleep that lasted so long that Patrice, Laura, and I were truly worried that the dog would expire. Yet just before we retired for the evening, we witnessed King Standwood walking near the east gardens, with his dog. The dog was trotting along as vigorously as ever as if nothing had ever overcome him."

"And so the puzzlement of the strange stupor that overcame every would-be champion before me…" Stavos prodded.

"Well, you heard that Cedric man," Evony continued. "He confessed to having murdered the first prince to try to champion my twelve cousins…to tossing his body in the river. I know Kathleen, and all of my cousins of Abawyth. No doubt they suspected or even perhaps had sure knowledge of the fate that befell the first man who tried to help them. Thus, rather than risk lives of others, my heart is certain that the strange stupor that overcomes every man who tries to help them is Kathleen's tonic…that my cousins would rather have remained slaves to Ewan Happer's heinous Midnight Masquerade than to have risked another life."

Stavos nodded, smiling with approval of Evony's assumption. "I can see that such compassion and self-sacrifice are at the core of your cousins' souls. It is evident in not only their endurance of such a vile situation as the Midnight Masquerade for their mother's sake but also what you have riddled out concerning this tonic."

"Then you believe me?" Evony asked. "You think that my guess where Kathleen and the strange stupor of Abawyth Castle—"

"Is spot on, love!" Stavos exclaimed. A frown of concern puckered his handsome brow a bit then. "And why wouldn't I believe you, Evony?" he asked. "I have believed everything you have confided in me thus far. So why think that I would hesitate, even for an instant, in doubting you now?"

Evony glanced away from him a moment. "Because, Prince Stavos, what I am about to tell you may seem so implausible and fantastic…"

His hand on her knee thrilled her so thoroughly that she quite forgot what she was about to tell him in the very midst of telling him. Looking back, she found that Stavos's smile had returned.

"Evony…were you not listening only a moment ago when I asked you why you would think I would ever doubt you?" he asked her.

Evony smiled, biting her lip with delight in owning his trust—and his touch. "I was listening," she assured him. "It's only that…at times I cannot believe that a man such as you found such instantaneous trust in believing me. After all, as you said, we've only known one another for a matter of days."

He leaned forward, gently caressing her cheek with the back of his hand. "Evony, I think our souls met long before our eyes—or our bodies or our minds. I trust you, Evony. I believe every word you say. I see your strength and wisdom—the alert and quick manner in which you discern things that others would not even recognize. Tell me this implausible, fantastic thing you have tell…for I can see that you believe it is something I need to know, in order that I may champion this kingdom and yours. And trust *me* now, sweet Evony, that my preeminent quest has become first and foremost to help *you*…even before your unfortunate, manipulated, nearly enslaved cousins."

She could not help herself then—she had to touch him! Evony was so compelled to embrace him in that moment—to feel the warmth that radiated from him, body, mind, and soul—that before she could think another thought, she leaned forward, throwing her arms around his neck and melting against him as she felt his arms embrace her in return.

He must champion her! As Stavos held Evony's soft, desirable body in his arms—as he inhaled the now familiar and heavenly fragrance of her hair and skin—he again silently vowed that, even if he were to fail in thwarting King Standwood and Ewan Happer, even if he were to fail in assisting Queen Raina to regain her throne and Queen Charmaine in regaining hers, if he were to fail the twelve princesses of Abawyth, none of it would seem as destructive and heinous as failing the woman he loved. And yes—he loved her! It was unfathomable, yes, that he could have found, in only a matter of days, the only woman who could ever truly own his heart and soul. If he failed Evony, then nothing else would matter to him—not his own kingdom, not the throne he should one day inherit, nothing.

Thus, he would not fail her. He would die first. And so, with one last inhaling of the beautiful perfume that was Evony's essence, Stavos said, "Tell it all to me, Evony. Tell me all I need to know to champion you."

Though she wanted to cling to him forever—though her heartbreak at knowing what she was about to tell him could be construed as treason but also understood as confiding in the man who would be the spouse of a princess of Abawyth—though tears threatened to erupt from her eyes at the thought of Patrice or one of her other cousins lingering in his arms the way she did now—Evony knew what she must do. And she did it.

Forcing herself to pull back from Stavos, to leave the warm safety of his strong arms, she began, "The tunnel, Stavos—the one my cousins and I used to escape the castle the night I was told that King Standwood could not be trusted and that he, in fact, was the cause of our misery and peril—I know it is the path you must take, the path that the first prince who attempted to solve this mystery must have when he followed my cousins to the Midnight Masquerade. And you must be prepared to keep the greatest secret you have ever kept when you follow it as well…if even you do." She sighed before continuing, "I do not know what, if anything, as yet, you plan to tell my cousins of what has transpired. But if you decide to allow them to linger in innocence until King Standwood is thwarted, you may find yourself in the tunnel, Stavos—the tunnel wherein the largest bulk of Abawyth's wealth is hidden."

"What do you mean?" Stavos asked. "And before you begin, I must tell you this, Evony. I have reasoned that I may indeed allow your cousins to linger in innocent ignorance until I face Standwood tomorrow. I do not want them in danger, and if they know we have your mother safe here, they may become so overwrought with emotion that one or more of them might inadvertently offer Standwood some sign that something is afoot. I will explain in more detail in a moment. But because I do plan to wait before telling them all, I may indeed allow them to travel to the Midnight Masquerade."

Evony's brow wrinkled, however. "But…but, Stavos, surely by now Ewan Happer knows Cedric is dead and that my mother and aunt are no longer his prisoners. Why then would he think that my cousins would continue to—"

"He will not tell your cousins that he no longer has their mother, Evony," Stavos explained. "I saw him only this morning. Though he was obviously unsettled, when I asked him if the Midnight Masquerade would be accessible tonight, he told me that indeed it would…and that he wondered why I would doubt it. I answered that it was nearly time for me to travel on and that the lure of the Midnight Masquerade might just be the thing to convince me to linger one or two nights longer at the Hungry Horse Inn. Thus, he assured me all was as standard with the Midnight Masquerade as ever it was." He paused, sighed with disgust, and added, "The villain plans to keep the princesses in ignorance as to their mother's changed situation. Therefore, they will attend the dance tonight as ever they have been. And so will I…for I will not abandon them to any danger. I will attend as 'the patron of the inn with the deepest pockets,' as Happer refers to me. I will watch over them, Evony. I will keep them safe."

Evony nodded with full comprehension. She likewise understood that she must tell Stavos of the unique trove hidden in the tunnel, not only so that he would be prepared and not altogether astonished when he came upon it but also because she had an idea concerning it—a way in which Stavos might distract Standwood from inadvertently noticing that a handsome prince from another kingdom was about to crush his greed-driven, undeserved rule of Abawyth.

She inhaled a deep breath of courage—for again she thought that in the past, men had been hanged for revealing the great secret of Abawyth that she was about to reveal. Yet it must be done. Something whispered to her mind that it was a pertinent piece to the thwarting of her vile step-uncle.

"Assuming you will be able to avoid Kathleen's tonic and thus evade the stupor…" Evony began.

Stavos chuckled. "I promise not to drink anything out of Standwood's dog's water bowl, if that's what you mean."

"But what if she puts it in your food, your drink at a meal, or…or is able to somehow succeed in getting you to ingest it?" Evony asked.

Stavos's eyes softened as he looked at her with compassionate understanding. "I will not fall victim to the stupor, Evony. I promise."

Nodding and attempting to have perfect faith in Stavos's ability to evade Kathleen's tonic—that was, if Evony was correct in her conjecture of what was causing the stupor in the first of it—she continued.

"When you are in the private chamber shared by all my cousins, if you look closely at the floor in the very middle of the room, you will see a pattern inlaid in the stonework of the floor. It's difficult to see, for it's meant only to be seen from above—from the loft in their chambers—but it is there, and you'll be able to discern from the varying colors of the stone exactly where it is…a pattern in the shape of heart. When you stand in the center of the heart and face north, look to the stonework in the wall directly across from your position, and you will discern a small, heart-shaped stone inlaid in the wall. When pressure is applied to the heart-shaped stone, a small part of the frame surrounding the large hearth to your left will slide aside and reveal the entrance to the secret tunnel."

"But all castles have secret passages like this one," Stavos offered. "Why has Standwood not investigated this entrance to this passage before now?"

Evony felt a smile of triumph curve her lips. "King Standwood does not know of its existence."

"A king not knowing of one of his castle's secret passages?" Stavos inquired. Then grinning with sure understanding, he added, "But it is not King Standwood's castle, now is it?"

Evony shook her head and said, "No, it is not. It is the queen's, and obviously—though it is a terribly sad realization—my Aunt Raina did not trust her new husband enough to share the existence of it with him."

"Thank the heavens," Stavos sighed.

"Yes…thank the heavens," Evony agreed. "When the princesses leave by way of the tunnel, wait a moment or two and then follow them. But what I tell you now…in a manner, I am committing treason, for no one but members of our direct bloodline and spouses know that the passage is not only meant as a means of escape during attack or siege. It is also the hiding place of the great hoard of the kingdom's treasure."

Evony paused, expecting Stavos to be astonished at the revelation. But he merely nodded and urged, "Go on."

Thus she did. "As you enter the tunnel, all will be stone and mortar, rock and dirt at first, of course. But as you follow along the way, you will come to…well, it is a small forest of silver trees."

Stavos did arch one curious eyebrow then. "Trees? Growing in a tunnel void of light and—"

"Silver trees, Stavos," Evony explained.

"Silver trees?"

"Mmm hmm. The forest of silver trees is so beautiful that you will think your eyes are deceiving you at first, but they are not. The small forest of silver trees will be well lit by torch sconces built into the tunnel walls. It's like walking into a dream." She shook her head, amazed at the memory. "For you see, they are silver, Stavos—trees finely crafted of silver, literal silver. Their trunks, their limbs, even the leaves are fashioned from silver."

At that moment, both of Stavos's dark eyebrows arched—with pleased admiration. "Astonishing," he said. "And clever…to hide a kingdom's wealth so well…and yet so fascinatingly."

Evony nodded, glad that he was impressed. "It is very beautiful. I've often felt sad…and selfish that we are the only ones who can ever enjoy its unique and remarkable splendor. But…there is more."

"Is there?" Stavos said, smiling with expectation.

"Once you have passed through the silver forest, you will enter the golden vineyard," she explained.

Stavos chuckled. "A golden vineyard?"

Evony nodded. "Yes. The vineyard of gold is also aptly named…for it is, indeed, a vineyard composed of magnificent leafy vines, heavy with clusters of golden grapes hanging from them…all crafted from pure gold."

"Astounding!" Stavos breathed. "And surely, this is the end of Abawyth's hidden wealth."

Evony giggled and shook her head. "No. In fact, what you will witness next, and lastly, will quite possibly have you thinking that you are indeed dreaming."

"I admit to your having my rapt attention, Evony," he said. Winking, he added, "My rapt attention on something other than your pretty little mouth."

As a thrill of delight traveled through her, Evony blushed. Even now, when the end of their adventure together was so close at hand, he still flirted with her. It soothed her aching heart just a little.

"Well, a ways before the tunnel returns to being lined with stone and soil, there will be a length of…of…of…"

"Of?" he prodded.

"In our family, it is referred to as the promenade of diamonds," she rather mumbled.

"The promenade of what?" he asked—for Evony had lowered her voice in telling him of the promenade. She knew how surreal it all must sound to him—and yet it was the full truth!

"The promenade of diamonds," Evony repeated. "It is a short yet priceless venue—a diamond horde, a wealth of precious jewels, comprising mostly diamonds, brought by my great-grandfather when he returned from an ocean voyage he adventured upon as a young prince. There are sapphires, emeralds, and rubies as well, but we refer to it as the promenade of diamonds. They are embedded in the walls and ceiling of the tunnel...so thickly that you will not believe it when you see it! In the firelight of a lit torch, it's as if a million stars suddenly clustered together somehow. It's truly breathtaking."

Stavos puffed a sigh, obviously still astonished by Evony's reveling the existence of the secret treasure hold of Abawyth. "And all this wealth...this...this hoard of silver, gold, and jewels...all of this is hidden up so near to the castle, right under your uncle's villainous ignorance." Stavos smiled. "I find it wildly satisfying...don't you?"

"Yes," Evony answered with a measure of contentment.

"And does Elawyth...does your kingdom, being that it is, in fact, the sister kingdom of Abawyth, have such a trove hidden near its castle, as well?" he chuckled.

"Yes," Evony answered plainly.

Stavos laughed. "Brilliant!" he declared with appreciation to cleverness.

Evony nodded. "When the original kingdom was divided between my mother and my aunt, so was the wealth of the then larger kingdom of Abawyth. Thus, Elawyth does indeed have the same tunnel—the same means of escape if needed, the same means of keeping the kingdom's riches cached safely away."

Stavos raked a strong hand through his hair, and the gesture caused Evony to wish she could weave her fingers through the softness of it just once more.

"It's an incredible thing, Evony—the tunnel, the well-hidden riches of Abawyth and its royal family," he sighed. "It makes Ethiarien's simple guarded treasure rooms seem rather bland and dull and ignorant." He smiled at her, raking his hand through his hair again. But then his brows wrinkled with puzzlement once more.

"But…but I'm not certain as to why you've told me this. If all goes well, I may indeed be espoused to a princess who owns this knowledge…but as yet, I am not. So I am wildly curious as to why you've risked so much, forsaking a great privacy, to share this with me."

"Because I had a thought…a scheme…an idea that might help distract Standwood so that you may more easily overthrow him," she admitted.

But as Stavos sat looking at her expectantly, she still paused. What if he thought her contribution to the plot ridiculous—silly and childish?

"Yes, Evony?" he prodded, however.

Plowing forth quickly and with courage in knowing he had never doubted or belittled her thinking before, she said, "When you follow the princesses into the tunnel—if that is indeed your plan—as you follow them to the dance, along the way, as you pass through the forest, vineyard, and promenade, break off a small branch of silver leaves, collect a cluster of golden grapes, and pry a gem from the wall of the promenade. It's easily enough done. Then bring them with you when you confront the king. Tell him some fanciful, imaginative tale of magic and sorcery. Show him the silver branch, the gold cluster of grapes, the gem, and tell him you gathered these things while following the twelve princesses through a land of enchantment where my cousins are transformed into swans or some such thing…and fly about the world doing…something."

Stavos laughed. "A fairy tale. I tell him some unfathomable tale of adventure and riches—which will appeal to his greed, of course—and then, as he and whoever may be listening are rapt by my ludicrous fabrication—"

"And the princesses will also know you are with them, for they will know, simply by the story and your evidence, that you indeed have been in the treasure tunnel…that you know where they go and—" Evony added.

"And before he knows it, the trap will be set and too ready to spring for him to escape," Stavos finished. Again he smiled, laughing in admiration of her wit. "Oh, Evony," he began, "what a wondrous mind you have in that beautiful head of yours."

She blushed, again glad he still flirted with her—even though, on the morrow...

"I have the rest worked out," he said, interrupting her thoughts. "If I can manage to make contact with your aunt's captain of the guard this evening before I am locked in with the princesses, if he is truly as loyal to her as she believes him to be, if the remainder of the soldiers and guards of Abawyth are as loyal she says...then whether or not my father, brother, and their legion of Ethiarien guards arrive by morning, we will easily take Standwood." He clapped his hands with joyous anticipation. "Oh, to see that man's face when your aunt and mother are presented alive and well before him, knowing what he has done. It will no doubt be a moment I will relish for all my life."

"As will I," Evony admitted.

Stavos inhaled a deep breath of resolve and determination. Exhaling, he then gazed at her in silence for what seemed an eternity before speaking again.

"And now the moment has come, my little Evony Elorietta," he said, his smile fading. His eyes narrowed as he leaned toward her, and Evony knew this would be her last moment alone with Stavos Voronin. This would be the final time that she would see him before he would be betrothed to one of her cousins.

He opened his mouth to speak, but Evony could not have borne his words of parting in that instant. Therefore, she found herself unexpectedly babbling, "Choose who you will tomorrow when my Aunt Raina rewards you with your prize, Prince Stavos. But Patrice...I know you favor her, and she is...she will be a...she will..." Yet even for her sudden burst of verbose and well-intended advice, she found she could not tell the man she loved to choose Patrice as his wife. "I-I find I cannot speak the words, Stavos," she said as her tears finally won the battle over her resolve not to weep. "I-I cannot give you up so easily as that. I cannot watch as you...and yet I know your father sent you here to win the hand of one of the twelve Abawythian princesses, and…and I know you must follow his command. But I cannot…I do not want to watch you choose…I do not…I cannot watch you choose a wife from among my cousins, Stavos."

He pulled her from her chair with such force that it left her quite breathless—so breathless that when he stood, pushed her back against the wall, and ground a kiss to her mouth so driven and wanting with passion, Evony nearly fainted from its consuming command.

Instantly her arms were around his neck as she kissed him—her hands woven in the soft, dark velvet of his hair that she had so often dreamt of every night since meeting him. Her tears mingled with their mouths, salting their kiss with heartbreak and proof that she loved him.

Stavos broke the seal of their mouths a moment—captured her face between his strong, warm hands. His blue eyes aflame with emotion, he said, "Evony…tomorrow, if I succeed…if your aunt grants me the prize Standwood promised to the man who liberated the twelve princesses of Abawyth…you know, don't you, that were you an Abawythian princess—"

"Do not speak it!" she cried out, placing her small hand over his mouth. "Do not make such declarations that you would considering choosing me if I were an Abawythian instead of Elawythian. I cannot bear to hear you—"

But Stavos pushed her hand from his mouth. "That I would *consider* on it?" he asked, seemingly astonished—somehow offended. "How can you think that I would merely consider you?"

"Please, Stavos," she wept. "You don't understand. You see, that morning when Bromius reared and I fell…that moment I saw you, I…"

A startled scream escaped Evony's lungs when the pounding on the door began. Releasing her, Stavos turned, hand at his sword's hilt. "Who is there?" he called.

But the pounding continued. The noise of it had obviously alerted the others, for Queen Raina and Evony's mother burst through the door adjoining Miss Lovie's rooms, frantic in looking to Stavos.

"We are found out by Standwood!" Queen Raina cried, tears springing to her eyes. Evony watched as both her mother and aunt began to weep, Tressa and Mikol clinging to their mother's skirt as they trembled with fear.

Miss Lovie stepped toward the door, but Stavos roared, "No!" and strode to it. Bracing one strong hand against it, he called, "Who calls here at this home?"

The banging finally ceased, and when a strong, deep voice on the other side said, "Dillon Thoringil of Abawyth!" Evony's hand flew to her gasping mouth as her aunt collapsed in a faint—her final breath being a whisper, "Dillon has come to me!"

CHAPTER THIRTEEN

"Did you hear that?" the princess Laura said.

"Hear what, Laura?" Kathleen asked—though she and the others did pause in their scurry through the treasure tunnel of Abawyth.

"It came from behind us, Kathleen," Laura explained. "A sound…something unfamiliar."

"I heard it as well," Karamelle offered. "As if something fell or…or…"

"Perhaps we have been found out!" Abbitha exclaimed. "Perhaps King Standwood has sent an assassin to dispose of us!"

"Oh, you are far too imaginative, Abbitha," Victoria sighed with impatience. "Most likely a loose stone only fell from the ceiling or some such thing nature does to startle princesses who are miserable and overly suspicious as we are."

"Or perhaps a diamond or ruby worked its way loose from the wall or ceiling and tumbled to the ground," Patrice suggested.

Stavos gritted his teeth. How could he have made such a noise, even as small a noise as dropping the large diamond he'd pried from the wall, striking the cobblestone walkway beneath it? Normally he was perfect in his ability to stay concealed. But Stavos's mind had been distracted all the evening and night long—remembering Evony's obvious disbelief that he would consider her for wife were she an Abawythian princess, followed by Dillon Thoringil's arrival, Queen Raina's astonished swoon, and the manner in which all in the room could visibly discern that Queen Raina and her captain of the

197

guard were desperately in love with one another. He'd been preoccupied since the moment he'd left the beloved little hovel in the village and arrived at Abawyth Castle to fulfill his charge to solve the mystery of the twelve sleepy princesses. All he could think of was Evony—of the way she had kissed him the moment before Thoringil had arrived, as if she quite expected it to be their last kiss.

And because of his preoccupation, he'd gone and caused suspicion to rise in the princesses as he followed them through the tunnel to the Midnight Masquerade, after everything—after cunningly pouring the drink Kathleen had given to him into a vase full of winter greenery that sat on a small table and aptly feigning that the stupor had overtaken him—after having had to leave Evony in the hovel, without having had the chance to tell her of his feelings.

But suddenly his attention was arrested once more by the conversation between the princesses some distance ahead of him.

"I can't go on," Patrice said. Without warning, the princess Patrice simply sat down upon the ground in the tunnel. Stavos tightened his black cloak around his body and pressed himself against darker space on the wall, hidden in the shadows that the lit torches did not reach.

"What do you mean, Patrice?" another sister asked. "We have to go on, for Mother's sake!"

"How do we know Mother is even still alive?" Patrice began to weep. "I'm so tired, so scared all the time…and for what? That vile man has never allowed us to see Mother and Aunt Charmaine. What if he has killed them already and—"

"Patrice!" Laura exclaimed. "Do not even speak it! Mother has to be alive. She has to be! And Aunt Charmaine!"

"I feel as if I can't go on either," one of the younger princesses said, bursting into tears and collapsing on the tunnel floor next to Patrice.

"Nor I!" another said, following the same manner of collapse.

"Girls! My sisters!" Kathleen pleaded then. "You cannot give up! Mother's life depends on it. I know you are tired and…and…"

But then Stavos watched as Kathleen herself crumpled into a heap, weeping with bitter fatigue, fear, and heartache.

Abbitha and Karamelle exchanged glances and then also began to weep. The princess Victoria erupted into such sobbing that Stavos was certain all of Abawyth could hear her. One by one, the remaining princesses of Abawyth—so tired, so fearful, so abused, and so manipulated—melted into tears of hopeless despair.

Stavos had seen this response far too many times in soldiers—soldiers who never recovered fully, and never quickly. The princesses could not arrive at the Midnight Masquerade with red, weeping eyes. Furthermore, if they didn't regain their composure, bravery, and strength soon, they would not arrive at all!

Stavos had learned that often strategies had to be forked—changed and reforged. Thus, he made his decision quickly, for there was no time to ponder it further. Forward motion must continue—one way or another.

Stepping from his hiding place in the shadows of the promenade of diamonds, Stavos spoke. "Princesses of Abawyth," he began.

The simultaneous gasps—the expressions of fear and dread—he had expected them.

"Do not panic, please," he said as he pushed the hood of his cloak back to reveal his face. "It is only I, Stavos of Ethiarien, and I tell you, please calm yourselves—for at this very moment, both Queen Raina and Queen Charmaine are safely hidden away in the company of your cousin Evony and a fair number of castle guards."

"What?" came the concurrent exclamations of astonishment.

"Please, it is true, and I will explain, albeit quickly. But you must remain as calm as possible and keep your wits about you," he said.

"H-how did you get here?" Kathleen asked, obviously the most awed of all the princesses in seeing Stavos awake and in their presence.

Stavos smiled. "Your cousin Evony," he answered, "she riddled out what was causing the stupor that overtook the other men before me, and we conspired that I should avoid it." He nodded to Kathleen, adding, "Evony has told me of your great skills in alchemy, princess. They are very admirable, but as I said, not all can be revealed here and now, and quickly. But I will tell as much as I can…and then we must hurry to the Midnight Masquerade."

"I recognize your voice now," Patrice offered. "You are one of the men who attends the Midnight Masquerade. It is many times I have danced with you since you joined the dance several nights ago."

Stavos nodded. "Yes, princess, I have been in attendance…and these past two nights, so has Evony."

"So she did not flee the harm…the danger Standwood posed to her and her siblings," Laura said, smiling. She looked to Victoria and said, "I told you that Evony was far too brave and determined to simply run."

"That is true, Princess Laura," Stavos agreed. "Your cousin Evony Elorietta has championed you all beyond that which I have time to express just now. So please, trust me in that I know her…and that she chose me to champion you from here forth."

Each princess stood, straightened her posture, and brushed tears from her cheeks.

"Tell us, Prince Stavos," Kathleen instructed. "Tell us what you can…and what we must do. If Evony has chosen you as champion, then we know that a champion you already were when you met her…else she would not have sent you."

Stavos nodded, bowing. "Owning Evony's trust is perhaps the greatest honor I have ever known. Now please, we must be swift."

As Stavos told the twelve princesses of Abawyth as much as he could of what had transpired and what must yet transpire if Standwood were to be thwarted and the royal families of Abawyth and Elawyth saved, he admired the strength he saw returning to the countenance of each and every princess before him. It was an admirable strength—not so resilient and profound as Evony's perhaps, but unique and admirable all the same.

Standwood would be thwarted. Stavos knew it more assuredly than ever he had before. Standwood would be thwarted, the queens restored to their thrones, and the princesses would finally find respite and rest—*all* of them. Especially the one princess who had captured Stavos's heart for her very own.

Evony could not find sleep. Her mind was so stricken with wondering what was transpiring at the Midnight Masquerade, even for her lingering fatigue she could not rest.

So many tormenting questions plagued her. Would Stavos spend such an important evening as this—the evening just prior to his conquering the charge given him by his father—dancing with Patrice? That was assuming, of course, that he had avoided the stupor inflicted by Kathleen's tonic. And *that* was assuming Evony had been correct in her assumptions. Would Ewan Happer somehow discover that it was Stavos who had killed Cedric and stolen the queens away? Would he wonder where Evony was—the new girl he had hired to dance at the Midnight Masquerade, absent on only her third night? Would King Standwood become suspicious? Would the captain of the guard, Dillon Thoringil, have the queen's guard ready when Stavos needed it? Would Stavos's father and brother arrive in time with Ethiarien soldiers to offer further power in Stavos's and Queen Raina's defense?

It was a torture of the mind! The fact was that Evony had decided to sneak away and attend the Midnight Masquerade, in case she were needed—but also to be with Stavos. But her own mother, her brother and sister, Miss Lovie, and her Aunt Raina were firm in support of Stavos's demand that Evony stay at home. Her part was done, and she had done far more than anyone could have ever imagined. It was up to Stavos now—Stavos, the queen's guard, and the allies riding from Ethiarien. And so she had remained behind, trying to accept that she was now in a different sort of peril—that they all were—and that they must allow Stavos to accomplish what he had come to accomplish and more.

But still she thought of Stavos—tossed and turned, wept and cried for missing him and for having to give him up. She owned regret as well—the very sort Stavos had told her he was brought up to avoid—for she had not let him speak his mind in their last moments alone—in those blissful, painful moments as they shared their final kiss before Dillon Thoringil arrived.

Evony's mind turned to Thoringil a moment then. He was a tall man, as tall as Stavos—young, handsome, strong, and very capable in appearance. And he was in love with the queen of Abawyth, and she with him. It was so obvious as her aunt's dashing captain of the guard entered the room and instantly dropped to his knees in a gesture of worry over her having fainting—in an palpable panic to revive her and know that she was well. It was likewise obvious that Evony's aunt was just as in love with the captain of her guard. As her eyes fluttered open and Queen Raina beheld the handsome face of Dillon Thoringil, such was the resplendence in her countenance that the room fairly lit up with its radiant light.

Evony wondered how long her aunt had loved Dillon Thoringil. She wondered whether she loved him before she married Standwood. Evony and her mother had often talked of the sadness of the fact that Queen Raina had chosen to marry for the supporting strength marrying another royal would give Abawyth rather than marrying for love—or in the very least happy companionship. But Raina was a wise steward over her kingdom and feared the people would doubt her and think her weak of mind if she did not marry a man of royal lineage.

Yet it was devastating to think that within just ten months of making the decision she did, Raina had nearly lost not only her kingdom but also her life. Therefore, when everyone in the room saw the powerful emotion Raina and Dillon Thoringil felt for one another, there was astonishment.

Though nothing inappropriate transpired between them—no physical affections that would have been frowned upon between a married woman and a man who was not her husband—it was there, hanging heavy in the room as apparent as if it had been a woven tapestry.

Thus, Evony's heart began to ache for her aunt as well. What could be done now? Standwood was her husband. And would her Aunt Raina be able to order the execution of the man to whom she was married, even for the fact that he plotted to have her murdered? And if he were executed, what then? Annulment and scandal? It was clear to her that just as Evony could never have the man she loved more than her own life, neither could her aunt. The knowledge was yet another painful burden.

And so, after many hours of torment of mind, thorough exhaustion enveloped Evony at last. But even unconsciousness offered no respite from her anguish, for even as she slept the sleep of a woman worn near to the bone with worry, fatigue, and unfamiliarity of tasks, Stavos haunted her dreams as assiduously as he haunted her every waking thought. Yet there was one respite for Evony: in her dreams, Stavos lingered in kissing her forever, loved her, and kept her. In her dreams, Evony belonged to Stavos. In her dreams, she did not have to give him up.

CHAPTER FOURTEEN

Evony's mind was spinning, as if she were trapped in some sort of whirlwind that was spiraling her and her family, and even poor, dear Miss Lovie, through events that were the stuff of dreams—and nightmares.

Just before the sun had risen, Evony had been wakened by a quiet knocking on the door. Her heart leapt in fear at first, for having been wakened from the deep sleep and dreaming her body and mind had found at last, her first thoughts were of danger—her next of Stavos.

Quickly rising from her bed, she hurried to the door and asked, "Who is there?"

Expecting to hear Stavos's beloved voice in response, she was surprised, as well as disappointed, when the answer came, "Dillon Thoringil, your highness."

Still, as everyone who had been wakened by the knock on the door gathered with interest, hope, and even trepidation, Evony herself was so desperate for news of Stavos and his quest that her trembling hands could hardly lift the bolt and work the latch.

In a moment, however, the captain of the Abawythian guard stepped over the threshold and into the room.

Evony held her breath. What news did he usher? Had Stavos been successful? Had he avoided the stupor and…

"Your majesty," Dillon Thoringil began, bowing to Queen Raina. "My queen, all is well with your champion, Stavos of Voronin."

There was an audible sigh of relief in the room as everyone exhaled held breath.

"He has sent word to King Standwood that he has solved the mystery surrounding the strange lethargy plaguing the princesses and that he will reveal what he has discovered to the king at noon today," the captain said. The striking man smiled as tears of joy began to spring from the eyes of Evony's mother and aunt. Even Tressa and Miss Lovie wept.

But Evony sensed a deep contradiction had taken residence in her bosom, for she did not weep, though the announcement should have sent her to her knees with overwhelming emotion. Yet the truth was so plain before her now: at noon, Stavos would report to Standwood, and shortly thereafter Standwood would be taken away in shackles at the very least. Then her Aunt Raina would return to her people, address them as their restored and beloved queen, and give Stavos his choice of a bride from amongst her daughters. Hence, for all the joy and hope Evony did feel in hearing of Stavos's success and that his own strategy was playing out in perfection, there was one hundred times the measure of heartbreak in her to accompany it.

"I have communicated with Prince Stavos," Dillon began, "and he has instructed me to bring you in secret…all of you to Abawyth Castle, immediately," he added, nodding to each one in turn—even Miss Lovie. "There you may prepare yourselves to witness the moment Prince Stavos tells his tale to Standwood. Prince Stavos has instructed that you should be well fed and dressed in the manner of the monarchy, so that when the time comes and you are revealed, my queen, and you as well, Queen Charmaine, you will appear before your subjects as strong and unaltered as possible."

"But how will you get them into the castle, Captain?" Miss Lovie asked then. "No doubt King Standwood has guards placed everywhere."

Dillon Thoringil smiled at the kindly woman. "Yes, he does, mistress," he answered. "And all are loyal to their queen…not the vile man who has attempted to steal her throne."

And so it was that Evony now found herself standing before a looking glass in one of the Abawythian queen's private rooms. For an instant, the reflection gazing back at her seemed as unfamiliar as a stranger. Her beautiful princess's gown was white and embellished with a delicate gold brocade. Her hair was clean and dry, thoroughly brushed, and loosely piled and pinned atop her head in soft, swirling curls. Her aunt had insisted that both Evony and her mother—and even little Tressa—have their necks and wrists adorned with sparkling, gem-bestrewn jewelry from her personal collection. Dainty diamond earrings tear-dropped from her ears, and her slippers were some of the most comfortable she had ever worn.

But as Evony stared at herself in the looking glass, knowing that this was the princess of Elawyth she saw, her heart longed for the little hovel and the hidden identity that had brought Stavos to her. She wondered where he was at that moment—wondered if he had taken a moment to waste a thought on her behalf. Oh, certainly he had; she knew him well enough to know that. Yet glory and legend were at his doorstep now—and a new bride. So she knew that his thoughts of her would grow few and far between, if they hadn't already.

"You look beautiful, darling," Evony's mother said, stepping to stand behind her. Gazing over Evony's shoulder at her image in the looking glass, she added, "All will be well, Evony, my love. Truly. This monstrous horror we've all endured will be behind us soon enough, and then we must sort out all that we have learned from our suffering and discern how best we can each use it to benefit others. Each experience we have in life teaches so many things, my Evony—even, and most especially, the unpleasant and painful ones."

"I know, Mother," Evony said—and she did know it. Her mother had ever taught her that all experience—good or bad, pleasant or ghastly—helped to shape one's character and way of thinking. But in that moment, Evony could not imagine that any good would ever come to anyone from her heart being broken.

"He is a superior man, Evony," Charmaine said, kissing her daughter's cheek. "He possesses a rare and heroic soul. Therefore, do not doubt him for a moment, darling. Stavos will always make the right choice."

It was the first time in all her life that Evony doubted her mother's intuition and wisdom. Of course Stavos would make the right choice! He would choose the Abawythian princess that would be the best queen for his people, the best friend and companion for himself. Evony was disappointed in her mother, and it was an unfamiliar and unhappy feeling. Couldn't her mother see how heartbroken Evony was? Couldn't she see that her daughter was in the worst misery of her life? Or was it that her mind was still so battered and beaten from enduring the prison in Ewan Happer's secret room that she had become blinded to the unhappiness of her eldest daughter?

Evony loathed herself instantly. How could she think such selfish and unkind thoughts? Where Evony had endured weeks of misery in hiding in Abawyth, in worrying, in doing without the comforts she was accustomed to, her mother and aunt had been locked up in utter darkness with only straw for beds. Her cousins had been enslaved as women who danced with strange men through the entirety for the night, and all to line the pockets of the vile Ewan Happer. Her own brother and sister had suffered—and even Miss Lovie, for she had put her own safety at risk by helping them. And then there was Stavos, who had trusted her almost instantaneously—who had followed her instructions and believed her words, saved her mother, her cousins, her kingdom, saved her young brother from possible death. Stavos had warmed her heart, her mind, her soul, and even her body—had saved her life from a bitter death of freezing.

Yet here stood Evony Elorietta, gazing into a looking glass, wearing a gown that might have fed an entire family for a week. There she stood thinking only of her own pain and loss. And so she ceased in pitying herself and began to humble herself with self-disgust.

"You're right, Mother," Evony said then, forcing a smile. "Stavos will make the right choice." She turned then, throwing her arms around her mother in a loving embrace and adding, "And he deserves so much happiness for having saved us all, doesn't he?"

"That he does, darling," Charmaine said, kissing her daughter's cheek again. "And he will have it, I am sure."

There came a soft knock on the chamber door.

"Come in, please," Charmaine called.

The door opened, and two men dressed in armor bearing the symbols of Abawyth entered. "Captain Thoringil has sent us to escort you to the main courtyard, Queen Charmaine."

"Of course," Charmaine said. "Come, Evony. We must don our cloaks and cowls and gather Mikol, Tressa, and their Miss Lovie at once."

Quickly snatching up the two heavy black velvet cloaks that lay on the bed, Evony's mother offered one to her.

As Evony fastened her cloak at her throat, her mother excitedly whispered, "This day will live in tales told forever, Evony—the day that Prince Stavos of Ethiarien thwarted the evil Standwood Warde and returned Queen Raina to her people."

"Yes," Evony agreed as she assisted her mother in placing her hood over her head. "Prince Stavos will certainly pass into legend today." And she knew he would. In a matter of minutes, Stavos would indeed become a legendary champion. Within the hour, Stavos would step into folklore—and out of Evony's life.

The courtyard was filled with people. All had come to see the only candidate to accept King Standwood's charge to solve the mystery surrounding the twelve princesses of Abawyth and avoid being overcome by the strange stupor. All had come to hear Prince Stavos Voronin of Ethiarien report to King Standwood on what he had discovered.

Early that morning, after Prince Stavos had exited the chambers of the twelve princesses in full health and consciousness, announcing that he had been successful in uncovering what had plagued the kingdom's beloved princesses over the past month, rumors had begun to circulate. All of Abawyth village was alive with talk, as well as all who lingered in any capacity in Abawyth Castle.

Thus, the excitement and anticipation of the multitude gathered in the castle's front courtyard was nearly tangible as Evony stood cloaked and hooded among the vast gathering. Dillon Thoringil had followed Stavos's instructions to the letter—meaning that, though the missing queens of both Abawyth and Elawyth were in attendance, they stood apart from one another in the crowd, surrounded by Abawythian soldiers dressed as commoners. Likewise, Evony, her brother, and her sister also stood apart from their mother and aunt, yet well guarded. Captain Thoringil had explained that he and Prince Stavos has agreed it would not be wise to have six cloaked and cowled figures standing together in the crowd, for it would, no doubt, draw too much attention for Standwood as he took to the bower overlooking the courtyard to address the people. Hence, Evony stood, one hand grasping Mikol's at her left, her other grasping Tressa's at her right.

It was cold out, even for the noonday sun positioned high overhead. Evony shivered a bit—not for the current cold condition of the day but for the memory of the morning she'd nearly frozen to death. Yet as she thought of Stavos's caring for her—using the heat of his own body to warm hers, to save her life—the memory caused such a scalding and blissful satisfaction to rise in her that she was not even aware, for a time, of the cold in which she stood waiting in that instant.

Thoughts of Stavos brought tears to Evony's eyes, but she was determined to stand strong—to resolve herself to accepting that, though Stavos had been led or brought to her by some divine, intervening hand, he had not been brought for her but rather to save the thousands of lives that would have suffered were her aunt and mother truly lost, leaving Abawyth and Elawyth ruled by Standwood's greedy, self-serving power. It was true, and Evony knew it. If Stavos had not come, thousands would have suffered—not simply her own siblings and her cousins but all those who dwelt in the sister kingdoms. Stavos was indeed a champion—a superior hero and rescuer to so many—and Evony knew she should give thanks for the rest of her life for being an instrument in helping him to save so many.

These are the thoughts she forced to swirl in her mind as she waited for King Standwood and Stavos to make their appearance to the people. Not thoughts of her love for Stavos or her deepest wishes and dreams that he would love her in return—*could* love her in return—but thoughts of all that would be blessed by his willingness to champion them.

Suddenly, a hush fell over the crowd for a moment, as King Standwood's pinched-lipped herald stepped onto the bower above.

"Citizens of Abawyth, and all who have come to hear your king today," the herald began. Stepping to one side of the bower, the herald called, "Your beloved and great King Standwood, accompanied by Prince Stavos Voronin of Ethiarien."

The crowd offered some applause, but it was nothing akin to what it should have been—for King Standwood was far from beloved.

"My people," Standwood greeted. Evony frowned, disgusted by the expression of arrogance plain upon Standwood's face. "I have brought to you a champion, at last!"

With these words, there was indeed a glorious uproar among the people. King Standwood stood smiling, nodding his head and mouthing thank you.

"The fool thinks the people are cheering for him and not Stavos," Mikol said all too loudly.

"Hush, darling," Evony quieted him. "I know. He is full of himself near to exploding."

"Yes, yes," King Standwood chuckled. "I know you are grateful to me. I know it, my people."

Though she stood with Evony and the children, Miss Lovie, being a villager, had no need of a concealing cloak or cowl. Therefore, as she glanced to Evony, Evony could clearly see the disgust plain in Miss Lovie's expression.

"I know that you all suffered with me as I suffered in losing my beautiful queen some months back," Standwood began. "And I know that when my twelve daughters were shortly thereafter stricken with a strange lethargy and despair, you were each as concerned as I. I know that you placed your hopes for their recovery firmly on the shoulders of each man who has tried to heal them or to discover what plague had overtaken them. And like you, I knew despair each time failure was all that resulted. But, my people, I have at last discovered a champion for our princesses—one who has somehow owned the strength of body to evade the stupor that took so many before him. I give to you, my people, my most recent gift you all…your champion and the champion of your princesses, Prince Stavos Voronin of the kingdom of Ethiarien!"

There was such an uproar of delight and cheerfulness that it was nearly deafening. Yet Evony smiled, for the sound the crowd was making mirrored the strength of the feelings that rose in her heart at the mere mention of his name—and at the sight of Stavos at last again, when he stepped forward on the bower.

"Good and kind people of Abawyth," he began. Glancing aside to King Standwood, he continued, "King Standwood allowed me to attempt to solve the mystery surrounding your twelve sleepy princesses…and that I have done!"

The crowd once more erupted into such sounds and shouts that Evony's body actually shook from the power of it.

Once the people had settled, it was Standwood who spoke next. "Prince Stavos has agreed to reveal to me, and to us all, exactly what he discovered last night while staying watch over my twelve daughters."

"*His* twelve daughters?" Mikol again exclaimed with contempt.

"Sshhh, my brother," Evony soothed. "All will be righted soon."

"And so, Prince Stavos," Standwood said, looking to Stavos, "let us now hear what you are the only man to know…all of us."

At that, Evony watched as her twelve cousins were led from the castle and onto a raised platform that had been constructed just below the bower. The sight was haunting, for it looked disturbingly as if the twelve princesses were being led to the gallows.

"You may begin, Voronin," King Standwood said. "Let us hear what has made our princesses so weak and unworthy these past months."

"Unworthy?" Miss Lovie exclaimed then.

Evony looked to Miss Lovie, shaking her head with understanding, yet warning that they should all be still, lest they be discovered and Stavos's secret strategy forfeit.

"King Standwood, last night, after I was shut in with the twelve beautiful princesses of Abawyth, I thought all was as plain as porridge," Stavos began. "Each of the princesses readied herself to retire…or so I thought. But as I watched over them, I saw a mist begin to grow in the room."

"A mist?" someone called from the crowd.

"Yes," Stavos answered. "It was like a fog, only brown in color, and it began to blur my vision."

"The stupor!" someone else called out.

"Quickly, I took hold of a nearby drapery, covering my face with it and breathing as slowly as I could…and as shallowly," Stavos continued.

Evony smiled, for the crowed was enthralled to perfect silence—and so was King Standwood. Stavos had the villainous, unworthy king of Abawyth placed exactly where he wanted him to be, and pride in Stavos's wisdom caused her bosom to burn and swell with satisfaction.

"Then, as the strange mist dissipated, I began the pretense of having been overcome by the stupor that had vanquished all the men before me," Stavos said. "Once the princesses thought I was unconscious—for they each in turn kissed me sweetly on the mouth to ensure that I was indeed insensible—well, that, my good people and king, was when my adventure truly began."

"They each kissed him?" Evony heard herself mutter with jealous disappointment.

"Hush, Evony," Mikol scolded then. "I want to hear everything."

"Through the one eye I had managed to keep open just a slit, I watched as the princesses began to float, their feet hovering inches above the floor," Stavos wove his tale. "All at once they swirled together, as if a wind funnel had taken hold of them. Faster and faster and faster they spun, and I began to realize that if I did not throw myself into the midst of the fascination, it would not matter whether I had avoided the stupor…for my journey would end. This is what my instinct shouted; thus I stood and hurled myself into the midst of the swirling princesses. And it was wise thing I did, for no sooner had I entered the wind than all thirteen of us were swept away…up and out through an opening that suddenly appeared in the ceiling. It was as if the very wind were carrying the princesses to a place I could not fathom. And as we traveled, we passed through many wondrous lands. First, we passed through a forest—so flocked in beauty that my eyes nearly could not behold it, for this forest was made entirely of silver."

King Standwood joined the crowd in gasping with astonishment. Yet when Stavos reached into a satchel hanging at his side and produced a small silver branch of leaves, all again grew silent.

"I present this to you, King Standwood," Stavos said, "a branch of silver leaves that I broke from a tree as we passed through the wondrous silver forest."

King Standwood accepted the leaves, frowned for a moment, and then smiled. "Are you a jester or a prince, Voronin? For any jeweler could craft such a thing."

"Do you think I endeavor to deceive you, King Standwood?" Stavos asked. "If so, then inquire of the princesses."

Standwood's smile faded. Leaning over the bower, he shouted, "Kathleen!" He did not even use her proper title—only angrily shouted her name. "Is this true? Did you indeed pass through a forest of silver last night?"

Kathleen straightened her posture. "We did," she answered.

Again the crowd gasped.

Standwood's expression of doubt disappeared, to be replaced by a frown.

"No doubt he is wondering where the silver forest is that he might steal it away for himself," Mikol grumbled.

"But that is not all, King," Stavos continued. "As the wind funnel began to slow, it blew us this way and that, until we entered a vineyard, your majesty…a vineyard crafted solely of gold."

Stavos drew a golden cluster of grapes from his satchel and offered it to King Standwood. Standwood's eyes boggled like a mouse's as he inspected the grapes.

"They are, indeed, solid gold in composition," King Standwood verified to the people as he held the cluster of grapes high over his head. "Is this true, Laura?" Standwood called down from the bower. "Was there a golden vineyard?"

"Yes, King…there was," Laura answered.

The crowd began to flitter with the sounds of gossip and speculation. But when Stavos drew a large diamond from the satchel, holding it out toward the people, they were silenced once more.

"But lastly, King Standwood—and perhaps most astonishing of all—was a mountain of precious gems, diamonds in particular," Stavos said. He handed the diamond to Standwood, who shook his head with obvious admiration.

However, in the next moment, Standwood looked to Stavos again, his eyes narrowing with suspicion. "Are you trying to make a fool of me, Ethiarien prince?" he asked.

"Oh, not at all, sire," Stavos said, his voice thick with mockery. "I have only done what you commissioned me to do, your majesty." It was Stavos's eyes that narrowed then. "To solve them mystery of the twelve sleepy princesses. And it is solved, King Standwood. I assure you, the mystery has been solved…all of it."

"Then where is this forest?" Standwood shouted as his temper began to rise—for it was obvious he still believed Stavos was mocking him. "This vineyard and mountain? If it is true, then I shall have it, and if it is not…then you shall have the hangman's noose, Voronin."

"Ask your princesses, Standwood," Stavos growled.

"Abbitha, Karamelle! Victoria! Is this true?" Standwood bellowed. "All of you, answer me. Were you taken through this silver forest, vineyard of gold, and…and space of diamonds?"

"We were," the princesses chimed in unison.

But Standwood had had enough of fairy tales. The growing indignation and fury on his face was evidence of it.

"If you have endeavored to make a fool of me before my subjects, Voronin—" he began.

"Oh, but, my king," Stavos interrupted, "I can prove that the mystery has indeed been solved, for I have the ultimate and undeniable proof with me—proof that your princesses were indeed plagued by a wickedness beyond imagination, that they were held enslaved, in fact…and that they were not alone in their enslavement."

"Enslaved?" Standwood shouted. "I demand proof now, Voronin! Prove that you know the truth of why the princesses were plagued with fatigue and despair! Prove it now, or my guards will have your head."

Stavos smiled, bowed, and said, "Of course, your majesty. Please, come with me—down from the bower and to the place where the princesses stand, and I will present the proof you ask for."

Standwood glared at Stavos. "Proof of this silver forest, golden vineyard, and diamond mountain as well?"

"If it be the desires of the Fates, yes."

Standwood turned on his heel, bellowing, "Bring him down with me! We will put an end to this lunacy once and for all!"

Even Evony was trembling with trepidation. What would transpire when her Aunt Raina was revealed to Standwood—when the true depth of his wickedness was divulged to the people? Surely there would be violence and danger, for the Abawythians might take it upon themselves to punish the villain.

Glancing about her, Evony attempted to discern which men were Abawythian soldiers in the crowd and which were not. Were any of the men from Ethiarien? Had Stavos's king father and prince brother arrived in time to assist her aunt's guard in protecting her?

Stavos and Standwood had reached the platform where Evony's twelve cousins stood waiting. As Standwood turned to face the crowd, he demanded, "Where is your proof, Voronin?"

"Good people of Abawyth," Stavos said then as he turned to address the multitude that had gathered, "your twelve princesses, they are not ill. They are not overcome by some disease that cannot be named. They have been enslaved by wicked villainy. Each night, your princesses leave Abawyth Castle and make their way to the Hungry Horse Inn in your woods nearby. There they dance all night with strangers…men who pay for there company."

A loud gasping and exclamations of disbelief rose up. But Stavos nodded to Dillon Thoringil, standing to one side of the line of princesses on the platform.

"The owner of the Hungry Horse Inn forced your princesses to dance at a vile, secretive ball known as the Midnight Masquerade," Stavos announced.

Evony watched as the captain of the guard then took hold of the man's arm that had been standing just off the platform near him. The man, wearing shackles at his wrists and ankles, was Ewan Happer himself.

"This is the villain who enslaved your beautiful princesses," Stavos continued, "treated them as if they were no more than horses to be bought and sold!"

As the crowd erupted with anger, Evony looked to Standwood. Though he still stood straight and arrogant, much of the color had drained from his face. He stood staring at Happer, as though gazing upon the reaper himself.

"But there is more, good people!" Stavos shouted over the angry crowd. "For are you not curious as to how this miscreant could force your princesses into such circumstances?"

Naturally the crowd quieted down—grew silent.

Again Stavos nodded to Dillon Thoringil, who in turn nodded to someone in the crowd.

Evony watched as men escorted her mother and aunt to the center of the courtyard. Both were still cloaked and their faces hidden by cowls.

"Here is Ewan Happer, King Standwood," Stavos growled. "I believe you know him…for did you not contract him to abduct and murder your queen as well as her sister, the queen of Elawyth?"

"How dare you accuse me!" Standwood roared. Gesturing to Happer, he said, "I do not know this evil man! I have never seen him before! And you shall lose your head for such accusations toward me…*me*…Abawyth's king!"

"Yet how could Ewan Happer force the twelve princesses to dance with strangers night after seemingly endless night? How could Happer force royalty to work for him, in order to line his own pockets with money?" Stavos growled. "Are you not curious, King Standwood?"

"No," Standwood stated—though the pallid hue of his cheeks and the trembling that began in his lips said otherwise.

Evony watched as four men escorted her mother and aunt up onto the platform.

"Well, I will tell you anyway," Stavos said. "And further, I will tell your people." Turning his full attention to the crowd again, Stavos said, "This man you have been forced to call your king plotted to take not only the Abawythian throne but also the throne of her sister kingdom, Elawyth. This man you have been forced to call king contracted the villain Ewan Happer to abduct and kill Queen Raina and her sister, Queen Charmaine of Elawyth!"

"Bind him! Chain him to the walls of the dungeon!" King Standwood roared. "He shall be executed this very day for his accusations against me." Yet not one guard, not one man in all the crowd or in armor or uniform, moved to do the king's bidding.

"Did you not hear my orders?" Standwood shouted. He turned to look to Dillon Thoringil. "Captain!"

The handsome captain of the guard strode across the platform toward King Standwood, while the crowd watched in astonished awe.

"Yes?" Dillon Thoringil spoke.

"I am king," Standwood growled. "And I command you to draw your sword and run it through the traitorous body of Stavos of Ethiarien. Now!"

"No," the captain of the guard stated.

"What?" Standwood exclaimed in astonishment. "I am your king, man! Would you die for Voronin? For I will kill you myself if—"

"Enough of your huffing and puffing, Standwood."

The crowd grew so silent at the sound of the queen's voice that the softness of butterfly wings in motion might be heard.

Evony's heart was pounding with excitement as she watched her aunt turn toward the people of Abawyth gathered in the courtyard and push the concealing cowl back from her face.

Gasping and every sound of astonishment and awe erupted through the throng! And as Evony's mother then unveiled herself as well, more sounds of joy than Evony had ever heard in all her life rose up like a song to heaven.

"Please! Please, my people," Queen Raina shouted above the noise. "Please! Hear me." The crowd quickly obeyed, and Raina said, "What Prince Stavos of Ethiarien has told you is the full truth. Standwood contracted Ewan Happer to abduct and kill my sister and me. But Ewan Happer disobeyed Standwood's commands and kept us alive…held us prisoner in secret these past months. We could not escape to come to you." Looking back toward her daughters, she added, "Or even to our beloved children." Queen Raina brushed a tear from her cheek and continued, "Can you forgive me, my people? Not so much for being taken from you…as for making a heinous decision that caused you trouble and pain. I chose to take Standwood Warde as my husband and king, because I thought the royal alliance would strengthen us all, us as a kingdom. But I was wrong. I married for convenience…when I should have married for love." Queen Raina looked to the captain of her guard and smiled. "Had I followed my heart instead of my head, you would not have had to endure Standwood's malice and evil, my daughters would not have had to endure the results of it, and my sister, her children, and her kingdom would not have had to endure it. Thus, I stand before you now, penitent of having married for position instead of love. And I promise you this…that once Standwood is taken from—"

"How can you be alive?" Evony heard Standwood roar. He had drawn his sword and was wielding it toward Queen Raina, intent on striking her. "You should be dead! You will be dead! Abawyth is mine!"

Before anyone could move, Stavos pushed the queen of Abawyth into the arms of the captain of the guard—and then plunged his own sword in Standwood's chest.

Gripping Standwood's hair at the top his head in one powerful fist, Stavos Voronin of Ethiarien shouted, "You will never threaten the queen again!" Then pulling Standwood toward him as he simultaneously pushed his sword through the man's body until only hilt and handle remained—the long blade protruding from his back—Stavos growled, "And now, Standwood Warde, here is your proof that the mystery of the twelve sleepy princesses is solved…and that the villain is vanquished."

Pulling his sword from Standwood's body, Stavos let the dying man fall to the platform floor.

Turning to face the throng of Abawythians who stood mouths agape in awe, Stavos said, "Abawyth…forget your villains, and rejoice in the deliverance of your princesses and the return of your beloved queen and her sister!"

CHAPTER FIFTEEN

Evony stood unable to move, even as everyone around her rejoiced. Could it have all happened so quickly? Could King Standwood truly be lying on the platform dead? Was she really witnessing her cousins, each embracing their mother in turn, weeping tears of relief, joy, and happiness? Was it Miss Lovie standing on the platform as Mikol and Tressa clung to their mother?

Even when the sound of what seemed a thousand galloping horses began to echo through the winter air—even as the gates of the courtyard were once more opened and the armor-bearing king of Ethiarien and his younger son rode into the courtyard with a legion of Ethiarien soldiers at their backs—still Evony could not move. She found she was frozen, just as if Stavos had never saved her from the winter's cold two days before. Evony stood stunned to paralysis with overwhelming awe.

In fact, it was not until the people of Abawyth began chanting that her mind began to escape from her state of shock. What were they saying?

"The champion's reward! The champion's reward!"

Evony looked back to the platform—watched the Ethiarien king and the younger prince of Ethiarien greet Stavos, kneel before Queen Raina, and even tousle Mikol's hair. Still the crowd was calling for their champion to be recognized. And in the next moment, as her aunt turned and asked the crowd to quiet, Evony knew that the moment she had dreaded since first seeing the handsome, charming, capable, strong, and heroic Stavos Voronin had arrived. Her aunt would give Stavos his choice of her daughters as his bride.

"My people! Oh, good and gracious people!" Queen Raina exclaimed. "Yes, we Abawythians have much to celebrate, and no one more than I...for I have my life, my sister's life as well. I have my very life, as well as the happiness and safety of my daughters for which to thank our beloved champion, Stavos of Ethiarien. Therefore, I will not pause in keeping Standwood's word, that whoever should manage to solve the mystery of the twelve sleepy princesses of Abawyth should have his choice of my daughters."

Evony gritted her teeth, hoping that doing so would keep the sour contents of her stomach from escaping through her mouth. She was trembling, not from the cold but from painful heartache. Whom would he choose? It would be Patrice, and she told herself she should be happy for Stavos—for Patrice was kind and loving. But she thought death would be easier to endure than watching Stavos choose his bride. And yet she found her feet would not move. She was as frozen as stone—could only watch as events unfolded before her—as the man she loved chose another woman to take as his bride.

Queen Raina turned to Stavos, even as several Abawythian guards lifted the body of Standwood Warde and carried it from the platform. "Come here, girls," Raina said, motioning to her daughters that they should line up before her.

"Come along, darling," someone said—and Evony felt a warm hand clasp hers. "You must do your duty, Evony." It was her mother's voice, and Evony turned to look at her. "You are a princess of Elawyth, a niece to Queen Raina, and cousin to the twelve princesses. You must join us on the platform."

But Evony shook her head as tears filled her eyes. "Mother...I-I cannot," she wept. "I cannot stand to watch him choose. You know that."

"You must, darling," her mother said, smiling with compassion and teary sympathy.

Evony nodded and slowly followed her mother through the crowd and to the platform. Dillon Thoringil took first her mother's hand to assist her up onto the platform and then Evony's. As she stepped up to the platform, her cowl slipped down, revealing her tear-streaked face to all who looked on.

Yet Evony straightened her posture, fixing her attention on a tree in the courtyard some ways beyond the platform. She would endure. It is what royals did, after all. They did not marry for love, but they did endure—and anything they were expected to endure.

"My prince," Evony heard her aunt begin, "I will waste no time in rewarding you for all you have done for me, my family, and our kingdoms. Accolades will follow, I promise you that. But for now, you must have your prize. Therefore, choose your bride, Stavos of Ethiarien. Chose whom you will to share your life, your kingdom, and your heart."

The tree at which Evony was staring was old. It was gnarled and misshapen, weathered, and it looked so cold standing there in the winter air. Evony thought for a moment that she was akin to it—cold, stiff, and sad.

"Thank you, your majesty," Evony heard Stavos respond.

Evony did not even move to brush the tears from her cheeks, for her arms felt as stiff and frigid as the limbs and branches of the old tree in the castle courtyard. He would choose now, and she would be forced to hear his choice.

"Queen Raina…Father," she heard Stavos said, "I chose the princess to be my bride the moment I saw her. And though I risk offering offense to you, Queen Raina, and though I risk forced abdication of my claim and responsibility to the Ethiarien throne…I choose Evony Elorietta of Elawyth as my bride…as my prize for playing some part in the thwarting of Standwood's evil that threatened Abawyth."

Evony could not breathe! She was certain she would faint!

"You would abdicate your position as first in line for the throne, son?" Stavos's father asked.

"I would," Stavos answered.

"And you would marry for love instead of position, Prince Stavos?" Evony heard her mother ask.

"Only love, Queen Charmaine," Stavos answered. "I will marry Evony Elorietta, or I will not marry at all. May I have your daughter's hand, Queen Charmaine? And will you not take offense at my choice of the princess of Elawyth instead of a princess of Abawyth, Queen Raina?"

"Of course I will not take offense, Stavos," Evony heard her aunt say.

"And yes, of course you may have Evony's hand, our prince," Evony heard her mother respond.

"And there will be no abdication, son," Ethiarien's king chuckled. "But I must meet this Evony for myself…for I am astonished near to collapse that a woman has managed to claim the heart of my son who once swore never to fall in love."

"Then meet her, Father," Stavos said.

He was there then—standing before her, smiling at her, brushing the tears from her cheeks. Evony shook her head as she watched Stavos drop to one knee before her.

"Will you accept me as your husband, Evony Elorietta?" he asked. "Your friend, companion, comrade, and lover?"

Evony blushed as audible sighs of delight lifted from the women of the crowd to float away on the cool winter air.

Yet before Evony could loose her astonished tongue long enough to answer him, Stavos continued, "Will you be my bride…my wife and mother of my children? Will you come with me to Ethiarien and lie warm and soft in my arms every night forever?" He stood, taking her face between his strong, warm hands. "I love you, Evony. You do know it, do you not? I thought that perhaps you didn't, and so I meant to tell you the last time we were together, there before the fire in your sweet little home. But we were interrupted and—"

"This cannot be true!" Evony sobbed. "I am brokenhearted at having lost you! You cannot truly be standing here before me asking…you are meant for a princess of Abawyth, not me."

"I am meant for you, Evony," he countered. "And you for me. You know that. Do not be so brave in all this—brave enough to do all that you have done to save your family and two kingdoms—and then doubt that I was not sent here by some divine hand for the sake that we are meant to be lovers. I know it. I have never doubted it. And I am sorry that I did not recognize that you doubted it. I meant to tell you last evening before I came to Abawyth Castle, but—"

"Tell me now, Stavos," she managed to whisper at last. "I want nothing…nothing but to be your wife, to belong to you…to be loved by you the way that I love Stavos Voronin of Ethiarien. Tell me now and—"

"I love you, Evony Elorietta," Stavos simply said. "Marry me, and I will spend my life making your happiness and keeping you warm. I promise."

Evony smiled at him—traced his lips with one finger. "I will marry you," she said. "Of course I will marry you and go with you to Ethiarien. But, Stavos, in truth…I am quite cold at the moment…and uncertain as to whether my feet may carry me to—"

Oh, the perfect bliss of his warm, moist mouth blended to hers! Evony did not pause in returning his embrace or his kiss when Stavos gathered her into his arms, kissing her with a hungry, unguarded passion that sent the onlooking crowd to roaring with cheering accolades of approval.

There was much yet to be explained, much to be healed and soothed in the kingdoms of Abawyth and Elawyth. Ewan Happer would be dealt with, and Evony's cousins would mend their heavy hearts and weary bodies from being pawns in the Midnight Masquerade—for they were strong. Her mother would rejuvenate, and so would her aunt, and Tressa and Mikol were safe at last. Even dear Miss Lovie was secure once more. Villains had been thwarted, kingdoms and peoples saved. Thousands of lives had been lingering in looming danger and misery and were now safe one more.

But Evony thought of nothing in those bliss-filled moments. For her, there was only Stavos—the euphoria of being in his arms, of being warmed by the wonder of his kiss, and the knowledge that their love would be infinite and everlasting.

EPILOGUE

Oh, how enchanting the summer nights were in Ethiarien! As she lay under the starlit sky, Evony couldn't imagine ever not recognizing and appreciating their warmth and beauty. Closing her eyes a moment, she listened—listened to the song of the crickets in the nearby hedgerow, the gentlest of breezes as it quietly played among the wildflowers and grass. The crackle of the fire Stavos had laid earlier in the day and Evony had lit only half the hour before added a sense of security and the mellowing fragrance of pinewood to the balmy air.

For a moment, she allowed her thoughts to travel back to summer days spent in Elawyth. Though they were warmer than winter and spring days, they were not so comfortable that one could lie in the grass under the moon and stars and simply savor the serene tranquility of the evening. But Evony had quickly discovered the summer nights in Ethiarien were the stuff of dreams. And though she felt a twinge of guilt at not missing Elawyth's or Abawyth's cool summer nights, she quickly dismissed it—for who would fault her for relishing such a moment as this?

Ponderings of Elawyth and Abawyth drew Evony's thoughts to the fact that it had been near to a month since the sister queens, Raina Thaybwyn Lardosean Thoringil and Charmaine Thaybwyn Elorietta, had rejoined the two kingdoms into one. While the city of Elawyth remained, it was no longer its own kingdom but a simple city—a part of the kingdom of Abawyth as it had been before.

Queen Raina and her king, Dillon, ruled Abawyth with wisdom and sympathy. Evony's mother, Charmaine, had been more than merely willing to give up the throne of Elawyth and allow it to fall under Abawyth's rule once more, for Charmaine longed for a simpler life than being queen allowed. Furthermore, it had been agreed upon by Raina and Charmaine that Mikol would inherit the throne of Abawyth. After all, he was the only male heir between them, and it was Queen Raina's desire that her nephew rule the kingdom one day, for she saw greatness in him—just as everyone else did.

Evony wondered a moment if Miss Lovie had managed as yet to keep Tressa from scampering through the village like a puppy each day. From her mother's letters, Evony had come to understand that Tressa had a love and sympathy for the people in Abawyth that was unusual and unmatched. It seemed Tressa was forever finding those in need in the village and running home to the castle to seek assistance for them. But she had taken to running off to the village without informing her mother or Miss Lovie. Therefore, Miss Lovie had become quite worrisome over Tressa. Still, Evony's mother had spoken with Tressa, asking her to please take Miss Lovie with her anytime she ventured into the village. Evony smiled as she thought of Tressa and Miss Lovie skipping off on errands of compassionate kindnesses together. She only hoped Tressa would not tax Miss Lovie's abilities too much. Perhaps she should write to Tressa herself—encourage her to be mindful of Miss Lovie's age and need of respite.

Images of Camille and Lillian Teche entered Evony's mind next. Their cruel mother—realizing she had abused the princess of Elawyth and knowing she had been somewhat accomplice to Ewan Happer's diabolical Midnight Masquerade—had abruptly decided to move to a distant kingdom, abandoning her daughters and her seamstress shop in Abawyth. Queen Charmaine commissioned Camille and Lillian to make a new wardrobe for Tressa, who had grown near an inch since Evony and Stavos left Abawyth and hardly had a gown that would fit her. Evony's mother, her aunt, and all twelve of her princess cousins had been delighted by the gowns, and

Camille and Lillian were now kept quite busy at the castle as two of the newest royal seamstresses of the regal family. Patrice had written to Evony, ensuring her that Camille and Lillian were happy in their lot and compensated very generously for their work. It eased Evony's mind to know it, for they were two young women deserving of comfort and peace.

So very much had transpired over the past six months. At times, Evony could not fathom how much change and living of life could take place in such a short time.

But now the day was long over, and Evony did not want to think of the fleeting passage of time. It was a warm summer's night, and the full moon hung like a silver coin midst a midnight sky full of stars that winked and twinkled even more brightly than the promenade of diamonds in the tunnel leading from Abawyth Castle.

He would join her at any moment—Stavos—Evony's beloved husband. He would return from his final meeting of the day with his father and brother over matters of the kingdom, and they would lie together in the cool evening grass as they had ever night since summer began. Bound in one another's arms, they would discuss the events of the day or any other thing that they were prompted to discuss. But in the end (for it was ever the same), their talking of the kingdom and its people would give way to their desire to think only about one another.

Evony heard Stavos's footsteps as he approached. Opening her eyes, she sat up where she'd been lying in the grass and smiled as he sauntered toward her. Oh, he was magnificent, this Prince Stavos of Ethiarien! At times Evony could not believe how attractive he was; from his broad shoulders to his long, muscular legs, he was indeed the archetypal male. As he reached her, joining her in sitting on the ground, the light of the fire caught in his eyes, and their sapphire blue outshone the moon and stars combined.

"Forgive me, wife," Stavos said, bending over to kiss her cheek with affection. "Have you been waiting on me long?"

"No," she answered, "though I would wait forever just to see you coming through the dark toward me the way you did just now. You're very handsome in the moonlight, you know."

Stavos smiled. "Hmmm...what is it you want from me, princess?" he teased. "Such flattery must be accompanied by a want."

Evony sighed as she studied him a moment. "Perhaps I find you so irresistibly attractive in the moonlight because it was under the moon and stars that we shared our first kiss, Prince Stavos."

But Stavos's handsome brows arched. "You are speaking of your first night as a masked woman at the Midnight Masquerade," he said, "the night I paid Ewan Happer two gold pieces so that I could have half the hour to relish the flavor of your sweet mouth." He kissed her lightly on the lips and then added, "But that was not our first kiss, Evony...or have you forgotten?"

Evony shook her head. "Oh, I could never forget the first time you kissed me, my prince...there in the dark of the hovel in Abawyth, as you were taking your leave. But that kiss was not what the one at my first Midnight Masquerade was, now was it?"

Stavos grinned at her, slipped a strong, warm hand around her neck, and agreed, "No...it was not."

"For the first of it, I was so astonished and bathed in bliss that you had kissed me that I had not opportunity to properly respond to the first kiss you blessed me with," she explained. "So I count the one at the Midnight Masquerade as our first *shared* kiss."

"Oh, I see your point, love," Stavos mumbled. "For once you began returning my kisses that night in the woods...well, shall we say that you have no idea what thoughts were taxing my mind that night."

But Evony giggled as Stavos placed a kiss to her shoulder. "Oh, we have been married six months, Stavos Voronin. I think by now I have somewhat of a notion at least of what thoughts were taxing your mind that night." She laughed a moment and added, "We women truly are quite innocent to some things concerning men. To that I will admit."

Stavos pressed a soft, alluring kiss to her mouth. Then he said, "The stars and moon are unusually brilliant tonight, it seems."

Suddenly, however, as Evony had come to know it often happened, a swift and powerful emotion washed over her as she looked him. And in that moment, she did not want to talk of stars and the moon, or of matters of the kingdom—or even the very romantic and adventurous past she and Stavos shared. All at once, all she wanted was to tell him what was in her heart.

Therefore, taking his face between her hands, she gazed into his beautiful blue eyes and said, "I love you, Stavos. I love you more than you can fathom. I love you so deeply...so severely...so perfectly. Thank you for coming to Abawyth, Stavos...for what would my life be if not for you?"

Stavos smiled. "Perhaps I should be tardy in meeting you more often," he teased, "if I am to be met with such emotional assurances of adoration."

"But I'm terribly serious, Stavos," Evony assured him. "What if you hadn't come? What if—"

But his hand over her mouth and his quiet, "Shhh," stalled her worried rambling. "I did come, Evony," he told her. "And we did meet that day in Abawyth. So do not worry yourself with what ifs, love...for they do not matter a whit. Not a whit. Life goes forward, not backward. I did come to Abawyth, and you did trust me with all your secrets. The queens were saved, the mysteries solved, and the villains thwarted. But most important, you and I found one another. So what does it matter, these what ifs? What does it matter when you're here with me on a warm summer's night, when the grass is cool and fragrant and the crickets and frogs are making their melodies for the benefit of our enjoyment? What does it matter— those things that never happened—when you're here in my arms, knowing that I am truly about to ravage you...when you know that in a matter of a few more moments, we will be consumed by our mutual passion, hmm?" He brushed a strand of hair from her cheek, laid her back in the grass, and kissed the tip of her nose once before letting his lips linger at the hollow of her throat. "What ifs do not matter when events have already passed us by, Evony. All that matters is this: perhaps threats, near tragedy, and hardship brought us together, but nothing…nothing will ever divide us from one another."

Evony smiled at him, lovingly tracing the outline of his mouth, the space where his whiskers ended and his lips began.

Stavos smiled, asking, "Why do you do that? Caress my mouth there?"

Evony offered a slight shrug in response. "I-I like to feel the space around your lips. Why? Does it not please you?"

Stavos chuckled. "Oh, it pleases me, love. Indeed it pleases me."

"So no more what ifs of the past, is that it?" she asked him.

"No more what ifs of the past," he confirmed. "Only what ifs of the present and future."

"Such as?" she asked as she ran her fingers up through his soft, dark hair.

Stavos lowered his voice. "Such as…what if I keep you here in the warm night air 'til sunrise? And what if…what if I allow all the thoughts that were taxing my mind during that first shared kiss we owned under the moon in Abawyth to turn to action, instead of mere thoughts?"

Evony giggled—sighed as Stavos kissed her neck. "Well then, I see your point concerning what ifs, my lover. So show me that some what ifs are desirable where others are not. What thoughts are taxing your mind tonight?"

"Thoughts of my love for you, of the taste of your mouth, the feel of your soft skin beneath my palms," Stavos answered.

Evony sighed. "Then what if you do keep me here 'til sunrise, my prince?" Cupping his face between her hands and pulling his head down so that she could place a long, alluring kiss of temptation to his mouth, she whispered, "I love you, Stavos."

"I love you, Evony Elorietta Voronin," he mumbled against her lips. "And as for it being a matter of what if I keep you here 'til sunrise, that what if is already in the past…for I *will* keep you here 'til sunrise. That I promise, love…and you know that I never break a promise."

"I do know it," Evony whispered as Stavos's mouth claimed hers with further promises of the sunrise finding them yet lingering in each other's arms.

AUTHOR'S NOTE

It all started when I was somewhere between six and seven. My mom subscribed to the Let's Pretend story record club for me. Oh, it was marvelous! Every few weeks, I would receive (via the US Postal Service) a brand-new Let's Pretend story album. Each album included dramatizations of two different fairy tales—one fairy tale per side on a 33-rpm, black vinyl record album. I'm telling you, it was the stuff of dreams!

I had loved fairy tales for as long as I could remember. In fact, when I was very little, there was a Snow White album my mom would check out for me at the local library. It was fantastic in its own right, read by some woman with a Brrrritish accent and enhanced with sound effects like wind and rain. But when the Let's Pretend series began arriving—wow!

Each fairy tale was verbally dramatized by a troupe of actors and wonderfully enhanced with sound effects as well. Oh, how they intrigued me! Each Let's Pretend episode was approximately twenty minutes long and enthralled me from beginning to end. If one of those 1970s Let's Pretend vocal performers walked up behind me today and said anything at all, I would recognize them at once! My little sister loved them too—and eventually so did my daughter. Even when Kevin and I got our first CD player back in 1990, I kept my turntable for years and years and years, simply to continue listening to my Let's Pretend records.

Years went by, and my turntable ultimately gave up the ghost. But when my daughter, Sandy, received a turntable for Christmas the year she was maybe fourteen, Let's Pretend returned to our house—that is, until she got married, moved away, and took her turntable with her. Yet all hope was renewed one Christmas when Kevin gave me a turntable with the ability to sync up with my computer. At last I could once more listen to my Let's Pretend records—and I did! I loved those story records as a child, and I'm not too proud to admit that I still do!

My favorite Let's Pretend album included Cinderella on side one and a fairy tale I had never heard before on side two: the Twelve Dancing Princesses.

Admittedly, Cinderella was my favorite Let's Pretend dramatization—because it was hysterical! The wicked stepsisters were a roar! In one of my favorite scenes, the wicked stepsisters, Fanny and Louisa (I'm serious...*Fanny* and Louisa), are getting ready to try on the crystal slipper:

"Oh, be still, Louisa! You won't be able to get so much as one *toe* into the glass slipper! If anyone can wear it, *I* can!"
"*You?* With *those* feet?"

If only you could hear their voices! They were hysterical!

However, as I said, I'd never heard the Twelve Dancing Princesses before receiving my Let's Pretend albums. From the moment I first listened to it, the story of the Twelve Dancing Princesses wildly intrigued me! First of all, it was new to me. But mostly it was the trip from the castle to the enchanted ballroom and dance that held my fascination—a forest of silver leaves, a forest of golden leaves, and an avenue of diamonds! With my mind's eye, I could see everything—the gowns, the dancing, the lake the princesses had to cross to get to the dance. I could see Prince Merrily of Flower Kingdom, stealthily sneaking along behind the princesses as he followed them to the dance, appropriately concealed in his invisible cloak, of course.

(Okay, now I just have to say it—because I know you're already thinking it too, the way I always did, even when I was little. Really? Prince *Merrily* of *Flower* Kingdom? Were they serious? I still can't get over that! But then again, I guess Prince Hottie with a Naughty Body from the Kingdom of Buff 'n' Studs wouldn't have been appropriate for story dramatizations geared toward children. But still—Prince Merrily? Yikes!)

Anyway, I was so intrigued with the story of the Twelve Dancing Princesses that it instantly became one of my favorite fairy tales, ever! Naturally, there was always one dilemma that bothered me about the story—that being the fact that only one princess could win Prince Merrily's heart (though it was implied that the other eleven princesses would find love with the princes that had been spirited away to the enchanted dance). Still, I figured it all worked out in the end and enjoyed the story of the Twelve Dancing Princesses until my Let's Pretend record was so worn I had to balance a penny on top of my turntable's head shell (the part that held the needle) so that the needle would dig deeper into the vinyl and not skip during play.

Hundreds of years later when I became an author, I was determined to one day write my own telling of the Twelve Dancing Princesses for my friends—you know, fixing up all the things my Let's Pretend story record may have lacked. And the number one thing was—you guessed it—kissing! Seriously, how could they not let Prince Merrily and Princess Hyacinth kiss? (Yes, Prince Merrily fell in love with Princess Hyacinth—you know, so she could fit in perfectly as the queen of Flower Kingdom.)

So about three years ago, the story of *Midnight Masquerade* began whispering to me in the quiet hours of the night and early morning. *Midnight Masquerade* would be my telling of the Twelve Dancing Princesses—only with kissing. And yet I couldn't seem to really sink my teeth into the story—just couldn't get my mind into it. My heart was there, and the basic plot, but I just couldn't find my groove where *Midnight Masquerade* was concerned. Even after I started writing it, I ended up shelving it for a time. I think I was feeling overwhelmed by the responsibility of retelling of one of my favorite fairy tales ever—and by the burning desire to make it as fun for my readers as it was for me.

And then, about the time that I had first shelved *Midnight Masquerade*, another author published her own version of the Twelve Dancing Princesses. Naturally, I kept myself from reading it, wanting to save it for later, when my own version was finished. I did, however, send it to my sister (who is also a fairy tale fanatic like me—probably due in part to those same Let's Pretend records).

So my sister read this other author's version, and guess what? "I love it!" she gushed. "It was the best retelling of the Twelve Dancing Princesses I've ever read!"

Well, that did it. *Midnight Masquerade* stayed shelved. I was discouraged and thought that since it had already been retold so well, my retelling simply would not stand up. I tried to put *Midnight Masquerade* out of my mind and went on to write two other books instead.

But *Midnight Masquerade* would not leave me in peace. Thus, about a year later, I opened the dusty old computer file I'd begun to work on and started once more. But then—you guessed it—*another* version of the Twelve Dancing Princesses was published that year! It had a gorgeous cover and wonderful title, and again fearing that reading this version might derail my own a bit, I didn't read it. Rather, I sent it to my sister. Wanna know what she said?

"Oh my heck! I *love* this version! It is by far the best version of the Twelve Dancing Princesses I've ever read!"

I promptly closed that already dusty old computer file named *Midnight Masquerade* and went on to write *Untethered*, *The Bewitching of Amoretta Ipswich*, and *One Classic Latin Lover, Please*.

Still, the story of Evony and Stavos would *not* stay silent. Even while I was writing *One Classic Latin Lover, Please*, it was there, always picking at my brain—always! Hence, I figured it was time to finish *Midnight Masquerade*, no matter what! When I have a story constantly pecking at my subconscious and conscious, it's almost impossible to move beyond it.

And so I blew the proverbial dust off the old computer file and began again. But all the while I was trying to get back into writing *Midnight Masquerade*, those other two retellings troubled me—the ones my sister had *loved* more than any! They kept me uptight, unsettled, and awash with feelings of inadequacy. And when one of those authors wrote another book based on the fairy tale, I really went into fits of anxiety and despair about *Midnight Masquerade*. To let the world read my version when so many other retellings were simultaneously hitting the market—yikes!

(As a note of reassurance to my little sister—I'm glad she loved those retellings because I wanted her to enjoy them! And if she ever gets around to reading *Midnight Masquerade*, I hope she loves it too! But it comes with a warning: I'm fairly certain my version is far different and kissier than the others.)

Yet I was too far into *Midnight Masquerade* now to shelve it a third time. Plus, it had already been advertised as "Coming Soon" over a year before. And so I just kept letting my favorite quote from Eleanor Roosevelt play over and over in my head: "You gain strength, courage, and confidence by every experience in which you really stop to look fear in the face. You are able to say to yourself, 'I have lived through this horror. I can take the next thing that comes along.' You must do the thing you think you cannot do."

It's that last line of the quote that I love so much—"You must do the thing you think you cannot do." It helps me through a ton of situations in life. So I began repeating it to myself while I was writing *Midnight Masquerade*, and it helped.

But I found that, in the end, it was something else that would pull me through: a group of ten-year-old children.

You see, Kevin and I team-teach a little class on Sundays for a couple of hours. It comprises an entertaining conglomeration of fourteen kids who are ten, turning eleven this year. In fact, only recently have I come to the sure understanding that these kids have done so much more than inspire me to finish *Midnight Masquerade*. They've healed me—successfully cured me of a terrible social phobia I've been secretly battling for about six years. No kidding.

I think the basis of the beginning of my SP (acronym for social phobia—because I just hate looking at the words spelled out!) started about twelve years ago but didn't conquer me until about five or six years ago. It was a slow process, in truth—not something I just woke up with one day but something that did eventually find me pretty much socially disabled.

I know, I know. Everyone always exclaims, *"You?"* when I confess this to them—because I've always been pretty good at hiding my true feelings and fears, of *not* wearing my heart on my sleeve, of *not* wanting to bring other people down just because I'm struggling. Know what I mean? I truly believe what Anne Shirley once said: "It's not what the world holds for you. It's what you bring to it." It's honestly against my core nature to be a pessimist, a Debbie downer. But I'm telling you one thing: social phobia is nearly debilitating, and at the height of mine, I'm surprised I didn't have a stroke or two.

My SP began to peak about 2009, I think. I would start to panic if someone recognized me somewhere and wanted an autograph, or if anyone asked me to do anything that required being in front of people, talking to new people, or attending social events. Even if people from my past happened upon me, I would go into this state of panic combined with just plain low self-esteem and self-worth. It was awful—and so *not* who I had always been! It was very unfamiliar and very frightening. Yet stress, criticism, and my poor self-image because of my "plumpness," combined with having to be in the public eye at times, had finally taken its toll on me. And to make matters worse, I began to really, really, really dislike myself because of it.

Perhaps the worst incident—the pinnacle of my desire to become a hermit and never go out in public again—happened in August of 2011. It had been a rough year already; a lot of good things had happened and were happening—big events—and yet lots of stressful things were going on as well. In just one week in June, our family attended a big meet-and-greet and then came home to my son Mitch's wedding to his gorgeous Mallory just three days later and to my daughter, her husband, and their son moving down to

Albuquerque just two days after that. The entire year leading up to June had been packed with similar events as well. It was the craziest year we had known since 2006 (and *that* was one for the books!).

Although being with supportive friends at the meet-and-greet helped me emotionally, the travel and sleep deprivation exhausted me. There were some huge emotional highs and lows with the wedding happening right on the heels of our return, and then helping with Sandy and Soren's move. To make matters even more stressful, that was the year that my book *The Trove of the Passion Room* was delayed!

Furthermore, just as I thought there might be a slight reprieve from demands and stress, one of my best friends found that her first little grandbaby had been born at only twenty-four weeks gestation. To make a long, horrible, tragic, painful, heart-wrenching story brief, the sweet little baby born in July passed away three weeks later in August. A viewing and funeral services were held. Keeping in mind that I do not handle loss well, especially because I tend to feel very deeply everyone else's sorrow and despair, our family attended the viewing of our good friends' little granddaughter. My body and heart were wracked with sobbing all through the viewing and funeral. For a long, painful hour, I watched friends and relatives enter the quiet, peaceful room where the viewing was held and lovingly smooth the baby girl's little white crocheted dress, so lovingly crocheted by her great-grandmother, as she lay in the tiny casket.

And then it was time for the funeral. Still sobbing and wondering how I would ever make it through a funeral of a child in the first place—especially one that included four musical numbers and seven speakers and was scheduled to last about two hours, *before* we all made the trek down for the graveside service—I walked into the chapel where the funeral was being held and was recognized—not as my everyday self, but as my author self. And when the funeral services ended two hours later and I was still sobbing and a wreck, Kevin and I paused, letting the other attendees exit first. Kevin knew this was not a day I was up to anything social, so we waited until the chapel was cleared before making our way toward the doors and exit.

I thought we were home free until a sweet, kind, well-meaning woman stepped in front of me and said, "You're Marcia Lynn McClure, aren't you? I know this isn't the best time, but I'm your biggest fan!"

The lady who approached me following the baby's funeral couldn't possibly have known all of what was going on. Still, the incident really sent me into a downward spin—a twist that found me tightening up socially even more than before. Christmas pretty much found me a nervous wreck and not wanting to ever step foot out of the house again—not even for Christmas shopping!

I had hit the wall—bottomed out—had enough. I was to the point that Kevin would have to really push me to even go to the grocery store—and when I did, I would break out in horrid nervous sweat that left me looking like Elvis in concert! I tried my best to battle through the social phobia, but to no avail. It just wasn't getting any better.

Then, in February of 2012 came a request for Kevin and I to team-teach this little Sunday class of kids. I was entirely freaked out, at first—totally unable to even feel comfortable in a room full of children! Keep in mind, I've always, always, always loved working with children—they're so loveable and hopeful and cute and funny and entertaining and fun to spoil. But I was legitimately at the bottom of my bucket of social functioning.

And yet the moment I walked into that room and met those children for the first time, I began to love and adore each and every one, individually. They were cute, funny, sweet, and just somehow soothing to my soul. Slowly, slowly, slowly, the kids began to draw me out of my hermit shell. They reminded me how enjoyable people really can be, how wonderful laughter is, how important the little things in life are. Slowly, slowly, slowly, I began to recognize that parts of me were starting to emerge from the hermit shell. I found that the overwhelming desire I had always owned to do impulsive, fun little things for friends and strangers was beginning to return. And though it took me a while (about six months) to embrace the fact—or even to fathom how I used to go about doing the fun things

I used to take such wild delight in—by November of 2012, I had begun to remember.

Much to Kevin's chagrin, I began to plan what Kevin and I would give to each of the kids in our class as our Christmas gifts to them. Some of the kids were newer to our class, and I didn't know them as well—and boys are always hard for me because they seem to like only money, expensive electronics, and food, right? Still, I found that I had a wonderful time preparing our gifts for the kids we'd grown to love so much. I mean, I always have fun preparing Christmas offerings for my own kids and close friends, but this was different—my chance not only to try and please each child independently but to convey to each one just how cherished they were to Kevin and me—to let them know that Kevin and I really, truly, sincerely care for them—unconditionally.

Yet as Christmas edged ever closer, I began to become nervous again. Presenting gifts to these kids meant actually talking to them out of the realm of our Sunday class—of speaking to their parents even! I knew that maybe the gifts I had chosen weren't spot on for each child. But I just tried to remember how fun it is to be nine years old and get *anything* that's a surprise. And to my own astonishment, I made it through! Whew! I even managed to speak to some of the parents, finally realizing that they weren't going to eat me alive. I still used up an unusual amount of antiperspirant during that time, but I lived through it and realized I was beginning to poke my head up and out of my dungeon of freakiness.

This is already way too long, so let me cut to the chase. I've gotten to know the parents (especially the moms) of our Sunday class kids now. I've gotten to know the kids even better than before, and I began 2013 with even more determination to escape my dungeon of freakiness. So I began sending a little thing here and there to each of our Sunday class kids—things like a type of candy I knew he or she favored or a meme that reminded me of one of them. I began sending random things to random friends and acquaintances the way I used to do too, keeping a little note to myself in my journal every week entitled, "This Week's Random Fun Things!" These things were for *my* benefit, so that *I* would know that someone knew they were being thought of kindly, not forgotten, even for as busy as I was in writing *Midnight Masquerade*. I never send anything too fancy—just a CD, a book, some candy—something I wanted to send just because I want to let them know I'm thinking of them.

How does this have anything to do with my writing *Midnight Masquerade*? Well, there's one little girl in our class, Kathleen, who looks like the actress who played Princess Tamina in Disney's movie *The Prince of Persia*. Well, when I'd first started writing *Midnight Masquerade*, I had named the eldest of the Abawythian princesses Catherine. Yet that caused a problem—because every Sunday, I would inadvertently refer to Kathleen as Catherine! I explained to little Kathleen exactly why I kept messing up her name, and she was very kind in not being irritated with me.

I continued to write *Midnight Masquerade* and continued to flub up and call Kathleen Catherine. But then I found that the problem bled over into my book; I kept typing "Kathleen" instead of "Catherine." Then one morning the solution hit me square in the face…finally! How could it have taken me so long to see the solution? I hopped up, hurried to my computer, and promptly went through my *Midnight Masquerade* Word document and changed all the references to Princess Catherine to Princess Kathleen instead! After all, Kathleen *did* remind Kevin and me of a princess in the first place, right?

Naturally, the process of changing Princess Catherine's name to Kathleen led me to think, *Hmm. Why don't I just name some of the other princesses of Abawyth after the girls in my Sunday class?* How fun would that be? Well, I can tell you this—*way* fun!

It was just like receiving a shot of adrenalin or a magic motivation elixir. All at once, *Midnight Masquerade* didn't seem like such a chore anymore! It was fun again, my mind opened up, and I was able to write without so much stress!

Historically there's always someone or something that inspires my story. You may not know it, of course, but it's true. For instance, the six swans that swim in the lake in *Shackles of Honor* are representative of a group of friends I still cherish and was very close with at the time I wrote the book. Certain characters in *Untethered* are modeled after two members of my Party Posse (the ladies who help me, support me, and basically carry me through author events). The hero, Maxim Tanner, in *The Trove of the Passion Room* endures many experiences that were based on experiences one of my sons had at the hands of aggressive, forward teenage girls when he was in school. It seems I can't really sink my teeth into a book unless I do have a real-life person, place, or experience to inspire me.

Therefore, my little Sunday class princesses—Abby, Kara, Kathleen, Laura, and Victoria—became my little inspirations— Princess Abbitha, Princess Karamelle, Princess Kathleen, Princess Laura, and Princess Victoria! (Abbitha and Karamelle are our nicknames for Abby and Kara). Suddenly, each time I thought of the twelve princesses of Abawyth, I thought of the sweet little princesses in our class.

Of course, we have boys in our class, as well—true heroes in the making! Andrew, Brigham, Cody, Dallas, Dillon, Hayden, Jonas, Keagan, and Max-Slash-Kyle. (Max-Slash-Kyle's name is really Kyle, but Kevin and I took to calling him Max-Slash-Kyle the very first day we met him because he resembles our daughter-in-law's brother, Max. Several kids that moved into the area and became members of our class later were terribly confused for a while because the schoolteacher would call Max-Slash-Kyle "Kyle" during the week, but Kevin and I would call him "Max-Slash-Kyle" or simply "Max" on Sundays. It seems for weeks after first moving in, Dillon, Victoria, and Andrew weren't sure if Max-Slash-Kyle's name was Max or Kyle!) Each dashing hero-to-be in our class intrigues and inspires me—so many different personalities and yet all of them sharing that quality of heroism. So the heroes-in-the-making boys in our class lent inspiration to my writing in *Midnight Masquerade* as well. As I've always said, I never know from whence inspiration will come! It seems that, more often than not, it just pops up from what seems like the most unlikely direction.

I'm not going to candy-coat it: for the majority of the time I was writing *Midnight Masquerade*, I allowed too many circumstances to beat me down, cause me to doubt myself, and view writing a story I'd always wanted to write not as fun or a gift to my friends but as an albatross around my neck. But then I started calling Kathleen Catherine—started doing silly, random things for friends—and it all changed—all of it. Not just my feelings about the book but my nearly debilitating social phobia began to dissolve as well. I still struggle sometimes, but I can feel myself ever so slowly returning to someone akin to who I used to be.

I just realized something else! I used to love, love, love to sew! Not clothes (other than for my daughter when she was little) but just fun stuff for friends. A few months back, I begged Kevin to go dig all my sewing stuff out of the storage tubs in our storage area. Believe me, it was not an easy task, for I hadn't sewn since we moved back to New Mexico four and half years ago. But then, in April, when I started planning Christmas gifts for the kids in our Sunday class, I thought, "How fun would it be to make individualized pillowcases for each one?" You know those pillowcases that are so popular now, the ones with the three contrasting fabrics? How fun would it be to make an owl-themed pillowcase for the little owl collector in our class? Or a basketball-themed pillowcase for the basketball nut in our class, right? Well, starting the pillowcases led me back to quilting! And so, therein lies another area in which a unique group of kids helped inspire me to healing—because working on my pillowcases and quilts is an easy, brainless, soothing project for me. I find it calms me down and gives me a goal that's very easily obtainable. And in the end, once a project is finished, I have a wonderful little something to give to a family member or friend that hopefully lets them clue in to how much I adore them!

I'm not sure why I chose to include all this personal information in the *Midnight Masquerade* Author's Note. Is it pertinent to giving you any insight into the actual process of writing the book? Nope. But maybe someone who's struggling with similar mountains of tribulation in life might glean a little hope in knowing that help and healing can come from the most unfathomably day-to-day venues of life—from just something funny a child might say or a sweet note from a little ten-year-old girl or realizing that one of the boys in your little Sunday class is already so handsome, charismatic, and charming that your husband dubs him "Most Likely to Appear on a Season of *The Bachelor* Someday." Simple things, kind people, are more often than not what get us through—heal our emotional wounds and allow us an escape from our dungeons of gloom, despair, and just plan freakiness.

In truth, *Midnight Masquerade* is not the book I originally intended it to be. So much stress before and while I was writing it, coupled with the fact that I kept trying to force it to be more vast and detailed than I originally planned when I just wanted to write it for fun, eventually led me to doing just that—writing it for fun, instead of trying to create a work of fiction that could hang with all the other versions out there. Therefore, I hope you enjoyed it, that it was just a fun read for you, something that swept you away from your own stress and pressures.

Let's go back to Prince Merrily of Flower Kingdom. (Really? Prince Merrily?) Stavos—now *that's* the name of a prince we'd all want to save us from hypothermia! I almost named him Stamos, but my original goal for *Midnight Masquerade* was to give it a sort of Russian feel. I wanted a cold place in your imagination—somewhere we'd all just want to escape from. I had even gone so far as to choose names for the twelve princesses of Abawyth that were derivatives of the names of the Russian Romanov princesses. I was always so very interested in the tragic story of Czar Nicholas II and his family. It's a terrible, brutal, haunting story, and my original intent was to pay tribute to the memory of the Romanov family via some of the names in *Midnight Masquerade*. But I found it kind of made me too sad. Additionally, I wanted Stavos's kingdom to be warm, for Evony's sake. It's the reason for the warm/cold theme throughout the book. I wanted Evony to be mesmerized by the warmth Stavos emanates. It's kind of a metaphor for love, I think.

As for Evony's name—personally, it's one of my favorites! I can't even remember where I found the name Evony. But Evony's last name—her royal surname, Elorietta—I stole from my friend Jean!

Jean is an angel, a mentor, a true, loyal, and enchanting friend. Elorietta is her maiden name and comes with *quite* a history. Jean is a princess in her own right, but the alliterative name, Evony Elorietta, just seemed to have a fairy tale ring to it. And you already *know* that I love alliteration!

I really just hope you enjoyed *Midnight Masquerade*. It is, after all, only a simple retelling of a lesser-known fairy tale my sister and I loved when we were kids. We still love it! And for my sister's birthday, I'm sending her two things—the second installment of the other author's Twelve Dancing Princesses books (hoping that she calls me and says, "Oh my heck! I *loved* it! This was my favorite retelling ever!) and, of course, something else I know she'll love almost as much, *The Smurfs* edition of Monopoly!

~ Marcia Lynn McClure

Midnight Masquerade

Snippet #1—This is random, but I think one thing that really stalled me while writing *Midnight Masquerade* was this: right in the midst of the most difficult parts of the book to write, I gave up my favorite stress snack, peanut butter with milk chocolate chips. I had gotten to where I ate peanut butter with milk chocolate chips together every day—multiple times a day—especially when writing. Well, with high blood pressure, high cholesterol, and the fact that I was turning into just one big, roly-poly fat globule, I decided to give up my favorite snack and worse vice. Well, after six months of enduring a life without peanut butter and milk chocolate chips, guess how much weight I lost? Not one single ounce! Still, in the end, I figure my cholesterol should be better, right?

Snippet #2—Guess what one of the best perks to finally finishing this book is? Yep! I *finally* get to read all those other versions of the Twelve Dancing Princesses that my sister *loved* more than any other version she'd ever read!

Snippet #3—If you're curious and would love to hear the Let's Pretend audio version of the Twelve Dancing Princesses that set me on the path to my love of that fairy tale, just go to the website http://www.artsreformation.com/records, scroll about halfway down the page, and you'll see a list of Let's Pretend stories' MP3s that you can listen to! Fun, right? Oh, dear Prince Merrily and his Flower Kingdom. You'll love it! And be sure and listen to Cinderella too. Fanny and Louisa—ah-ha-ha!

Snippet #4—If you'd like a couple of children's book versions of The Twelve Dancing Princesses to share with your daughters, nieces, sisters, and moms, my two favorite version are by Ruth Sanderson and Marianna Mayer with K.Y. Craft as the illustrator. Both include excellent text with *fantastic* illustrations.

Snippet #5—I've had my own version of Cinderella in mind for about ten years. I plan to start writing it in 2014. But no pressure, right?

Snippet #6—The other two fairy tales I've retold for myself and my friends are Snow White (which has always been a lesser favorite fairy tale for me) as *Saphyre Snow* and Beauty and the Beast as *The Whispered Kiss* and *Divine Deception*. I plan to write retellings of *Cinderella*, *Little Red Riding Hood*, and *1001 Arabian Nights*, at least. Ha ha! That's a ton, right?

Snippet #7—Agnes Teche is named after Edward Teach—a.k.a. Blackbeard, the pirate. In my mind she looks like a female version of Blackbeard.

Snippet #8—You know Cedric, Ewan Happer's henchman? Yep—named after the bellhop in *Home Alone 2*! Not sure why. The guy just popped into my mind one day. Of course, henchman Cedric looks nothing like bellhop Cedric. My brain just operates on "Random" most of the time.

A Special Dedication and Thank You to…

- Abby—for your wide-eyed expressions, sincere and contagious laughter, and soft, sweet reading voice. You gladden my heart and vanquish my worries.
- Kara—for your lovely smile and peaceful countenance, your radiance and warmth. You warm my very soul.
- Kathleen—for your eloquence, unwavering faith, and sincere care and concern for others, especially me. You inspire me to go on and encourage me to endure.
- Laura—for being a soothing balm of tranquility and guardian angel to my spirit.
- Victoria—for being comfortable in your own skin and making me laugh when laughter is what I need most.
- Andrew—for so many moments of amusement that leave me laughing to myself for weeks and weeks. You lift my moods and keep me smiling.
- Brigham—whose smile, turned-up nose, and bright, expressive eyes give me a window into heaven. Thank you for watching over me (i.e., what you said one day when I was weary: "Now you go home and take a nap…because I'm taking care of you.")
- Cody—for a radiant countenance that cannot be overlooked and lends brightness and contentment to my world.
- Dallas—for wisdom, an astonishing memory, insight, unwavering support, and respect. You are a true mentor in my Hero's Journey.
- Dillon—an archetypal hero in the making, the sometimes brooding, always charming "guy the girls get up and go to school for in the morning." You have dissolved a measure of my anxiety and lightened my anxious heart more times than you know.
- Hayden—for Fu Manchu mustaches with one little Starburst, recognizing my silly movie quotes, and simply giving me so many moments to giggle over.

- Jonas—for that adorable bobblehead gesture you do and for big, sincere smiles and merry eyes that encourage, entertain, and enlighten me.
- Keagan—for your rare sensitivity to the feelings of others, particularly to me. You are a giver of compassion, and I thank you for all you have gifted me.
- Max-Slash-Kyle—for being my "culinary" kindred spirit, in all things salty, sweet, and delicious! And for the little way you have with talking out of the corner of your mouth when mischief is in your mind—it makes me happy.

And now, enjoy the prologue of
The Whispered Kiss—
another beautiful romance
by Marcia Lynn McClure.

PROLOGUE

Antoine de Bellamont sat trembling in the presence of the dark Lord of Roanan. How could plucking one bloom from a rose vine have found him thus?

"And what explanation do you offer for your thievery, man?" The dark lord's angry voice boomed, echoing through the grand hall like a violent, threatening storm.

"I-I would hardly call it thievery, milord," Antoine replied. "One bloom from such a rose vine as that on your eastern wall…it is merely a trifle."

"You trespassed upon my grounds and stole from me!" the dark lord roared. "'Tis thievery as the law deems it—plain and simple! And that without reckoning for the trespassing, for which I may take the liberty of killing you!"

"But surely, milord—" Antoine began.

"Silence!" the Lord of Roanan barked.

Antoine swallowed the hard lump of fear in his throat. He fancied his heart had been residing there since the moment he was escorted into Roanan Manor House.

He watched the man sitting in the shadows before him. Enormous in stature, the dark lord's size alone was enough to intimidate. Yet with the angry voice and a character apparently void of any compassion, the Lord of Roanan was no less than terrifying. Antoine wished for a moment he could see the man's face more clearly. Similar intimidation he had never known. Even for his trade as a merchant, he had not known such a threatening presence as now sat before him, half hidden in shadow. Still, in the next moment, Antoine de Bellamont was grateful he could not make out the man's countenance—his features. Better to leave the devil's face a mystery.

"I asked for an explanation, and you have given me none. Only feeble excuses," the dark lord said. "What explanation do you offer, thief? I ask this for the last time, so speak the truth. I will know if you are in earnest…or a liar as well as a thief."

Again, Antoine swallowed hard. He reached up with one trembling hand to brush a lock of silver hair from his forehead. Perhaps the truth would set him free.

"I am a merchant, milord—Antoine de Bellamont—from one day's ride south of here, in the port town of Bostchelan," he began. "Do you know it?"

"Of course I know it, you imbecile!" the dark lord growled.

"Forgive me. Of course, sire," Antoine continued. "A merchant I am. However, I have been informed just this morning by a messenger that my ships, all three, have been pirated—all cargo aboard lost as well."

"Pirated," the dark lord mumbled. "Thieves…such as yourself."

"No, sire, please. Only wait," Antoine pleaded. "I am penniless, destitute, and must now return to Bostchelan to my four daughters…all of whom will now suffer in great impoverishment."

"What has this to do with your own thievery? What has this to do with my rose?" the dark lord demanded.

"I am returning to my daughters, milord," Antoine explained. "Of the four, three are quite spoiled, I am reluctant to admit. I have pampered them, given them anything they required or desired."

"Then you prove yourself an imbecile as well as an appalling parent," the Lord of Roanan said.

Antoine nodded, though he was loath to agree with the angry man. Antoine knew himself to be a good parent. Hadn't he given his daughters everything they had ever desired? What made a good parent if not that? He suspected such a cruel man, as sat cloaked in shadow before him, had no children. What would such a dark lord know of parenting? Still, he was fearful, and agree he must. And yet a vision of Coquette entered his mind then—Coquette, who asked for nothing, expected nothing. Coquette, for whom Antoine had plucked the fateful rose.

He continued his explanation, gazing with pleading eyes into the shadows hiding the man's face, "Yet there is one daughter, my little Coquette…she is unlike her sisters. When I asked her what I might bring back for her from my travels to Roanan…she asked only for a flower—a rose, that she might gaze upon its beauty in remembrance of her dead mother."

"How touching," the dark lord growled. "I see you put the little one on the same path as the others…the road to ruination by way of spoiling her."

"No," Antoine said. "Coquette is not little. I only call her little because she is so very precious to me. Coquette is this month twenty and one."

"Twenty and one and begging for a flower?" the dark lord mumbled. "Is she malformed? Why has she not wed? Why have none of your daughters yet wed? Methinks were they wed, your destitution would not matter so much and your thievery may have been avoided."

"My daughters, all four, are very beautiful, my lord…Coquette most of all," Antoine explained. "But I fear I have found no suitor worthy of any of them, particularly Coquette."

The dark lord was silent. Antoine hoped pity for his daughters would keep the man from exacting any punishment for the stolen rose.

"A sad, emotive story indeed, merchant," he said at last.

Antoine smiled, relieved. He felt hope rising—hope of being released, of avoidance of peril.

In the next moment, however, the dark lord stood, drew his sword, and slammed it down on the table between them. Antoine gasped, startled and terrified.

"I am not without compassion," the Lord of Roanan growled. "Therefore, I will give you your own choice. Do you know the laws of Roanan pertaining to thievery?" he asked.

Antoine swallowed, the beaded perspiration on his brow beginning to trickle over his temples. Indeed, he knew the laws.

"Amputation, milord. Amputation of...of the hands," he stammered. Pain pinched at his wrists as he looked at the steel blade drawn before him.

"That is correct, merchant," the dark lord said. "I may cut off your hands for stealing from me. Here and now, without pause, I may do it, and the law would not question."

"Please, milord!" Antoine began, panic rising in him like a killing fire. "Please! How...how would I provide for my daughters? How would I live without my hands?"

"Where were these thoughts before you stole from me, thief?" the Lord of Roanan asked.

"Please, sire, please," Antoine begged, trembling as he watched the man raise his blade. "You...you spoke of a choice. You...you said you would give me my own choice. What choice did you speak of?"

Sword yet in hand, the dark lord turned his wrist this way and that, the sword, the glint of the steel, catching the dim light. "It is very sharp. An excellent weapon. The cut will be swift and clean, I assure you," he said.

Antoine gulped, terror and fear as he had never imagined rising in him. "What choice do you speak of, milord? Please! I beg your mercy!"

He heard the dark lord inhale deeply, releasing the breath in one long, slow exhale.

"Your hands or your daughter. The one you favor...the good one, the unspoiled one. What did you call her?" the dark lord asked.

"Coquette," Antoine whispered.

"Yes, that was it. The only daughter who will not care you are destitute, merchant. The daughter for whom you stole from me. I will take her hand in marriage instead of yours from your arm here at my table. I will wed her, for I am in need of an heir. I will even restore your trade to you. Three ships? Is that what the pirates took from you? Then I will give you three ships and this as well."

Antoine's eyes widened as the dark lord drew a black velvet purse from his coat pocket and tossed it on the table. The sound of the purse landing on the table echoed through the grand hall, and Antoine knew it held a great sum.

"Seventy gold pieces, merchant. Payment for you daughter," the dark lord said. "Or I can take your hands." A triumphant chuckle emanated from within the shadows as the Lord of Roanan continued, "But I am not a monster. Thus the choice is yours. I will cut off only one of your hands here and now—whichever one you choose—and you may seek the aid of the physician in Roanan. I will have you brought to him as soon as the deed is done, in fact. You will surely survive and be able to continue to provide for your daughters—perhaps not in the manner to which they have become accustomed, but provide for them you may all the same. Or…you can give me something in return for the thing you stole from me…your daughter."

"You…you would leave me both hands and restore my ships and trade?" Antoine asked. Perhaps it was good fortune, not bad, that led him to pluck the rose.

"In return for your favorite daughter as wife," the dark lord growled.

"Still, Coquette," Antoine hesitated, "sh-she has done nothing to deserve such—"

"No. She has not," the Lord of Roanan confirmed. "And yet you consider it, do you not, merchant?"

Antoine moistened his lips as he gazed at the velvet purse on the table before him. He must have his hands, both of them! Such a deformity was surely not comely, not to mention the pain of amputation. Further, however would he provide necessity for his daughters without one or the other? And how would he provide necessity for them without his ships? Surely he could not be expected to kneel to hard labor to provide for them. Even yet, hard labor would not provide for their extravagances.

"Still…she is my daughter," Antoine whispered, reaching for the purse.

He startled and yelped as the sharp blade of the dark lord's sword bit into the table near his hand.

"Make your choice, merchant, for my patience is wearing far thin," the dark lord growled.

Antoine moistened his lips again. It was not a hard choice to make. Coquette, angel that she was, would never be happy knowing her sisters were not. His ships and trade restored! Why, with seventy gold pieces, he could return to Bostchelan a wealthy man and fill the list his daughters had given him—all but Coquette's request.

"What of the rose, milord?" Antoine asked then. "May I…may I retain it and present it to Coquette if I choose to give her over to you?"

There was silence as the dark lord seemed to consider his request.

"Yes," he growled.

"And you will treat her well?" Antoine asked. He would not have Coquette treated poorly—at least, not too poorly.

"No," the Lord of Roanan answered. "I am the Lord of Roanan. I will take from her what I will when I will! She will serve me as I deem she should."

"But she is kind, milord, her spirit as beautiful as her image. I-I…" Antoine stammered, still staring at the purse on the table.

"However," the dark lord interrupted, "she shall want for nothing. Any possession she desires, she shall have. This I promise you."

Antoine grinned. Triumph! His ships and trade restored, his hands still attached to his person. There was no question! He knew the choice Coquette would want him to make. At least, that is what he whispered to his conscience.

"Agreed," Antoine said. "I will keep my hand that I may provide for the three daughters left to me. You have promised to provide for my fourth, and though I am loath to give her over to you, it is the only choice before me."

"Is it?" the dark lord mumbled.

"But of course!" Antoine exclaimed. Oh, how relieved he was! "One daughter that I may keep my hand and provide for the other three?"

"I warn you," the dark lord began, his voice low and resolute, "I will have an heir…no matter what manner of treatment it may cost her. And once my heir is born, I will put her off as I would an old dog."

"But Coquette is strong, my lord," Antoine explained. "The strongest and bravest of my four daughters. She can stand whatever treatment of her you see fit."

The dark Lord of Roanan was silent for a time—such a time that Antoine feared he had only been in jest, feared he did not truly intend to restore his trade and ships to him.

"Bostchelan is one day's ride from Roanan," the dark lord said at last. "If your daughter is not here by the sun's set the day after next…then I will ride to Bostchelan myself, cut off your hand, and you shall have no ships nor trade."

"Agreed," Antoine said, fairly leaping to his feet. He moistened his lips once more, nodding toward the purse on the table. "And the purse, milord?"

"Take the damned purse, merchant!" the Lord of Roanan roared. "And watch the port at Bostchelan for three ships to come to you."

Antoine reached out and gathered the purse into his hands. Carefully, eyes wide with excitement, he placed it in the pocket of his breeches.

"Thank you, Lord of Roanan…for your mercy," Antoine said, bowing low.

"Thank your daughter for my mercy, you coward!" the dark lord shouted. "Be gone! Be gone, before I change my mind and run you through before me!"

"Yes, at once, milord," Antoine said.

He turned, fleeing from the great hall of Roanan Manor House. As he fled, he smiled. What luck! Surely such luck was not so simply applied. His ships returned! Seventy gold pieces in his pocket!

"Merchant!" the dark lord shouted.

Antoine stopped. He considered his chances of escaping through the open doors before him. Yet they were still twenty or more feet in advance. Two guards stood before them as well. He could not escape, and thus he turned.

"Yes, milord?" he choked.

"The rose," the dark lord said. "The purse you have, but you have neglected the rose."

"The rose?" Antoine asked.

"Godfrey," the dark lord ordered, "give the fool his damnable rose!"

Another man stepped from the shadows. Antoine had not noticed this man before and surmised he must have been standing near to the Lord of Roanan the length of the ordeal.

The man, older yet robust in appearance, lifted the rose from its resting place on the table. In his excitement over the purse of gold pieces, Antoine had completely forgotten the presence of the rose.

With the regiment, rhythm, and timing of one of the king's soldiers, the man named Godfrey strode to Antoine. He stopped short before him, clicking his heels together and extending his hand with the rose.

"I thank you," Antoine said.

"Remember, merchant," the dark lord called as Antoine hurried for the open doors and freedom, "by the sun's set day after next— she will be here or I will come for you."

Godfrey watched the merchant flee down the great steps of Roanan Manor House. Such cowardice! He could not believe he had witnessed it. The merchant had sold his daughter for the price of three ships and a purse of gold pieces. What kind of man valued his own hand and trade over a child?

Turning, Godfrey returned to his master's side.

"And what think you of it all, Godfrey?" his Lord of Roanan asked.

Godfrey shook his head and answered, "An abomination. I could never have imagined such cowardice in a father."

"Oh, there is more there than mere cowardice, Godfrey," the Lord of Roanan growled. He was silent for a moment and then asked, "And what think you of your master who threatened to cut off a man's hand for the sake of a stolen rose? What do you think of your master, who barters for a woman simply to acquire an heir?"

Godfrey was silent. He knew his master well. He knew his master better than his master knew himself. But that knowledge he would keep silent.

"I am in your service, milord," was his response.

"And so you are," the Lord of Roanan said.

Suddenly, the dark Lord of Roanan stood and returned his deadly blade to the scabbard at his hip. The sound of steel being sheathed echoed through the still darkness of the great hall. A moment later, the room echoed again, this time with the triumphant laughter of the dark lord himself.

"What fate has gifted me such sweet reckoning as this, Godfrey, I ask you?" the tall, dark, and fierce lord asked.

Godfrey looked to his lord, glad to be in servitude to Roanan's master and not indebted to him. He thought of Antoine de Bellamont. The merchant's choice was cowardly. Godfrey knew, even as he looked at the powerful, calloused man before him, he would have let both his hands be severed rather than see a daughter married to such a man as his lord appeared.

"I ask you, Godfrey," the dark lord said again, stepping from the shadows, "which fate would wink upon me long enough to gift me this?"

"I know not, sire," Godfrey answered. Detestation and amusement blended together in his master's eyes, the result of a fierce flame of loathing.

He considered his lord and the rarity of the smile he now wore. Smiling out from the dim-lit room, the perfect white of his teeth flashed like a lion's. The dark brown waves of his hair framing his face and falling to the vast breadth of his shoulders only further accentuated his intimidating appearance. Large in stature, powerful in body and will, and as hard-hearted as the devil himself, the Lord of Roanan was not to be trifled with, and Godfrey felt ill at ease with no better answer to give his lord.

"That is true, Godfrey," the dark lord chuckled. "I forget myself, for you have no knowledge of the man who has only just sold his daughter to me for the price of a small merchant fleet. No knowledge of the merchant and no knowledge of the daughter."

"No, sire. 'Tis true I do not," Godfrey admitted.

He watched his lord's eyes narrow as he growled, "'Tis true you do not, Godfrey. Yet I have. I have a knowledge beyond cognition, and I am fated to have my reckoning." His lord fell silent, eyes narrowed, brow puckered into the most scathing of frowns.

Godfrey startled when, in the next moment, his lord slammed one powerful fist upon the table.

"We must make haste, Godfrey," the dark lord commanded. "Two days hence I shall be expecting my bride."

"Yes, sire," Godfrey said with a nod.

The dark lord quirked one eyebrow in Godfrey's direction. "You doubt the merchant will keep his word," he said.

"He seems a coward, milord," Godfrey admitted.

"And a coward he is," his master replied. "And it is why I know he will sacrifice his daughter for wealth, rather than his hand for her sake."

"Yes, milord," Godfrey said, his own wrist aching at the thought of his lord's sharp blade.

"Then let us make haste," the dark lord said again, "for I am to be wed. And thereafter, my heir will be conceived at last."

"Yes, milord." Godfrey nodded, lowering his eyes as his master passed.

He watched his lord determinedly stride from the room, his long legs swiftly carrying him toward the grand staircase.

"Well," Victoria whispered as she stepped from the shadows, "fate indeed. What fate would find us with our lord taking a wife?"

Godfrey released the anxious breath he had been holding. He turned to Victoria, shaking his head in disbelief.

"I know not, madam," he said.

Victoria was the housemistress of Roanan Manor House and had been Godfrey's confidant for near to four years since his arrival. It was often they sat in contemplation of the mystery who was their master.

"I know of seven women who have offered to…to bear his heir, legitimate or otherwise, in the course of this past three months alone! And yet he refuses every one. Some know fathers more wealthy even than he is," Victoria offered in a whisper.

"There is yet no remarkable gossip in the village of any wicked dalliance with women where my lord is concerned," Godfrey said. "None other than the common gossip, of course."

"Though I myself have seen many a chambermaid and serving wench near to begging for his applied kiss," Victoria told him.

"That is true," Godfrey agreed. "Still, if he were of the low moral character of other titled men, we would hear of it. Yet the mystery of his anger, his hatred, and constant loathing of others—"

"Of women," Victoria corrected. "One does not serve in this house and yet avoid awareness of his loathing of women."

"His distrust of women, perhaps?" Godfrey offered.

"And yet he would wed a woman of no acquaintance or consequence…a merchant's daughter?" Victoria mused.

"A ruined merchant. A cowardly one at that," Godfrey mumbled.

Victoria sighed, shaking her head. "He confounds me." She raised her eyebrows, her eyes widening as she added, "Though I was not at all certain he would not chop the man's hands off right before our eyes!"

"I believe his desire was to do so," Godfrey said.

"I believe it was," Victoria agreed. "But he would not." Godfrey heard Victoria's sigh of relief. "And now?"

"And now," he continued, "now we wait for our new Lady of Roanan to arrive. For our lord will not look back once he has set his path."

"No. Indeed he will not," Victoria whispered.

Godfrey felt his eyes narrow as he gazed out the open doors of Roanan Manor House. How he pitied the girl whose father would sell her. How he worried for the girl who must endure an existence in the clutches of the powerful and apparently heartless Lord of Roanan.

My everlasting admiration, gratitude, and love…
To my husband, Kevin…
My inspiration…
My heart's desire…
The man of my every dream!

ABOUT THE AUTHOR

Marcia Lynn McClure's intoxicating succession of novels, novellas, and e-books—including *The Visions of Ransom Lake*, *A Crimson Frost*, *Untethered*, and *The Pirate Ruse*—has established her as one of the most favored and engaging authors of true romance. Her unprecedented forte in weaving captivating stories of western, medieval, regency, and contemporary amour void of brusque intimacy has earned her the title "The Queen of Kissing."

Marcia, who was born in Albuquerque, New Mexico, has spent her life intrigued with people, history, love, and romance. A wife, mother, grandmother, family historian, poet, and author, Marcia Lynn McClure spins her tales of splendor for the sake of offering respite through the beauty, mirth, and delight of a worthwhile and wonderful story.

BIBLIOGRAPHY

Beneath the Honeysuckle Vine
A Better Reason to Fall in Love
The Bewitching of Amoretta Ipswich
Born for Thorton's Sake
The Chimney Sweep Charm
A Crimson Frost
Daydreams
Desert Fire
Divine Deception
Dusty Britches
The Fragrance of her Name
The Haunting of Autumn Lake
The Heavenly Surrender
The Highwayman of Tanglewood
Kiss in the Dark
Kissing Cousins
The Light of the Lovers' Moon
Love Me
The McCall Trilogy
Midnight Masquerade
An Old-Fashioned Romance
One Classic Latin Lover, Please
The Pirate Ruse
The Prairie Prince
The Rogue Knight
Romantic Vignettes-The Anthology of Premiere Novellas
Saphyre Snow
Shackles of Honor
Sudden Storms
Sweet Cherry Ray
Take a Walk With Me
The Tide of the Mermaid Tears
The Time of Aspen Falls

To Echo the Past
The Touch of Sage
The Trove of the Passion Room
Untethered
The Visions of Ransom Lake
Weathered Too Young
The Whispered Kiss
The Windswept Flame